D1068745

MARY AND O'NEIL

MARY AND O'NEIL

JUSTIN CRONIN

THE DIAL PRESS

CRONIN
0001617776

Published by
The Dial Press
Random House, Inc.
1540 Broadway
New York, New York 10036

Library of Congress Cataloging-in-Publication Data
Cronin, Justin.
Mary and O'Neil / Justin Cronin.
p. cm.
ISBN 0-385-33358-7
1. High school teachers—Fiction. 2. Married people—Fiction.
3. Philadelphia (Pa.)—Fiction. I. Title.
PS3553.R542 M37 2001
813'.54—dc21
00-049377

Manufactured in the United States of America
Published simultaneously in Canada

February 2001

BVG 10 9 8 7 6 5 4 3 2 1

For Leslie

Contents

Nobody sees it happen, but it does. For suddenly, it seems, the woods are bare.

John Updike, "Leaf Season"

LAST OF THE LEAVES

November 1979

ARTHUR IN DARKNESS—drifting, drifting—the planet spinning toward dawn: he awakens in gray November daybreak to the sounds of running water and a great arm brushing the side of his house. *The wind,* he thinks, *the wind;* the end of autumn, the last of the leaves pulled away. The running water, he understands, was never real. He lies in the dark of the bedroom he shares with his wife, waiting for the dream to fade—a dream in which, together, they sail over a cliff into blackness. What else? A sense of water below, a lake or stream, Miriam's hand in his, of everything loosed from the earth; a feeling like accomplishment, shapes fitting together with mathematical precision, all the equations of the heavens ringing. A dream of final happiness, in which they, Arthur and Miriam, together, at the last, die.

Arthur rises, takes a wool sweater from the chair by his bed, pushes his feet into the warm pockets of his slippers. He draws the sweater over his head, his twisted pajama top; he puts on his glasses and pauses, letting his eyes, cakey with sleep, adjust. In the feeble, trembling light (The moon? A streetlamp? The day is hours off), he discerns the form of his wife, a crescent-shaped ridge beneath the blankets, and knows her face and body are turned away from him, toward the window, open two inches to admit a trail of cold night air. How is it possible he knows he is going to die? And that the thought does not grieve him? But the feeling, he believes, is just a tattered remnant of his dream, still near to him in the dark and cold of the predawn room, Arthur still, after all, in his pajamas; by breakfast it will recede, by lunchtime it will vanish altogether, dissolving into the day like a drop of iodine in water. Is it possible he is still asleep? And Arthur realizes this is probably true; he is fast asleep, standing in the icy bedroom, knees locked, his chin lolled forward into the downy fan of hair on his chest; he is, in fact, about to snore.

. . . To snore! And with this his head snaps to attention, his eyes fly open; he is, at last and truly, awake, dropped as if from a great height to land, perfectly uninjured, here. The living, breathing Arthur. But to be fifty-six years old, and dream of death, and not be afraid; this thought has somehow survived the journey into Arthur's encroaching day, hardening to a kernel of certainty in his heart. He shakes his head at the oddness of this fact, then at the coldness of the room, *Christ Almighty;* even in the dark Arthur can see his breath billowing before him like a cloud of crystals. Below the blue bulk of their bedding his wife adjusts herself, pulling the blankets tighter, as if to meet his thought; a hump disengages itself from the small of her back, travels the width of the mattress to Arthur's side, and vanishes with the sound of four paws striking the wide-plank floor. A flash of blond tail: the cat, Nestor, awakened from its spot between them, darts through the bedskirts and is gone. *Enough,* Arthur thinks; *onward.* He closes the window—a sudden silence, the wind sealed away from him— and departs the bedroom, shutting the door with a muffled snap. Behind it his wife will sleep for hours.

Downstairs, his mind on nothing, Arthur fills a carafe with water from the kitchen sink, pours it into the coffeemaker, scoops the fragrant dirt of ground beans into the paper filter, and turns on the machine; he sits at the table and waits. *Dear God,* he thinks, thank you for this day, this cup of coffee (not long now; the machine, sighing good-naturedly to life, exhales a plume of steam and releases a ricocheting stream into the pot), *and while we're at it, God, thank you for the beauty of this time of year, the leaves on the trees by the river where I walked yesterday, thank you for the sky and earth, which you, I guess, in your wisdom, will have to cover with snow for a while, so we don't forget who's boss. I like the winter fine, but it would be nice if it wasn't a bad one. This is just a suggestion. Amen.*

Arthur opens his eyes; a pale light has begun to gather outside, deepening his view of the sloping yard and the tangle of woods beyond. He pours the coffee, spoons in sugar, softens its color with a dollop of milk; he stands at the counter and drinks. *Not a bad one, please.*

Today is the day they will drive six hours north to see their son, a sophomore in college, lately and totally (or so he says, his voice on the phone as bright as a cork shot from a bottle: *totally, Pop*) in love. Arthur doesn't doubt this is the case, and why should he? What the hell? Why not be in love? He sits at the kitchen table, dawn creeping up to his house; he thinks of the long day and the drive through mountains ahead of him, the pleasure he will feel when, his back and eyes sore from hours on the road, he pulls into the dormitory lot and his boy, long legged and smiling and smart, bounds down the stairs to greet them. In the foyer with its bulletin boards and scuffed linoleum and pay phone, the young lady watches them through the dirty glass. Susan? Suzie? Arthur reviews the details. Parents from Boston, JV field hockey first string (again the memory of his son's voice, brightly laughing: *But her ankles aren't thick, the way they get, you know, Pop?*); an English class they took together, Shakespeare or Shelley or Pope, and the way she read a certain poem in class, the thrilling confidence in her voice cementing the erotic bargain between them. *(I mean, she looked right at me, Pop, the whole time, I think she had the thing memorized; you should have seen it, the whole class knew!)* And Arthur knows what his son is saying to him: *Here I am. Look.* And Arthur does: Susan or Suzie (Sarah?), fresh from her triumphs of love and smarts in the marbled halls of academe, banging the hard rubber ball downfield on the bluest blue New Hampshire autumn day.

Sounds above: Arthur hears the bedroom door open, his wife's slippered trudge down the carpeted hall, the mellow groan of the pipes as she fills the basin with water to wash. Arthur pours himself a second cup of coffee and fills a mug for Miriam—extra sugar, no milk—positioning it on the table by the back kitchen stairs. Outside the sky has turned a washed-out gray, like old plastic; a disappointment. For a while Arthur sits at the table and watches the sky, asking it to do better.

Miriam enters, wrapped in her pale-blue robe, and takes the coffee almost without looking, a seamless transaction that always pleases him. She sips, pauses, and sniffs at the mug.

"This is sort of old."

"I've been up awhile," Arthur says. "I'll make a fresh pot if you want."

"No, I'll do it." But she doesn't; she takes a place at the table across from him. Her face is scrubbed, her combed hair pulled back from her face; she does not dye it, allowing the gray to come on without fuss, nor perm it, the way so many women they know have done. Arthur lets his eyes rest there, in the whiteness of the part of her hair, thinking of his dream, a vague disturbance that no longer creates in him any particular emotion, as the widest rings on pond water will lap the shore without effect. (Something about a lake? He no longer recalls.) She holds the cup of old coffee with both hands, like a hot stone to warm them, resting there on the table.

"What time is it?" She yawns. "Is it six-thirty?"

Arthur nods. "I thought we should get an early start. We can stop for lunch at that place in Northampton."

"Not there." She shakes her head. "Do you remember the last time? Please. Let's stop someplace else."

Arthur shrugs; he doesn't remember what was wrong with the restaurant. "I thought it was all right," he says. "We can try that place across the street. Or we can pack a lunch."

Miriam rises, dumps her mug of coffee down the sink, and begins to make the pot she has promised herself. Arthur watches his wife, full of a great, sad love for her; he knows this day will be hard. Not the drive, which they have made many times; not seeing O'Neil, their son. Arthur understands it is the girl she dreads. She tries to like the girls he likes, but it is always difficult for her.

"We have to be nice, you know."

Miriam stops rinsing the pot. "Quit reading my mind."

"Okay. But we do." Arthur rises and goes to where she is standing, her hands resting on the edge of the sink. He wraps his arms around her slender waist and smells the beginnings of her tears—a sweet, phosphorescent odor, like melting beeswax.

"It's stupid, I know."

"I don't think it's stupid at all. Why is it stupid?"

"I feel like someone in a play," she says. "You know, the mother? That old bitch, can't let go, nobody's good enough for her boy."

"And you're right. Nobody is. And you're not like that at all."

A heavy sigh. Still, Arthur holds on.

"She's just somebody he met in class. We've been through this—how many times?"

"They're probably sleeping together."

Arthur nods. "Probably."

"God, listen to me." She shakes her head and resumes cleaning the pot. "You probably think it's just great."

Arthur doesn't answer. The cat comes nosing into the kitchen and coils first around Arthur's feet and then around Miriam's, asking to be let out.

"That goddamned cat," Arthur says. He kisses Miriam's neck, still warm with sleep and the sheets of their bed. "You know, I had the strangest dream," he says suddenly.

Still facing away, Miriam tips her head against his. "I think I did too. So. Tell me about yours."

Arthur lets his eyes fall closed; in this interior darkness, his wife's body pressed against his, her hips and his hips meeting— always the old rhythm implied, the metronome of marriage—he imagines he is asleep and tries to return to his dream, following it down a long hallway, a trick he has used before.

"I'm not sure," he says after a moment. "I've already forgotten."

"Was it a bad dream?" She is stroking his hair. "I heard you muttering."

"I don't know." Arthur draws air into his chest. "Some of it."

"What else?"

Arthur thinks. It is her voice he is following now; below him, without warning, he suddenly feels the tug of blackness, a yawning chasm as vast as a stadium. And something else: the smell of baking bread. He has never had a dream like this before, of this he is certain. The memory of it makes him feel strangely happy. He opens his eyes.

"I think you were in it." He shrugs at nothing; already the information is gone, as is his memory that she, too, has dreamt, and meant to tell him what. "I think you saved me from something, as usual. So it was a good dream."

She turns to face him then; her eyes still moist, she kisses him quickly and smiles. Up close he sees that her face is tired, and newly thin: his fault. Regret slices through him, and then, filling its wake, a pale and luminous awe. How many times has she performed this duty? He searches her gray eyes with his own. How many times has she been awakened from a sound slumber by a distant cry and made her fumbling way down a darkened hall, to wrap herself around a son or daughter whose arms flailed at nothing, saying, No, no, there's nothing to fear, none of it was real? He asks this, and for an instant he imagines that the children are asleep upstairs; but of course this is an illusion, a trick of time, like the pea that darts from shell to shell unseen, and so is in both places at once and also neither. No: it is morning in their kitchen, the children are grown and gone, O'Neil at college waiting for their visit, his sister, Kay—moody, mysterious Kay—married now and living her life in New Haven. The passage of years is amazing, a thing of wonder. He stands before it as, in the past, he stood outside the children's doors, listening to Miriam deliver the comforts he could not: a glass of water, a fresh blanket, Miriam holding the child's hand in hers to say, squeezing, See? *This* is real. How many times? A thousand? A thousand thousand? Count the stars in the heavens, Arthur thinks, and you will know that number.

"You're welcome," she tells him.

And their day begins.

Each of them has a secret. Here is Arthur's:

His secret is a letter, which he has delayed writing until this morning, at the office where he works—a letter he will never send. It is a letter to a woman not his wife.

Dear Dora, he writes.

How did it come about? Even Arthur doesn't know; could not say, precisely, how it is that on this morning in November he, Arthur, age fifty-six, a devoted married man for twenty-nine years, has fallen in love (is he? in love?) with Dora Auclaire. But he has; he does. Confusingly, he loves his wife no less because of it; he dares to think, knowing it to be a kind of arrogance—something terribly, destructively *male*—that he loves her even more. To think of Miriam is to think of himself, the span of his life and his children's lives, and to know what is meant by a common destiny. He is human, and therefore weak, but his weakness is for Miriam. He cannot look at her and not feel love, or the fear that comes with love: that someday one of them will be alone.

But Dora Auclaire: he has known her—how long? Ten years? Fifteen? Did they know one another when their children were small? Arthur allows himself the pleasure of thinking of her, and what she might be doing now, at ten-thirty in the morning on a Friday in fall at the busy clinic where she sees her patients: the young girls in trouble, the old men wheezing from years of smoking, the tiny babies who have cried, mysteriously, through the night. He sees her, moving from room to room—neither gliding nor marching, her stride merely purposeful—wearing her clean white coat with jeans and a sweater beneath (not much jewelry; earrings, perhaps, to complement her heart-shaped face, and a single silver chain), touching, advising, jotting notes on a chart in her fine, square print, before excusing herself to telephone the hospital in Cooperstown to reserve a bed for the teenage boy in the examining room whose two-day stomachache is almost certainly not caused by drugs, as his mother claims, but acute appendicitis. Arthur, at his desk four blocks away, sees it all. (And before he knows it, there is Miriam too: plunking a due-date card into the stamper at the checkout desk, refiling spools of shiny microfilm, pushing a cart of books, heavy with facticity, through the quiet, dusty aisles.) She is a lonely, spirited woman in her mid-forties, a physician and a widow with two young sons—a woman who could chop a cord of wood one minute and swab a toddler's throat the next—and Arthur loves her. He loves her strong, thin hands, and her gleaming stethoscope, and her sadness, which she does not wear around her like a shawl—some garment of mourning—but inside, in a deep place he cannot see but feels: the same grief that he would carry if Miriam were gone. Her husband, Sam, was a carpenter who restored old houses, and it was an old house that killed him; six years ago, on a bright morning in May (Arthur remembers reading of it in the papers), he stepped from the window of a fourth-story cupola of a falling-down Queen Anne on Devereaux Street, placed his weight on a ledge that turned out to be rotten with moisture, and down he went in a rattling rain of tools and equipment, forty feet to the packed-dirt yard.

The town of Glenn's Mills, New York—small, nondescript, economically marginal except for the retired cardiologists and downstate corporate attorneys who buy up and rehab the old houses—rests at the bend of a river once so polluted with tannery acids it was given the name Vinegar Creek. This is the town where Arthur has made his whole life. His law firm, a one-man outfit on the town's ten-block main street—trusts, wills, real estate, the occasional divorce—was his father's before it was his, and though in school Arthur had thought first that he'd like to be an engineer, and then an architect, and finally a big-city lawyer, he has no regrets about living a life that was, in the end, simply handed to him: The spring of Arthur's last year at NYU law his father, a two-pack-a-day Lucky Strike smoker, entered his office, removed his hat and coat and scarf, lit his first cigarette of the morning at his desk, rubbed his rheumatic hip once in the ice-cold room, and suffered a stroke of such lethal power that it succeeded in rearranging all the details of his son's world in one painless instant. By the end of the week twenty-six-year-old Arthur was meeting with his father's clients and scraping the mud from their boots off the carpet and finding that he liked it, all of it; the thousand choices of his life suddenly included the choice not to choose, and within a month he had canceled his plans to clerk for a federal circuit judge in Manhattan and was studying like mad for the bar. He telephoned the girl he'd been dating in New York—Miriam, finishing up her master's in library science at NYU—and invited her north for a visit from which she would return for only one semester to complete her degree; she found a job in the county library, shelving books and reading to children; within a year they married. If asked, Arthur would say he didn't so much begin his life as find it, like a wallet or a ring of keys he'd merely mislaid.

Now, for the first time in thirty years in this quiet town of trees and houses and shops—"Glenn's Mills, New York, Gateway to the Hudson-Mohawk Valley Region"; a town where the theft of garden tools from an unlocked shed makes the papers; where the same man who cuts your hair on Tuesday will run on Wednesday to extinguish the flames of your burning house; where the shopkeeper who catches your child pocketing a package of baseball cards will close up the store and drive the boy home (O'Neil, ten years old, claimed to have done it on a dare)—Arthur has felt this life, this pattern of meaning with its exchanges of goods and services and affections, disturbed, even endangered—all because he has fallen in love with Dora Auclaire. For it is her loneliness he loves, above everything else about her; when he sees her on the street or at a party, or he finds himself, on the second Tuesday of each month, sitting across from her in the small classroom at the high school where their novel-reading group meets, and listens to her voice—calm, precise, ironic—advancing some opinion, inevitably superior to his own, about *The French Lieutenant's Woman* or *Crime and Punishment* or *A Confederacy of Dunces* (and Arthur must confess: he almost never finishes these books, which tire and oppress him;

he keeps going only to see *her*), it is her loneliness that he hears, and it is her loneliness that moves him to love her. If he found her simply pretty or clever or sexy or generous to children, Arthur would know what to do: nothing. Do nothing, and let the sensation fade over time, like the buoyant happiness that lifts his heart after certain movies, or the delicious nostalgia he feels each November when the first snow falls, evening comes on, and he walks home through early darkness and a world drenched in the dreamy half-reality of new snow. (And wasn't there a dream he had this morning, something about flying, flying over water?) But he can't do nothing. The core of her life is loss—a forty-foot plunge on a damp morning in May—and somehow Arthur has zeroed in on that core, and trapped himself there.

The office is quiet; above the door to the waiting room—a dim, shabby space with battered file cabinets, an old plaid sofa, a coffee table dressed with stacks of wrinkled magazines, and the desk where his secretary sits when he hasn't given her the day off, as he has today—the clock reads ten forty-eight. He has canceled his appointments, meaning to use this wedge of time between finishing his work and leaving for New Hampshire (already he is running late; he should be out the door at eleven, to pick up their suitcases and feed the cat and hustle to the library to get Miriam, all before noon) to solve the problem of Dora Auclaire. But what is the problem, exactly? Isn't it true that he, Arthur, has made no serious mistakes, committed no unpardonable sins against his marriage? He looks at the page, the words he has written: *Dear Dora.* It is written on a yellow legal pad; its length seems suddenly absurd. How will he fill such a thing? He means to record what he feels, to give it shape, to make sense of it by setting it in words. Instead, he rips the paper from the pad, wads it in his fist, tosses it in the wastebasket behind his desk (a moment's worry—should he leave it there? But it says nothing, only a name . . .), and begins again:

Dear Dora.

The problem is that there is nothing to say, no story to tell and therefore finish; that nothing has, in fact, happened between them at all. And yet: like every secret Arthur's has a history, an arc of events. Pressed, he would trace this awkward, silent moment at his desk to an afternoon a little over eight months ago, when Dora came to see him in his office. He had done some work for the clinic before—a zoning variance for an addition, permits to build it, the odd dispute with a patient over billing—so when she entered, shaking her umbrella, and told him the matter at hand was personal, he was surprised, and interested; he wondered what it could be. There was some money, she explained, that she'd inherited from an aunt—not much, just $60,000—that she wanted to put away for the boys. Could he draw up some kind of . . . well. What did one call it? A trust? She said the word as if she'd only just learned it, though of course she knew just what she was asking. There were beads of rain in her hair, which she wore short, in neat layers, making a dark frame around her face. She liked the sound of it, she said, smiling at him: *a trust.*

He offered her a seat and set to work. And how was she? And the boys? (He remembered two: Josh, the younger but a strong kid like his father; his older brother, Leo, the more delicate, a boy who liked to read and taught swimming at the Y.) He drew up the papers at his desk. It was easy work, pure boilerplate, though just the kind of work he liked—putting money aside for children. Dora named her brother, a surgeon in San Francisco, as one trustee, herself as the other; she had already visited her broker and invested the money in a sensible mixture of zero-coupon bonds and blue-chip stocks. Her will was up to date, she thought, she'd taken care of that right after Sam had died—she said this last phrase quickly, almost as one word—though if it was not too much trouble would Arthur mind having a look at it? A thick envelope, full of folded paper: she had brought it in her bag.

And so on, through that afternoon and part of another, when the papers were ready to sign. He would call her, he said, when the documents came back from the brother in California; he could mail her a copy, or else she could come to pick it up, and of course he would keep one in his office, on file, *her* file. Fine, she said. Fine.

They looked at one another. Their time together was through. It's funny, she said then, buttoning her coat—and was she blushing? And was he?—it's funny how you can enjoy doing something like this, something so *mundane,* with someone whom you like. Did he know that sometimes—well, once or twice—she had thought that the two of them should have lunch? She liked what he'd said in reading group about that book—*Mrs. Dalloway,* that was it—about how every character in the story was alone, and either succeeded at it or failed. She'd thought it right then; the two of them could be friends, real friends who did things together. But how could he have known? She'd only just told him, of course.

Which was how it happened, though not then. He showed her to the office door—for a moment it had seemed possible they would kiss right there, an image so compelling, so completely disorienting, that Arthur quickly drove it from his mind—and a week later he telephoned her to tell her that the signed copies had been returned, and they agreed to meet for the lunch she had promised him, so that he could give them to her. The week of rain had become a week of snow, temperatures falling back into the teens though it was nearly April, and Arthur hurried the six blocks to the restaurant, wondering what he was doing. Was he doing anything at all? But when he arrived and saw Dora sitting at a booth in back, not at one of the open tables in the middle of the room, he knew. Without breaking his stride he stepped to the booth and slid himself into the narrow space across from her; he saw she was drinking tea. Her overcoat, heavy green wool with shawl lapels, lay over her shoulders. Her smile was almost a laugh. Was he late? he asked. No, no, she said, shaking her head. The window by their table was a wall of steam; someone, a child perhaps, had written something in the steam, fat letters now faded. She blew over her tea. The snow had kept her patients away for the day, she said. He wasn't late at all.

The restaurant was shrouded in a heavy white light, and nearly empty. They sat together an hour, talking and eating their lunch of sandwiches and soft drinks while the waitresses, two old women Arthur knew by sight but not by name, sorted steaming silverware and smoked long brown cigarettes at the counter. Arthur knew what was said about small towns, but as a lawyer, he'd found the opposite was true: everyone had something to hide. It was possible in such a place to live a kind of secret life, and if anyone asked, he could always say that he'd done some work for her. He'd been a lawyer long enough to believe that there was nothing simple about the truth, that it came in any number of forms, and this was one. They talked about people they knew, about the patients at her clinic and their sad stories, and about their children, as any two people their age, meeting for a meal, might do. She did not talk about Sam, though in a way she did; so many years, she remarked, looking around, since she had set foot in this place; she was glad to see it had not changed. With her practice and the boys besides, she said, it was all she could do to grab a quick bite at her desk. She gave a little laugh. Time moved quickly, did it not? And yet it sometimes seemed she had been doing things this way forever, pulling her life and her children's lives like a cart.

Then as the hour drew late, on the verge of their good-byes,

Dora reached across the table, found his hand with hers, and gently held it. Just that: Dora held his hand. Arthur felt himself raked, like the surface of a pond. Twenty-nine years, and he hadn't once done this, held another woman's hand; and yet people did it all the time, he knew; did it as if it were nothing. Arthur saw that she wore a watch with three gold hearts on either side of the face: one for each boy, and one for Sam. A gift: he knew this without asking. Mother's Day? An anniversary? It was the kind of thing he might have bought for Miriam; it was merely an accident that he had not. Her hand was warm, and a little damp. She brushed the back of his hand with her thumb, once, and then she let it go.

And yet the moment felt frozen, as if neither of them could leave it, like a room without doors. She pulled her coat around herself a little; her eyes darted to the counter, where the women were smoking and talking (Arthur's eyes followed; no, they had not seen), and then found Arthur's again, squinting. "Well." She tipped one shoulder and smiled uneasily. He realized only then that she hadn't worn her glasses. It made her eyes seem very large. "Was that, you know, all right?"

He didn't know, and also did. His mind had filled with a white emptiness, like a field of whirling snow—like forty feet of air. He heard himself say, "Yes."

When was this? March, a year ago. Arthur, in his office, sips his coffee, now gone cold. At eleven-thirty he will pick Miriam up at the library, and together they will leave for New Hampshire. Through the spring and summer he and Dora continued to meet, at his office or hers, or for lunch, always in plain view and broad daylight, and always under the pretense of work she needed done: a quarrel with the town over parking at the clinic, an old tax matter of amazing density and frivolousness, a meaningless dispute with a neighbor over a drainage easement. How did I get on so long without a lawyer, she said, how did I ever manage without you? One matter would be settled and before the ink was dry she handed him a fresh folder of papers, bringing the two of them together in a continuous flow of trivial tasks like a chain of silk handkerchiefs pulled from a magician's sleeve. Her pleased face said: *See what I've come up with?* Before this is over, she joked, I'm going to be your best client.

But what was *this?* And—the real question—why wasn't he, Arthur—happily married Arthur—troubled by it, or troubled more? In the past he had imagined himself having an affair—everyone did, you couldn't not *think* about it—but never like this, this affair that wasn't, quite. They held hands, not even really holding; she would rub his shoulder when he said he was tired, or touch his cheek with one finger, quickly, when another person might have stopped her hand in the air before his face. Each time they were together it happened, this touching, but only once, and never anything more. Yet it was also true that he had come, in some way, to rely on it; it did something for him that nothing else did. It made him happy, there was that, to be touched by another for no reason. But something else: it was as if, in those instants, he ceased to be who he was. His whole life became a memory, and not even of his own. Whose, then? He had met Sam Auclaire once, he believed, at the high school maybe—a play? parents' night?—or else merely seen him, striding out of the hardware store with a sack of nails in his hand, or driving his pickup, ladders lashed to a frame over the bed, through the streets of town. Arthur remembered a tall man, muscular, with curly blond hair gone an early, peppery gray. So that was his answer. Dora touched him, and the happiness he felt was not his own but Sam's, at being so terribly missed.

It went on like this into the fall. He never set foot in her house, nor she in his, and if anyone suspected (suspected *what?*), Arthur heard nothing about it. He told no one, because who was there to tell? His clients? The old women at the Coffee Stop? The man at the service station who changed the oil in his car? He wished for a brother, as he had many times in his life, but hadn't one; he worked alone, and had few friends that Miriam did not share. His life was like a small, comfortable room, every piece in its place. Only by being with Dora did he step outside of this room, though only for an hour or two, and never so completely that at the end of their time together he could not return to it, and to the life he understood. He wondered how long it could go on.

Then, two weeks ago, Arthur found himself driving with Dora out of town, to see a parcel of land she said she wanted to buy. The town had begun to feel close to her—that was the word she used, *close;* she had always dreamed of building a house and raising her boys in the country. She said she wanted to get his opinion, but her meaning was clear: things had reached a certain point between them. The afternoon was cold and bright, and they drove the fifteen miles south with barely a word between them. For the first time since she had come into his office eight months before, dripping with rain, Arthur felt truly afraid. In Domingo they found the unmarked dirt road that led to the property, which was marked with a large For Sale sign pocked with bullet holes. Arthur recognized the phone number on the sign; it was the number of the county clerk's office, in Harbersburg. On the phone Dora had told him that before the land had been taken over by the county for nonpayment of taxes, it had been a dairy farm.

In the parked car they changed into sneakers and then set out on foot. The land was level and moist—Arthur could hear running water somewhere—and they moved slowly through the shrubs and shabby trees, all of it tangled by brawny grapevine. It took him a moment to realize that the overgrown path they were following was the driveway, but once he saw this, other details emerged: rusted farm implements poking from the ground, gullies lining the pathway that had once been drainage ditches, a shape in the trees that he recognized as the cab of an old Willys Jeep, melting into the leaves and mossy earth. The scene disturbed and interested him. How long, he wondered, had it taken for nature to reclaim this place? Twenty years? Thirty? How much time was required? Then they emerged into a clearing—the trees opened above them like a hatchway, revealing a sky of radiant, shimmering blue—and found themselves standing at the edge of an immense pit. Of course: the house's foundation. The hole was some forty feet across, roughly square, and some ten feet deep. Its floor was irregular, long buried beneath a sea of leaves and debris. Again, Arthur's eyes adjusted. An old-fashioned nail-keg lay on its side, beside a rusted saw blade and a monkey wrench and the head of a hammer, half peeking from the dirt. The scene leapt into view. More saws, hammers, wrenches, an iron sledge, a workbench with a vise, all of it bathed in the brilliant sunlight. The basement was full of tools.

It was then, standing at the edge of the farmhouse's foundation, that Arthur felt it: a terrible fear, like falling, and then, in its wake, a deep and melancholy calm.

He looked up. Dora was standing beside him, gazing into the hole. He said, "This is something the two of you wanted."

She answered without raising her head. "What do you mean?"

"To build a house. Out here, somewhere." He took her gloved hand. "You and Sam."

Dora said nothing, but her face, paling, gave the answer. She had looked at this very place before, when Sam was still alive. They had stood right where the two of them were standing now. He imagined what that had been like, the hopeful feeling of it, and the sounds of their two boys tearing around the woods, somewhere nearby. It would have been when Leo and Josh were small.

"I really am sorry," Arthur said.

"Well, you're right. We did come out here." She shrugged, and gave him a distant and painful smile. "It was a long time ago, Art."

"No, I mean I'm sorry that I can't"—he stopped. He had approached the edge of something, and then he crossed it—"do this."

For a moment neither of them spoke. Wind moved in the trees, and the branches swayed.

"Oh, it's all right." Gently, Dora freed her hand from his—as gently as the first time she had taken it, across the table in the restaurant, months before. She folded her arms over her chest.

"I truly am," Arthur said.

She laughed, almost bitterly, though Arthur knew that, like him, what she felt was more like sadness. "What you are is relieved, Art. Still, it would have been nice, at least for me." She sighed then, deeply, and Arthur saw that her eyes were glazed with tears. With a long finger she brushed one away. "Forgive me, but I really liked being a wife. I was good at it, and I miss it. Maybe all I'm doing is remembering."

And that was the end of it. They drove back to town, and by the time they returned they were friends again, with things to do: Dora to fetch the boys at Scouts, and Arthur to phone Miriam (not here, they told him; she'd only just stepped out) and then drive out to the Price Chopper in Vermillion to do the shopping he'd promised her he'd do. He pushed his cart through the bright, busy aisles, the air smelling of the cold from the open freezer cases, and knew that he was saved. The thought filled him with an almost manic energy—for he also knew, now, that he would never be caught, nor would have to confess—and standing in the checkout line, jammed into the final gauntlet of movie magazines and candy displays, he found himself talking, almost babbling, to a woman one aisle over, a neighbor who had once baby-sat his children. Was his mother well? And the kids? *Yes, fine, though of course the nursing home did things, certain things he didn't care for; they wouldn't for instance let her out for walks when it was raining, which she had always loved, and his children, well, Kay was settling into married life, the usual bumps in the road but nothing serious, her husband, Jack, was still finishing his dissertation, Arthur couldn't even understand what the hell it was about, trying to teach, she knew how that went, and O'Neil was still enjoying school, running cross-country and thinking about maybe medicine, though he'd have to decide soon, however he and Miriam managed to pay for it, well, that was another subject entirely; they were driving up to see him in a couple of weeks, to meet his new girlfriend, from Boston. . . .* It poured forth from him. It disgorged, like the contents of his cart—flank steak, spaghetti sauce with pork and mushrooms, ice-slickened canisters of frozen juice, and all the rest, a hundred bucks' worth (for he had overshopped)—onto the cheerfully humming rubber conveyor belt. He wanted to talk, to tell his story; to sing it if necessary, like a hymn, or the tale of a traveler come home at last.

Now, two weeks later, Arthur sits in his office (ten fifty-two and counting; he really has to *go*), composing his farewell to Dora Auclaire. Since that day in the woods they have not spoken, though they have seen each other once, in passing. Tuesday last, three days ago: Arthur, hustling back from Lawson's Stationery with a package of pencils he didn't really need, his head down against a gritty wind, heard the toot of a horn, and knew it was for him. He raised his head in time to see the sticker-covered tailgate of Dora's old VW squareback as she passed (ERA NOW, No Nukes, Carter-Mondale '76), and over the seat, a wave. A greeting? A good-bye? He froze, thinking she might stop; when he saw she wouldn't, he raised his hand to return the wave, but she was already gone.

What he wants now, at his desk, the blank paper before him, is to acknowledge her, to finish the wave; he wants to put into words the happiness he feels, that he loves her but will never be with her, and that this love will therefore harm no one. His office is empty; the answering machine is on, the sound turned low. Behind him, beyond the windows of his office, cars pass in an almost continuous flow, washed pale by gray November; the last leaves tremble on their stalks; above his head hovers the yellow stain of his father's cigarettes, a ghostly halo that no coat of paint seems to cover for long. For some time Arthur simply sits there, his mind a perfect blank. Without realizing it he has nudged his consciousness to the edge of deepest memory, and his dream of 5:00 A.M. with its sounds of distant water and feeling of final flight. At last he takes a clean sheet of white paper—the legal pad was a mistake, of course—from the tray on his desk, selects a fresh pen, fat-tipped and forgiving, and begins again. *Dear Dora*, he writes.

The letter is one sentence long; he signs it, *love, Art*. His eyes rise to the old schoolroom clock above the waiting room door: 11:38. So, after all that, there is no time to mail it. He puts the folded letter in an envelope, writes Dora's name on it, places the envelope in his pencil drawer, and pushes it shut. *Late*, he thinks, *late*. Miriam will be waiting for him in the library foyer, clutching her books and papers and all her nervousness to her chest. The car needs gas, he will have to cash a check on the way out of town; they will arrive at the college in darkness, and there will be confusion about whether to eat dinner first, or check into the hotel, and then the question about restaurants, and if the girl will come with them, and her parents, if they are visiting too—a chain of uncertainties and potential disappointments all shouldered into motion because he, Arthur, is running late. (Not Suzie or Sarah: *Sandra*. He says the name aloud, to etch it in memory: "Sandra.") He wraps his neck with a woolen scarf, douses the lamps in his office and waiting room, slides into his trench coat—a gift from Kay at Christmas—and steps outside.

And this is when he stops—pauses and turns, his keys in one hand and his briefcase in the other, at the open office door. His back to the street, Arthur scans the waiting room, its blond oak paneling and sagging sofa and coffee table with magazines, everything perfectly still and frosted with dust; beyond, through the inner office door, his eye finds the mahogany desk where his father died, and his chair, cocked back on its springs where it came to rest when he, Arthur, stood at last to go. The image seems somehow apart from him, at once frozen and containing movement, like a photograph: the ghost of Arthur, rising. For an instant he imagines he sees this—sees him*self*—and a dark chill twists through him. *What in the world . . . ?* But it is nothing, just a trick of the light, of the time of day and his own need to hurry. He shakes his head once to dislodge this vision, steps onto the sidewalk and is gone.

Miriam Patricia Burke, née Braverman, age fifty-four—wife to Arthur, mother to Kaitlin and O'Neil; empty-nester, librarian, caffeine addict; attendee of conferences and symposia; taker of classes (ornithology, ballroom dancing, vegetarian cooking); registered Democract, former Jew, sometime jogger (you might see her, a lone figure humping her way along a country lane in her purple sweatshirt and pants); holder of degrees in literature (Barnard) and library science (NYU); daughter of the late Daniel Chaim Braverman and his beloved Alicia; sister and trusted counsel to siblings Monica (fifty) and Abraham (fifty-seven); a woman lately described by a man she met at a party as "a gal who did good and still looked it"—Miriam Patricia, Mimi to her friends, stands in the foyer of the Vinegar County Library and wonders if she is dying.

Two weeks ago: she discovered the lump in her left breast, by rolling over in bed. She turned, half sleeping, and a dark presence met her and then took shape, a mass the size and solidity of an acorn, pressed between the mattress and her rib cage. The awareness of it hurled her into consciousness, and a series of swift calculations to firm the moment into fact. She was in bed; it was seven o'clock; Arthur was away for the day, something about an abandoned farm, and had left for his office early, before she was even awake. She lay in bed, her brain spinning with terror—*Not this! Not this!*—daring herself to touch the place beneath her nightgown where the thickness was. So large! It met the tips of her fingers with something like an electric current. One in nine women; that's what they said. But what happened to them, those one in nine? It was more than panic she felt; it was death, making its way to her door.

And yet, as she began her day—the first day of her dying—a strange orderliness filled her, an almost fatalistic calm. She rose, washed, dressed. She sat down at the table (her cold coffee mug, by the stairs, was waiting, and a note: *Price Chopper? Anything? Call,* signed with the little sketch of a bear he always left for her), rose again, and treated herself to a breakfast of sausage and French toast, glazed with syrup and stamps of yellow butter. She expected not to want it once it was made, but found the opposite was true: she was unaccountably ravenous, and for the time it took her to eat her breakfast, that was all she did and thought about—sliced the toast into squares, the sausage into cylinders bursting with watery fat, forked it all onto her waiting tongue. She chewed, swallowed, reloaded; if she had been capable of it, she would have licked the plate. Then when she was finished she rinsed her plate and called her doctor and told him what she knew; by two o'clock he had his hand there, and told her not to be afraid. *"Concerned,"* he said, scribbling, not really looking at her. He was a plump man, bald and flatfooted, a doctor who actually still made house calls. She had known him for years, and now he wasn't looking at her. "I'd be *concerned,* for now."

There were other doctors then, and more appointments—the ultrasound and mammogram, and the visit to the radiologist in Cooperstown to read the films, then back to Dr. Bardin and the consensus that the surgeon was the next person to see. Serious medicine, she discovered, was a kind of maze, a series of hallways down which one traveled; at the end of each was a door which one opened, hoping to find it locked; but as long as they opened, one was forced to go on. And yet, somehow, through two terrified weeks, she has told Arthur nothing. On Tuesday next—four days from this moment in the foyer, waiting for Arthur to appear so they can drive to New Hampshire—the surgeon will evaluate her; the mass will be aspirated, and then there will be a surgical biopsy, and decisions to be made. Her story will come out. Why hasn't she told him? Her lies are not elaborate; it has proved simple enough to explain why she will be away for an afternoon, to let slip over breakfast or watching television in the evening some vague announcement about a meeting with the State Library Association in Ithaca or a booksellers' convention in Binghamton (Arthur, glancing up from his paper or the program, his eyes distracted, saying, *Well, okay, thanks for letting me know, why are you even telling me?*), all to account for the three or four hours it takes to drive to a new doctor and back, and of course the mileage on her car. She is saving him, of course, from her bad news, waiting until she knows something one way or the other; she is letting him live his life for now because she loves him. But the truth is—and she has to admit it—that the longer she remains alone with the knowledge of what is happening to her, the longer she herself is saved. Under the flat institutional light of the doctor's office there was "a mass" and a "cause for concern," there were "treatments" and "courses of therapy," the problem was confined to "the affected breast," which in turn was the property of "a white female, married, 54, no family history." (She had peeked at the radiologist's chart.) Nowhere, at no time, has she uttered the word *cancer*, nor heard it used. The breast was "affected." The mass was "palpable." The patient was "married." She, Miriam Burke, was something—some*where*—else.

But where? Outside, beyond the smoked glass of the library foyer, the sky is so white it seems to tremble, poised on the very edge of snow. Leaves whirl in the parking lot, nearly empty now of cars, a temporary oasis of calm tucked between toddler storyhour and the full-blown hurricane of the after-school rush. Miriam looks at her watch and sees that it is noon, on the button. Where is Arthur? She is already wearing her coat—she had expected to find him, waiting at the curb, twenty minutes ago—and the dry heat of the foyer has begun to close in on her, dampening her frame with perspiration. Should she go back in and call? And if no one answers—if he is neither home nor at the office— what then? For a brief moment she fears that something has happened—Arthur is not the best driver; he has seemed, of late, even more distracted, more airy, than usual—but then she realizes it is herself she is thinking of. Arthur is fine; Arthur is late. Sighing to hear herself sigh, she removes her coat, her hat, her gloves; finding then that her arms are too full, she puts the coat back on, leaving it unbuttoned, and checks her watch again. Beneath her coat and her white turtleneck sweater and her brassiere's gleaming apparatus of wire and lace, in the folds of skin where her left breast meets her rib cage, a bright point of cancer glows.

She is thinking, then, of her children, Kay and O'Neil, and of her daughter's wedding, fourteen months ago. A bright day in September: all the trees had just begun to turn, beneath a sky so vastly blue—blue like neon, so blue it seemed to buzz—it was impossible not to remark on it. (*Such perfect weather!* they all said. *And the sky!*) After the ceremony everyone drove back to the house, where a tent had been erected in the yard. The memory visits her in a series of pictures: Kay in her wedding dress, a full gown studded with small white stones; her husband, Jack, whom Miriam wishes to like but can't, handsomely serious in his gray morning coat; his hard-drinking relatives from St. Louis—nearly all of them were bankers or the wives of bankers, it seemed—smoking cigarettes and talking up a storm as the waiters in their black pants and pressed white shirts passed trays of cheese and crab puffs and tiny things on sticks; Arthur's mother, just recovered from gall bladder surgery, rising, somehow, against the tidal pull of age, to shuffle through a dance. From the sidelines she watched the tiny floor fill up—Jack and Kay, Arthur and his mother, the bankers and their wives—turned, then, to find O'Neil beside her, smiling, then taking her elbow in his hand. C'mon, he said. The band was playing something, she guessed, you could lindy to. I won't tell my shrink if you don't. You do dance, right, Ma?

She looked at him, pleasure filling her like water pouring into a vase: her grown son just back from his first two weeks of college, all smooth white teeth and rangy limbs, his eyes glowing with champagne. How had it happened? Why did she miss him so, when he was standing right there? She hadn't cried during the wedding but now it seemed she was about to; it was possible she would begin to cry and never stop, so she let him take her to the dance floor, place his hand at the small of her back, and steer her into and through the music—when had he learned to do this?—then spin her out to the ends of his fingers, catching her before she flew away. She saw herself, as if from the corner of her eye: a blur of blue dress, arcing like a comet's tail away from the sun's bright

heat and light; the boy in his gray suit, taller by far than she, hurl-
ing her outward and reeling her in again. As the song's last bars
approached he folded his arms over her somehow, catching her
weight as he tipped her back on one foot; her other foot rose, and
before she knew what had happened her full weight was in his
arms. Her hair skimmed the floor, blood filling her skull in a
dizzying rush; O'Neil, her boy, had his mama in a full dip. As he
returned her to a standing position she detected, around her, a
smattering of jokey applause.

As the next song began he tipped his head across the floor toward his sister and Jack, who was wiping the lenses of his heavy
eyeglasses on a handkerchief.

"Aw, he's not so bad, Ma," O'Neil said. He handed her a glass
of ice water; she hadn't even seen him get it. "You know? So it'd
be okay to lighten up a little. At least for Kay."

The remark startled her. Had she been so obvious? And it was
true, about Jack: he seemed rigid and fusty to her, not at all like
the boys Kay had dated in high school and then college—clever,
flirtatious, quick with a joke—and not at all like O'Neil or his
friends, whom Miriam adored. She drank the water O'Neil had
handed her, surprised to find how much she wanted it. No, she
couldn't quite bring herself to like him, much as she'd tried. From
the first day Kay had brought him home to visit, she had thought
it; his life was a train he expected her to board. She saw it all: the
old station wagon strewn with toys and the sacks of groceries in
back, the dry dinners with deans and visiting economists, the bur-
rowing claws of life on the margins of some small college town.
(And wasn't it also true that she, Miriam, had never really gotten
along with Kay? That love was one thing but getting along was
something else, and there had been, well, certain difficulties, certain unnameable tensions, between them? That this gap was the
very one Kay had chosen to fill with Jack? Making it, in the end,

Miriam's fault?) So, no. She didn't like him, not one bit. But more than this, she had forgotten—actually *forgotten*, if for a moment—that the party was her daughter's, not O'Neil's. The yellow stripes of the tent, the band's silly music, the crispness of the autumn air, and the calming presence of the waiters and waitresses gliding through the company with trays in their hands—she had forgotten that all of this has been called into being by her daughter's decision to marry Jack.

"Mom? Come in, Mom."

She looked up to find O'Neil, grinning and wagging his eyebrows. A waiter moved past, and she placed the empty water glass on his tray, trading it for a full one of champagne.

"Ammunition," she said then, and drank; she smiled back at O'Neil, who was drinking too. She thought about telling him to go easy on the champagne, but decided quickly not to. Beyond the walls of the tent it had begun to grow dark, blue afternoon bruising to black. One of the caterers was firing up the propane heaters that hung on poles in each of the tent's four corners.

"All right, hon." She put down the empty champagne glass. "The mother of the bride will go ask her son-in-law to dance."

"Now you're talking." He rolled his eyes. "I'm sure that will be, you know, interesting. Jack is an interesting guy."

"Very," she agreed, and touched his sleeve. "But I'm not doing it to make you laugh. For Kay, like you said."

And so she danced with Jack (O'Neil, solving a problem, appeared at that moment to take Kay by the arm and whisk her off across the floor); she danced with him not once but twice, and though he talked her ears off—all nonsense about his dissertation and his theories of wage and price controls, and which uncle was a partner in which St. Louis investment firm, as if she might someday have some serious money to spend in St. Louis—she found herself, for that time, liking him, almost, just as O'Neil had hoped. He was just a nervous boy, not really a man at all, uncertain how to dance with a grown woman or where to place his gaze and what to say to her while he did so (nothing; *Say nothing*, she thought). He was doing his very best, in other words, and what else was there to wish for? When it was over, he made a little bow, awkwardly hugged her; looking over her shoulder, he might have actually called her Mom.

The sound of a car horn: Arthur, idling at the curb, is waving to her from the wheel of the mud-spattered Peugeot. Miriam buttons her coat again and heads outside to meet him. Their suitcases are in the backseat, as promised, and a surprise: beside them she sees their old wicker picnic basket, with a wool blanket folded neatly on top. Greasy diesel fumes huff out the tailpipe and are whisked away into the autumn air.

"Sorry." He makes a flustered gesture with his hands. "I decided to pack a lunch. And I couldn't find the goddamn cat again."

"You and Nestor need to work some things out." She arranges herself in the front seat. "Anyway. You did find him? And left him some food? We're not abandoning him to the foxes, in other words?"

"He was under your dresser."

"Ah." She nods. "I see. *My* dresser. Sounds like a conspiracy."

"Mimi, I just got held up." His voice, though apologetic, is impatient too. He has been late for nearly everything his entire life; his voice says she should be used to it by now. "I said I was sorry. I had some work to do."

"So you did." She hears herself sigh; the urge to fight has passed. "Oh, it's all right, Art. I should be, but I'm not really mad at all." She leans over the gearbox and—why not?—kisses her husband's cheek. She knows this will surprise him, and it does; as she pulls away, Arthur reaches with his hand to the place on his face where she has kissed him.

"Now," she says, slapping her knees to tell him it's over and to get the car in gear, "let's go rescue our boy."

Arthur and Miriam, on the road; an hour of winding country lanes—woods and towns and gas stations floating by, everything denuded and bathed by a thin autumnal light—and then they join the interstate, a pulsing artery of commerce headed east into New England. In Albany they change places in the parking lot of a McDonald's—it is just after two o'clock—continue into Massachusetts and the Berkshires, and stop at a state park near Great Barrington to eat the sandwiches and drink the soup that Arthur has packed.

They arrive at the college after six, its great buildings ablaze with light. Despite the cold, students are everywhere. Doors and windows are open; music pours forth across the little town. They check into their hotel on the edge of campus and then telephone O'Neil in his dorm room. In the background Arthur can hear something like a party going on—loud voices, doors slamming, a girl laughing over the sound of a horn section and twanging guitars.

"Sorry," Arthur says, "we got a bit of a late start."

"What?" O'Neil says. "Will you guys shut the hell up? Hang on, Pop." There is a muffling silence as his son smothers the receiver to yell something over the music. When his voice comes back on the line, the music is gone. "We're all just cramming for midterms here. Very intense stuff."

"I could tell. Sorry we're late."

"Sounds like a story." O'Neil laughs at something Arthur can't see. "Mom there?"

"In the shower. Have you had your fill of fun already, or do you still want to eat?"

"When didn't I? The stuff they serve here is like army rations. Want to know what they gave us last night? Salmon loaf and pea-cheese sauce. We thought it was a joke, like Eat this, and that's what you'll do: you'll pee cheese-sauce."

"Lovely," Arthur says, laughing. "Bring Sandra, if you want. We're all pretty excited to meet her."

"Sandra who?" His son lets the question—a joke, Arthur realizes—hang for a moment. "Kidding. But she's got a rehearsal. It'll be just me, I'm afraid."

Thirty minutes later they go downstairs to find O'Neil in the lobby, sitting on the sofa and reading from a stack of alumni magazines on the coffee table. He has dressed up a little, wearing pressed khakis and a navy wool blazer with a slender black necktie hanging loose around his throat. But what Arthur notices first is the haircut. O'Neil has always worn his hair long, in loose curls that hang over his ears. All of that is gone, replaced by a spiky crewcut. Their boy rises, smiling at the sight of them, and catches them both in a long-armed hug.

"Honey," Miriam says mournfully. "Oh, God, I know I shouldn't say anything. Your hair?"

O'Neil grins self-consciously and runs a hand over his scalp. "It was funny, but I just woke up one day and thought: I have to get rid of all this hair. I actually skipped a class just to go to a *barbershop*."

Miriam reaches out to touch his hair but stops herself, stroking the air just inches from his head. "Well, it can always grow back," Miriam says.

"All the guys on the team are getting it cut like this now," O'Neil says. "Some of the girls too."

"I think it looks great," Arthur chimes in. "Very 1962. I think I had one just like it."

O'Neil smiles. "See, Mom? That's the idea."

The steakhouse where they usually go will be too packed by now with the parents' weekend crowd, so they agree to eat at the hotel, taking seats in the bar while they wait for a table. Miriam, pleading exhaustion, orders a club soda, and Arthur his usual Dewars and water; when the waitress asks O'Neil what he wants, he thinks a moment, and then asks for a club soda too.

"You know, the hardest thing for most of the guys on the team is not drinking," he says, chewing a mouthful of peanuts from a bowl on the bar. "They catch you, you're off, no question." He reaches into the inside pocket of his blazer and produces a photograph. "That's Sandra."

The girl in the photo is younger looking than Arthur expected, and a good deal prettier. The photo is of the two of them, standing arm-in-arm before a brick building that Arthur recognizes as O'Neil's dormitory. Her hair isn't brown, as he imagined, but a bright shade of blond that verges on red, a red that reminds Arthur of certain autumn leaves—though the picture, he realizes, was taken months ago, before the summer had gone. The grass at their feet is lushly green, and they are both dressed for warm weather and sunshine, O'Neil in his nylon running clothes, Sandra in white tennis shorts and a T-shirt. On her head, covering most of her hair and dimming her eyes and brow into shadow, she wears a baseball cap—navy blue, with a red *B* for the Boston Red Sox. The way the shadows fall makes Arthur think that the photograph was taken just before sunset, and the two of them are on their way to dinner, or to change for dinner. Sandra is small, the top of her head rising only to O'Neil's shoulders, and a bright splash of freckles dresses her cheeks and nose, which is button shaped and turned slightly upward as she looks into the photographer's lens. Arthur knows he should say something about how pretty she is, and when he does, his son smiles with happy relief.

"Sox fan, I see," Arthur adds.

O'Neil shrugs. "I guess. Really, she just likes hats. She's what you would call a hat person."

"She's in a play?" Arthur asks.

O'Neil frowns in confusion. "No. Well, she has been, but she isn't now. What gave you that idea?"

"You said she had a rehearsal."

"Oh. I did, didn't I." O'Neil nods. "Actually, it's a jazz band. She plays the trombone, if you can believe it. You'll hear her tomorrow night."

Arthur laughs at his son's embarrassment, though he also knows that this is exactly the kind of thing he likes about her. What does anyone like? Freckles, the curve of hair where she tucks it behind an ear, the sound of her voice when she tells a joke, her great, gleaming trombone in its velvet case. O'Neil has had girlfriends before, but this, Arthur knows, is different; he is entering the web, the matrix of a thousand details that make another person real, not just an object to be wanted. Beside him Miriam, looking at the photo, hasn't said anything.

"Hey," Arthur says, "the trombone can be very sexy."

"I don't know how she does it all," O'Neil says. "There's field hockey and band. She's starting this year, so next year she'll probably be varsity, and she's on the lacrosse team too. Then, she's, like, a straight-A student, doubling in bio and English, with all her premed courses on top of it." He shakes his head, amazed. "Some days it's all I can do just to get out of bed and go to class."

"Seems like she's a good influence," Arthur says. "Don't you think, Mimi?"

Miriam manages a smile and passes the photo back to Arthur, who hands it to O'Neil. "She sounds like a lovely girl," Miriam says.

"It's true," O'Neil says, and laughs at himself. "God knows what she sees in me."

They each have two drinks before they are seated at a table and order dinner. The hour is just nine, but already O'Neil is yawning. Every time this happens he apologizes and makes a joke about how they're not really boring him, it's just the running, all the workouts this past week for tomorrow's race.

"You don't really have to come," he says, smearing a piece of bread with cheese from a crock on the middle of the table. "We're going to get hammered, anyway. We're completely overtrained. You should go to the field hockey game instead. Sandra's just JV, but those girls are really *good*."

The food is so bad it's actually funny—everything over-cooked and drenched with heavy sauce—and in the end, O'Neil eats most of what's on his parents' plates in addition to his own. An amazing performance: he caps off the meal with a slab of chocolate pie while Arthur and Miriam share a pot of watery tea. They offer to drive him back to his dormitory, but in the lobby he changes his mind; the walk will do him good, he says, to help him digest all of it before the race, which is at one o'clock the next afternoon. Arthur goes up to their room and returns with a hat and scarf, to keep him warm on the walk home.

"I meant what I said," O'Neil reminds them, winding the scarf around his throat. "You really don't have to come. There's not much to see even if we do okay. You'll be pretty much just wait-ing around to watch me drag up the rear."

"We're here to be with you," Miriam says. She steps up and hugs him, quickly. "There's no way we're missing it."

From the doorway they watch him trot down the walk, head hunched down against the cold, not looking back.

"He's probably going to see her," Miriam says.

"Wouldn't anybody?" Arthur asks. "You saw that picture." He gives a little admiring whistle. "Holy moly."

A silence falls over them. Miriam hugs herself against the cold air moving through the open door. It is certainly cold enough to snow; under the lights of the hotel Arthur can see shimmering puddles of ice just beginning to form on the flagstone walkway. Finally she says, "I'm sorry."

"What for?"

"This morning." She shrugs. "In the car. All of it. I'm not being a good sport, am I?"

"You're the mom. You love your kids. There's nothing to be sorry about."

Upstairs, Arthur showers and puts on his pajamas, then sits in darkness on the edge of their bed. He feels a slight movement under the covers and turns to see that Miriam is laughing.

"What's so funny?"

It takes her a moment to speak. "Your *face*," she manages. "When you looked at that picture. You should have seen yourself." She rises on the pillows and touches his arm to reassure him. "I'm sorry, Art. It was just so funny."

Arthur climbs under the covers beside her. "She is pretty," Arthur says. "You know, I think she reminded me of you."

"No, she didn't," Miriam says. She turns and puts her arms around him. "You're very sweet, but you don't have to say that."

"Nothing sweet about it," Arthur says. He kisses her, and feels sleep coming. "It's true."

Arthur and Miriam, out of town: they awaken late, eat a breakfast of coffee and sweet rolls in the hotel lobby, then set out on foot to the campus to find O'Neil. It is nearly eleven; the day is bright and icy cold. Overnight, a mass of clear arctic air has moved in, and the effect is vaguely kaleidoscopic, all the colors and shapes of the town and campus at once less than real and somehow more. Above the college's stone entranceway a banner says, Welcome Parents, and beneath the bare trees and blue, blue sky, the wide lawn of the college's main quadrangle floats like a plate of ice.

They arrive at O'Neil's dormitory, hoping to surprise him

with a bag of muffins filched from the hotel breakfast buffet, but no one answers the door when they knock. A moment of confusion: Didn't they arrange to meet him here? Then, as they're leaving, they run into his roommate, Stephen, on his way back from the shower. They have known him for years; O'Neil and Stephen went to high school together, and though the college did not let them share a room freshman year, now they are together again. Stephen, who is tall and fair with a long nose and a hairline that's already receding, is wearing a terry-cloth bathrobe and carrying a plastic basket of toiletries under his arm. Behind one ear is a dab of shaving cream. He seems startled to see them, but after an awkward moment he hugs Miriam and shakes Arthur's hand.

"He left, like, an hour ago," Stephen explains. The door across from Stephen and O'Neil's room opens, washing the hallway with the smell of cigarettes and the sound of Steely Dan. Miriam recognizes the record—it is one that O'Neil played all through high school. A young woman Miriam doesn't know steps from the room in a silk dressing gown, says hello to Stephen, and heads down the hall to the showers, humming the song as she goes. Miriam tries not to look but does; her hair is a thick, glistening black, like a curtain of velvet, and the way she walks, her bare feet silently striking the hallway's green carpet, suggests that, beneath the gown, she isn't wearing anything at all. The smoke from her cigarette follows her like a laugh.

"I wasn't even awake yet, really, but I heard the door," Stephen says, yawning. Miriam wonders if Stephen is lying, to cover for O'Neil—did he even spend the night there?—but decides not to say anything about this. "You can probably catch him over by the grandstands. I think he thought you were meeting him there."

They leave the muffins with Stephen, who is biting into one even as he's saying good-bye, and head back out into the bright day. By the grandstands, a five-minute walk away, they find O'Neil in his sweats, milling around with the other members of the cross-country team. A few students and parents are already sitting in the aluminum bleachers, chatting and hugging themselves in the cold. O'Neil explains the course: five miles down trails through the woods that abut the playing fields, then up the hill into the middle of town, and back to the starting line. He hasn't shaved, and his hair, despite its length, seems disheveled, as if he had only awakened moments ago. On the other side of the field a fancy motorcoach is parked, and Miriam can see the other team stretching out in their shimmering violet sweatsuits. The race is thirty minutes away.

"God, why did you let me eat all that?" O'Neil is on the grass, sitting Indian style, though the bottoms of his running shoes are somehow together. He bends forward at the waist, his forehead dropping to his knees in a single liquid motion. "Never mind. My fault, right? The chocolate pie was definitely a mistake, though. I was up moaning half the night."

"Is Sandra going to be here?" Arthur asks.

"You know, I thought she would be, by now." He rises nimbly and does half a dozen quick hops on his toes. Miriam can practically feel the energy coiled in him, a spring about to release, chocolate pie or no. O'Neil scans the scene, looking for Sandra, and shrugs when he fails to find her. "I'm sure she'll show up. I told her you were coming, and if that doesn't get her here, nothing will."

"I'm beginning to think you invented her," Miriam says.

"Trust me, Mom." O'Neil smiles confidently. "I couldn't have made her up if I tried." Still standing, he spreads his legs wide, pivots on the balls of his feet, and drops one knee to the grass. "God, I feel just awful. At least it's cold," he says. "I'm better when it's cold."

O'Neil introduces them to some of his teammates and then to his coach—a surprisingly young man, not much older than the runners themselves, with a woolly beard and long black hair—and then shoos them to the grandstands, to wait for the race to begin. By the starting line O'Neil and his teammates have stripped to their shorts and tank tops and gathered in a tight circle around their coach, their bodies making constant small movements even as they listen to what he's telling them. They break apart then, each finding someplace nearby to go. Some jog in place, or stretch; others merely stand quietly, waiting.

"What are they doing?" Arthur asks.

Miriam watches. O'Neil is one of the quiet ones. Apart from the others, he has selected a spot fifty feet from the starting line, near a line of parked cars. His hands dangle limply at his sides, and his head is slightly bowed; even at this distance, she can see him breathe, and knows by the rhythm of his rising chest that his eyes, turned down, are closed.

"He's being alone with it," she says.

A hush has fallen over the crowd; everyone, parents and friends, has been led into this moment of silence, like a prayer before mass. The runners gather at the starting line.

"This is it," Arthur says.

Miriam looks to O'Neil, who has taken a spot in the middle of the line, between two runners from the opposing team. She knows at once that he will do well, better than he has ever dared imagine, that this day will be his. Her confidence is absolute; she knows this fact as certainly as she knows his name. She says it then—"O'Neil"—and as she does, the runners crouch, the gun appears from nowhere, and with a single report, they're off.

She rises to her feet. "Go!" she cries, and the two teams burst away. "Go! Go! Go!"

*

Arthur in the bleachers, thinking of Dora Auclaire: his son is running—the two teams are gone; in seconds they have flown over the field and disappeared into the woods—and yet his mind has drifted away from all of this, crossing two state lines and traveling half the width of New York State to alight in his office, where the letter waits in his desk. Unsent but sealed, it is, like his wave on the street a week ago, one more thing half finished. When he mails it, he knows, these many months of secrecy will all be over, and he can rejoin his life. And yet he has not done this. He was already so late another delay would hardly have mattered; he could have dropped it off at the clinic (no: he would have seen her, stopped to talk) or paused at the post office on his way home to feed the cat and pick up their bags. He could have, but didn't, and so here he is, thinking of her.

"Did you see that?" Miriam says. She is pointing across the field. "That kid tripped him. He almost went down."

"Where? What kid?"

Her tone is sharp; she lifts her eyebrows with impatience, and all at once he returns to her. Miriam. The race. A bright cold day in fall.

"The tall one, Art. At the starting line." She frowns incredulously. "How could you have missed it?"

He smiles; she knows he has no idea what she's talking about. "Well, no harm done. Or was there?"

"Sometimes, it's like your head is a big empty dance-hall, Art." She squeezes his arm. "No. No harm done."

As O'Neil predicted, for the next twenty-five minutes, until the runners return, they have nothing to do. To keep warm they walk around the infield, where students and other parents, about thirty of them, have gathered in little groups to talk and pass the time sipping hot cider from foam cups. For a while they fall into conversation with a man and his wife, parents of one of O'Neil's teammates, up from New York City for the weekend. Arthur wonders about Sandra, if she has arrived yet, but supposes she hasn't; O'Neil would have said so, even just to tease them, to make them guess. He is thinking about this and looking over the crowd to try to pick her out when a cry goes up.

Impossibly—so little time seems to have passed—the first runner has appeared at the edge of the woods. Like the point of a wedge he leads the other runners in a long arc around the field, a jostling mass of gold and violet. Arthur looks for O'Neil, doesn't find him, then does, about midway through the first pack, five or six runners off the leader. Everyone scrambles toward the finish line, where both coaches are counting out the seconds on their stopwatches.

"Where is he?" Miriam is saying. She bounces on her toes, looking over the heads of the crowd. "Where is he?"

"There." Arthur points, and then it happens, as it always does: all the memories he carries inside him of track meets and soccer games and piano recitals and class plays—twenty years of watching his son from the sidelines of playing fields and the back of dark auditoriums—suddenly organize themselves, like the plot of a novel or movie, leading to this moment. Excitement wells up inside him, a huge and desperate desire to see his son do well, a feeling so intense he would step out of his body if he could. He hears his voice, and Miriam's, the two of them yelling:

"Go, go, go!"

For the final moments of the race everything seems to slow. As the runners take the last turn around the field, O'Neil makes his move; he has kept something for the kick and in a burst he uses it, passing one runner and then another, his arms and legs moving in perfect headlong syncopation. Even so far away Arthur believes he can see his son's face, and the pain that is etched across it.

"Thirty-seven, thirty-eight, thirty-nine . . ."

The first runner crosses the line, the pack just steps behind. Arthur can hear his voice, yelling his son's name, and he is yelling still when O'Neil crosses the finish, a split second off third place. He expects his boy to collapse on the ground, utterly spent, but this doesn't happen. O'Neil slows to a stop, grinning, his chest heaving, his hands riding his slender hips, and then looks upward toward the bleachers, his eyes narrowed in a squint. Arthur, at the finish line, is about to call out O'Neil's name to show him where they are, but then O'Neil finds who he is looking for—not Arthur and Miriam, but a girl whom Arthur knows is Sandra. Somehow he has missed her; or perhaps she has arrived late, after Arthur had stopped looking. She bounds down the aluminum bleachers and at once is beside him.

Arthur hears Miriam whisper, "God."

"Steady," Arthur says, and takes her elbow. "Let's go see."

O'Neil is almost too euphoric to notice them. "Can you *believe* it? Fourth place." He shakes his head in utter amazement. "I've never done that well. Not even close. It was the last turn when I knew I could do it. I saw myself passing those guys, and then I just did."

He introduces Sandra, who shakes first Miriam's hand and then Arthur's, meeting his grip with a firmness that is at once surprising and completely natural. The last runners are crossing the line, and in the confusion Arthur has the chance to look at his son's new girlfriend—to examine her without seeming to. She is prettier, even, than in the photograph—her eyes are somehow brighter, bluer, her hair a truer shade of gold—but her beauty, Arthur decides, is not the kind that everyone would necessarily notice, nor something she herself is aware of, as some pretty girls are. She is wearing jeans and a wool cap, like a beret, and a puffy nylon ski jacket, navy blue and zipped to the collar against the cold; Arthur can see, peeking through the neckline, a pink oxford shirt with a threadbare collar that he recognizes as his son's—a shirt, in fact, that used to be Arthur's. He can tell she is as surprised as Arthur is that O'Neil has done so well, and that her surprise is part of his son's happiness; it is an unexpected gift he has given both of them.

When the last runners have crossed, the coach steps up and claps O'Neil on the back. "See what I'm saying? About the kick?" He puts his bearded face close to O'Neil's and thumps the middle of his chest with the butt of his fist. "You have to go *in*." He turns to Arthur and Miriam and shakes their hands again, as if meeting them for the first time.

"Your son ran quite a race," he says. "I don't know what you fed him last night, but do it again sometime."

Despite O'Neil's surprising finish the team as a whole hasn't done that well. Most have finished in the second pack, well behind the leaders. Their strongest runner, whom they were counting on to place in the top three, twisted an ankle out on the course and was forced to drop out. O'Neil points him out, an ordinary-looking boy hobbling around the infield with a sack of ice in his hand.

"I guess he didn't go *in*," O'Neil says. "To tell the truth, I can't stand that guy. He's a good runner, but that's not everything."

Arthur looks away from the boy and returns his gaze to O'Neil, who is putting his sweats back on and sucking a wedge of orange that someone has handed him. The pleasure he feels in his son, he knows, is something new. He is watching his son step into himself, into life. Suddenly Arthur knows that, from this day, the love that he feels for O'Neil will be a different kind of love. His son's transformation cannot be stopped, or hastened, or adjusted; the man he will become is already present, like a form emerging from a slab of stone. All that remains is to watch it happen.

"Let's celebrate," Arthur says. He turns to Miriam, realizing suddenly that he has almost forgotten she is there; he has forgotten Sandra, too, walking beside his son with their arms wrapped around one another's waists, like any couple.

At the edge of the field O'Neil stops. "Great," he says. "Well, actually, I should go back for a while." He tips his head over his shoulder toward the bleachers, where the two teams are still gathered. "It's the last meet of the season. Sandra has a game to get ready for too."

"That's right." Arthur gives her his best smile, though he is disappointed; he would like to have O'Neil to himself for a while. "Field hockey, right?"

She shrugs modestly. "It's just JV."

"JV nothing," Arthur says. "I hear you girls really kick some ass."

Sandra laughs at this, knowing, as she must, that she is hearing O'Neil's words played back by his father. They agree to meet instead for dinner, after her game, and that Arthur and Miriam will spend the day shopping in town. The question of Sandra's parents turns out to be no question at all; they are out of the country, she explains, sailing in the Caribbean.

"Did you notice the shirt?" Arthur asks later. They have returned to their room to change for lunch; they are planning to eat someplace nice, to make up for last night's bad meal at the hotel. Miriam is sitting on the bed, wriggling out of her jeans and into a pair of warm wool slacks. Arthur, at the mirror, slides the knot of his necktie to his throat.

"What are you talking about?"

"Sandra's." He can't say why he's brought the subject up; he wonders if he's being mean. "It's not important, I guess. Under her coat? A pink oxford, frayed at the collar." He shrugs, and resumes tying his tie. "I thought maybe it was one you gave me once."

Miriam flops back on the mattress to pull her slacks on the rest of the way. "I've never given you a pink shirt in my life," she says.

Miriam sleeping, dreaming of birds: a silly and disturbing dream, in which all the birds—ravens, parrots, sparrows, canaries—are wearing hats. Why are you wearing hats? she wants to ask. Do birds wear hats now? Was it always this way? She is in an empty room, she is at the hospital—not the one in Cooperstown, but a hospital from years ago—she is alone in a field of purple heather and can't find her children; the birds are responsible, the birds have taken them away. Arthur is beside her now. *See?* he is saying. *It is all so simple. The children are gone; they have flown away from you.* She turns then but it is no longer Arthur beside her; her father is there now, wearing a white shirt and suspenders to hold up his gray trousers. She breathes him in, a smell like the color blue. Pure happiness fills her, as if she has stepped into a beam of light. Daddy, she says, Daddy, I thought you'd died. *Oh, baby girl,* he says, and touches her wet cheek; *oh, baby girl, I'm sorry, I did.*

She awakens then in the half-dark room, a room she doesn't remember at all. Her mind is adrift, unfixed; she feels almost afloat. Across from her she sees a bureau with a porcelain washbasin and pitcher, and on the nightstand, a telephone, with instructions taped to the dial. The hotel, she remembers. She is at the hotel, in New Hampshire. It is Saturday. O'Neil has run his race—a sudden pleasure fills her, not only for his victory but the fact that she knew, in advance, that it would occur—and she and Arthur had lunch together after, and wine besides, and returned to their room for a nap. The clock on the table says that it is just past four; at six they will meet O'Neil and Sandra for dinner. Beside her Arthur softly snores.

What is wrong with me? she thinks. *Why can't I like this girl?*

She reviews, in order, O'Neil's girlfriends of the past: sweet little Ellen, whom he used to buy Cokes for at school dances; the vaguely Asiatic, exotically named Ione, almost certainly his first kiss (she had caught them, or nearly, standing too close and blushing at the bottom of the basement stairs); the girl who she has always thought of as "ninth-grade Nancy," plump and funny and without question the smartest of them all (at MIT now, she's heard, and *thin*); the blur of Betsys and Danielles and Sarahs and Elizabeths in the last two years of high school, when there was always some new voice in the kitchen on Saturday evenings and O'Neil, in so many ways, had begun to hit his stride. *Why can't I?*

She finds herself thinking, then, not of Sandra but of Kay, realizing that she hasn't spoken to her in at least two—three?—weeks. (Though if Kay wanted to talk, she could have called herself. And isn't silence, in its way, a good sign? That everything is well, that the ship is still steaming safely away from shore?) Disapproving, moody Kay. How like Kay to make Miriam feel so awful, suddenly, about everything, by doing nothing, by simply existing at the far end of a telephone line running from this hotel room to the apartment in New Haven that she shares with her husband, Jack—dreary, low ceilinged, and filled with obscure, unreadable books and rickety graduate-student furniture. What has Kay ever wanted except to be left alone? Even when she imagines Kay now, when she goes to the past to think of her child, she sees her at a distance; this little girl with curly brown hair, frowning at her dull and meaningless toys, waiting only for the moment when she could leave them all behind. It was as if Kay was born with a secret she was determined not to share, the secret of who she was. Of all the difficulties Miriam had imagined, this was the one she had never anticipated: that her child should seem not to love her, to acknowledge her as important and real. Other parents complained about their teenagers, how these sweet, cuddly children who had doled out love in generous heaps had, almost overnight, been reborn as intense and gloomy strangers who shrank from their very touch; how their bad hair, bad skin, bad moods, and bad friends were a symptom of some deeper, but one had to believe temporary, badness. On paper Kay was the daughter any mother would be proud of, a trouble-free honors student who spent her weekends reading fat Victorian novels and won a full ride early to Yale, tidy and polite, with a nugget of loyal friends whom Miriam knew less about than the inhabitants of a distant sun. It would have been a relief, almost, if Kay had run into some trouble: if she had missed curfew once or twice, come home in a daze smelling of beer or pot, or been caught smoking cigarettes behind the metal shop at high school; something, anything, to prove that she was angry and give her anger shape, a place at the table. But there was nothing. She lived in their house like a dowager boarder. There was no badness to complain about; there was just no Kay.

"Don't you like any of us?" Miriam had asked once, in despair. The insult was slight; Kay had declined, with her customary cool politeness, to go on a family picnic. She was fifteen, and had chosen to forgo a few hours of togetherness in healthy summer sunshine to finish a novel she was reading. (Not even one assigned for class; her homework, she confessed, was long done.) The car was packed. O'Neil and Arthur were waiting in the drive; Miriam had returned to the house half hoping to find Kay doing something wrong but had found her, instead, sitting at the kitchen table intently reading precisely the book she had professed a desire to read. The room was silent; not even the radio was playing. She had poured herself a glass of milk. At the sound of Miriam's voice Kay's eyes rose from the page, wearing an expression of bored concern that was, Miriam realized, completely parental. *What are you talking about?* her eyes said. *What on earth are you doing? I'm trying to read a book.*

"Don't take it personally. Of course I like you."

Miriam opened her mouth to speak, but what more was there to say? The disarming literalness of Kay's answer made anything else, any deeper probing, impossible.

"It's all right," Kay insisted. Her eyes returned to her book before she had even finished talking; she gave a little wave. "For goodness sakes, go have fun."

Now, ten years later, Miriam feels the humiliation of the moment afresh, how her fury and need had been twisted in on themselves, and turned into silence. She remembers almost nothing of the picnic itself; she remembers only this moment in the kitchen, and the one that followed, when she stepped from the house into the sunshine and surrendered to it, its blinding light and promise. *Fine. Fun. Read in the dreary kitchen if you must.* On the bed Miriam lets one hand rise to where the lump is; at the end of her fingertips she feels its firm, insistent shape, and allows her touch to linger there. (It could still, of course, be nothing; though wouldn't someone have said so, if it could be nothing? Whatever it is, it is not nothing.) Beside her, on the little bedside table, the telephone rests, unused.

She rises then, careful not to wake Arthur, pulls on a sweater and shoes and her coat, and leaves the hotel. Evening has fallen; the air is dry and very still, and lights are coming on. She walks alone to the center of town, toward the restaurant where she and Arthur had lunch, though that is not her destination. Horace Bullfinch, Glassworks: the sign hangs on iron hooks over the front door, its lettering crisply ornate, like the sign on an old-time apothecary shop. It is a large brick structure, half hanging over the dammed river, with a wheel that turns in the water beneath it. By the door, a wide glass window is fogged with steam.

She steps inside and finds herself in a large room with tables and chairs scattered about, and a counter for coffee and sweets.

On the far side she sees a wall of windows, looking out over the millpond, and beyond it a patio, with tables and chairs covered for the season. The room is empty except for a lone woman standing at the pastry counter, reading in the heat. Her eyes rise as Miriam enters; she nods, smiling emptily, and then returns to her magazine.

Stairs lead down to the basement. Miriam finds herself once again in a large room, though the space has been divided in half: a gift shop on one side, and on the other, behind a wall of thick Plexiglas, a demonstration area, where a man and a woman are working. Miriam sheds her coat and joins the small group of people who have gathered to watch. At either end of the space are two stone kilns, like bank safes, their interiors glowing with a churning heat; between, laid across long work tables, rest half-a-dozen long metal tubes. The process is a blur of detail. In the tiny work area the man and the woman move with a graceful and liquid surety, like a couple dancing, though they are dressed cumbersomely, for hard labor: heavy aprons and thick safety glasses, rubber gloves that reach to their elbows, denim jeans and shirts despite the heat that Miriam knows must be searing. Somehow they manage to maneuver their long poles in and out of the heat, from table to kiln and back again, never colliding with anything or with each other, but never speaking either. They are young, in their thirties; Miriam imagines—then is certain—that they are married. (No, she decides, not dancing; *cooking*. It is as if she is watching a couple cooking in a kitchen.) The woman wears her dark hair in a long, swinging braid, wonderfully thick, and has a strong, narrow face. Behind her goggles her eyes are calm, and shine with the reflected light of the kilns. In and out of the fire she guides her rods, a half dozen at her command, spinning them with quick intensity as they cool. As Miriam studies her, she holds one to her lips, puffs out her cheeks, and expels a steady exhalation of breath. At the other end of the tube a bubble appears; Miriam finds herself exhaling, too, a breath that she realizes she has been holding in anticipation. The bubble expands to the size of a Ping-Pong ball, then a tennis ball; its surface gleams with the wet translucence of a baby's fingernails. It seems perfect to Miriam, and yet the woman is not satisfied. Examining it, she frowns, then worries it quickly with a knife before reinserting it into the fire.

It is then that Miriam notices the small display table in front of the Plexiglas wall, and on it a solitary glass pitcher, no more than four inches tall, with a wide curling lip. The walls of the pitcher are voluptuously thick, like the cream that the pitcher itself is intended to hold. A tented slip of paper beside it bears the price: *$50.00*. Fifty dollars for a cream pitcher. She knows why she has come; she will buy the pitcher, as a present for Kay.

But in the gift shop the saleswoman tells her that they're sold out; the last cream pitcher is the one on the table, and not for sale. She offers to take an order for her—she can have the pitcher in just a week or two, the woman explains, certainly in time for the holidays—but Miriam shakes her head, no. The point is to have it now, to feel the pure pleasure of coveting something and receiving it immediately, in one smooth transaction of discovery; waiting even a week or two, she knows, would break the chain. She has resigned herself to leaving the shop empty handed—she has put on her coat and scarf—when something else catches her eye. On a shelf above the sales counter she sees a display of glass musical instruments, the size of Christmas ornaments. A guitar, a saxophone, a tiny, jeweled flute: each is miraculously detailed, made of a brittle, paper-thin glass like the skin of ice on a puddle just frozen. In all her life Miriam has never seen anything like them. She dares herself to peek at one of the dangling tags: *$140.00*. Astounding, she thinks. But it could be a thousand. In her heart she has already bought one. Who is it for? For O'Neil?

For Kay? For herself? Miriam finds the one she wants and lifts it gingerly from the shelf. She is surprised, and not surprised, to find that it weighs nearly nothing. The saleswoman stands silently beside her, wearing an expression of pleasurable expectancy that Miriam knows must be a mirror of her own. In her open palm she holds out the glass trombone for the woman to see.

"A gift," she says.

The evening's guest list expands: A phone call to O'Neil's room to tell them they're on their way, and now his roommate, Stephen, will be joining them, and his new girlfriend, Eliza—the girl from across the hall, with the black hair and silk robe and morning cigarette.

"None of their folks came up for the weekend," he explains to Miriam. "They're like little orphans."

In the background Miriam can hear laughter, and then Stephen's clear voice, reciting a line from *Oliver Twist:* "Please, sir, I want some more." In his hammy cockney accent the words come out as "Ple-*suh*, I want sum-*moa*."

"They're a sad sight," O'Neil says. "Besides," he whispers, "I sort of already made the offer."

"Did Sandra win her game?"

"That's the spirit, Mom. Yeah, a real blowout. She scored twice, and took a good one in the shins. I'll let her tell you all about it."

At O'Neil's dormitory everybody piles into the big Peugeot, the girls in the back seat, O'Neil and Stephen stretched out like oversized children in the wagon's cargo compartment with the jumper cables and bags of sand. The mood of the group is exuberant; Miriam wonders if the four of them have been drinking, and then wonders why she is wondering; it's a party, it's fine if they have. Turned in her seat, she chats with the girls about the hockey game—Eliza is on the team too—and listens to their gossip about other people she doesn't know, their coaches and teachers and classmates. Eliza, it turns out, is also from Boston; in the dark car her teeth shine very white—the white of china—and she laughs easily, more easily than Sandra, who seems, beside her, a figure of almost mysterious calm.

"I always knew O'Neil would have cool parents," Eliza says.

"You hear that, folks?" O'Neil calls from the back. "You passed."

Eliza lights a cigarette she has taken from her purse and opens her window to exhale a trail of smoke.

"Hey, you're freezing us back here!" O'Neil says. "Pee-ew!"

Eliza turns to Sandra. "Did you hear something?" She passes the cigarette back to Stephen, who takes a drag and hands it back, over his shoulder.

"What part of Boston are you from?" Miriam asks Eliza. Then, to Sandra, "Did you know each other before?"

The two women look at each other, and then, puzzlingly, burst into laughter.

"We're cousins," Sandra explains.

At the restaurant Miriam waits with O'Neil and his friends in the bar, while Arthur goes to find out about their table. When the two girls leave for a minute to go to the ladies' room, and Stephen is ordering drinks for everyone at the bar, she takes O'Neil's elbow.

"I wanted you to know," she says, "I think Sandra is just great."

"Well, she likes you too." He smiles and rocks back on his heels. "It's no big deal, Ma."

She wants to tell him about Sandra's present, stashed in her purse, but decides to let it be a surprise. She hasn't even told Arthur about it. With his friends along it will probably have to wait, anyway.

"Of course it's a big deal. If she's the one you like."

O'Neil shrugs, embarrassed. Stephen returns from the bar and hands each of them a drink: club soda for Miriam, a beer for O'Neil. The season is over.

"I know you don't like the haircut," O'Neil says. "I didn't tell you, but it was Sandra's idea. She's kind of nuts about short hair."

"And hats," Miriam says. For the evening Sandra has traded in her wool beret for a flapper's doeskin cap, pea-green, the front brim folded up and away from her forehead.

O'Neil laughs and holds up a finger. "Right. Don't forget hats."

By the time they get to the table, it is after eight. Sandra is due back at the college at nine-thirty, to help the other band members set up for the dance in the ballroom, so they all order their steaks and eat quickly, everyone talking and drinking and eating at once in the crowded restaurant. Miriam was disappointed, at first, when she learned that Eliza and Stephen would come along—that her time with O'Neil would be diluted in this way—but now she thinks better of this; it is good to see him with his friends, a part of something entirely his own. The four talk easily, finishing one another's sentences and laughing at jokes before they've ended, and though Sandra is the quietest one, Miriam can tell that she is, in some ways, the center, the planet around which they turn. When the conversation drifts too far into their college lives, it is always Sandra who leads it back to Arthur and Miriam, asking them questions about O'Neil or their stay in town, and always at a moment when this will seem natural. Stephen is the comedian, O'Neil the straight man who lets him shine; Eliza is the gay one, in love with her own beauty and the power it possesses. She flirts openly with O'Neil and even Arthur, but always offers something small—a sparkling glance, a touch of the hand—to Stephen, to remind him she's with him. Miriam knows that this is what her son has wished for: to show her and Arthur the new family he has made.

The last of the wine is being served when Miriam looks up to find Sandra's gaze upon her. A slightly too-long moment passes; then Sandra smiles.

"Let's thank our hosts," she says to everyone. Expressions of gratitude float over the table as goblets are raised. Miriam feels her face grow warm: how lovely to be thanked. But her pleasure goes deeper than this. These aren't children talking, but grown-ups. Their thanks are genuine, something they've chosen to offer.

"Let's not forget about your race," Arthur adds.

O'Neil laughs and lifts his glass. "Fourth place. The highlight of my career."

When they're done, Miriam whispers to Arthur to flag down their waitress so they can pay the bill, but it turns out he's already done this. Somehow he has slipped his credit card to the waitress and signed the bill without Miriam—or anyone—even noticing. As they're getting ready to leave, Miriam pulls Arthur aside in the vestibule. "Eliza was right about you," she says.

Arthur looks at her. "How's that?"

She takes his arm and winks. "*Very* cool."

Back at the college Sandra excuses herself to run ahead to the ballroom, and by the time the group arrives, they see her up on the stage with the other members of the jazz band, getting ready to play. Tables are spread out across the room where students and their parents are gathered; already a line has formed by the beer keg. The room is decorated with crepe paper and streamers and, over the stage, a large blue-and-gold banner, identical to the one at the college's front entrance, that reads, Welcome Parents. A mirrored ball hangs from the center of the ceiling, spangling the floor and walls with a confetti of colored light.

"You'll see, Mom," O'Neil says happily. He loosens his tie and nods at the stage, where Sandra is talking to other members of the brass section. She is easy to pick out, even in the darkened room, because of her hat. As Miriam is watching her, she brings her trombone to her lips, pumps the slide three or four times, and releases a single, crisp note. "They're really very good."

The room fills up with parents and students. Onstage the band readies itself to play, testing their instruments with random notes that tense the crowd with anticipation. Then there is a pause, the bandleader raises his arms, and the music begins. After just a few phrases Miriam knows what she's hearing: "In the Mood."

She pulls Arthur close to speak over the music. "My God." She laughs. "Just how old do they think we are?" But the band, as O'Neil predicted, is very good; already she can feel their precise rhythms moving through her. Why did she not think of this? A night of music: it's what she needs.

"Come on." Arthur steers her with a hand at her spine. "Let's dance."

She dances with Arthur, then O'Neil, then Stephen. A wonderful energy fills her. Song after song—"Satin Doll," "Sentimental Journey," "Something's Gotta Give," "Chain of Fools"—the dancing continues without rest. When the band finally breaks at nine-thirty, Sandra appears to drink a soda and dance with O'Neil—a DJ spins records to keep the party going—and then the band takes the stage again, kicking off their second set with a tart blast from the horn section and the theme from *Hawaii Five-0*. A wonderful, surprising, joke; whole tables rise to their feet and take the floor again.

The evening roars onward, a party so unexpectedly marvelous it cannot be refused. All through the second set Miriam dances; she cannot recall an evening when she danced so much, not for years and years. Arthur to O'Neil to Stephen and back again;

when the band pauses between songs, she gets herself a cup of beer—just awful, thin and warm as dishwater, but somehow perfect—and stands off to one side to catch her breath and watch.

Then O'Neil is at her side. His face is flushed with pleasure, his brow glazed with sweat. He takes her by the hand. "Ready?"

"No, really. I'm exhausted."

He laughs incredulously, and gives a little pull. "I won't take no for an answer."

"I just need a little breather, sweetie."

"I don't believe it." He frowns, though not seriously. "Well. The next one, okay? With Sandra up onstage we're one girl short."

She nods. She cannot help herself; how marvelous, she thinks, to be called a girl. "The next one."

She watches O'Neil head back into the crowd; she realizes that for the first time that evening, she is alone. And yet she does not feel alone. The wonderful music, the spinning lights, all O'Neil's friends there (for more have arrived; he seems to know everyone); she has the uncanny sense of stepping into his life, and all the promise it contains. With her eyes she searches the open floor again and finds O'Neil dancing with a dark-haired girl she does not recognize; she sees Arthur dancing with Eliza, and Stephen, a solitary figure at the base of the stage, swaying his hips and pumping his fist, a beer in one hand and a lit cigarette in the other; she sees Sandra swinging her trombone back and forth in time to the music's joyful rhythms. She knows that O'Neil has left her, that his life has begun, but the thought does not grieve her. It is as if time has thrown off its moorings, revealing all—that she, Miriam, has disappeared. She thinks of her father, gone twelve years, and her mother, too, sleeping her way into death not long after, as if it were not possible for her to remain in the world without him. A hole had opened; she had only to step through. After the funeral, the second in a year, Miriam walked alone through the Brooklyn apartment, not so much missing them as marveling at their absence. The places they had been, had sat and stood and walked and slept and eaten: fifty years of life in this place, and now they were gone. And yet their presence was vivid, palpable—a thing not seen but felt, like a parting of air. It was as if she were walking through the rooms of memory. She is remembering this, and watching too; the music stops—not the end of a song, merely a break in the action—the dancers stop in their tracks, and she sees O'Neil, the dark-haired girl swung out to the very tips of his fingers, throw back his head and laugh. The words, half remembered, form in her head. *See? It is all so simple. The children are gone; they have flown away from you.*

And this is when she feels it—the first pain. What she has experienced until now has been more of a presence, a sense of something *there*. It was this awareness that brought her fingers to her breast to find the lump two weeks ago. But now, at this moment watching her son and his friends dancing, her mind adrift in the past, a tiny ball of fire ignites within her. It rockets through her body with a nauseating rush, leaving her hands and feet tingling, her brow glazed, her throat constricted with bile. The room lurches below her; she reaches one hand outward to brace herself, but finds nothing to hold, to stop her fall. The wall, she thinks. The wall will save her. Three more steps and she is there.

Then someone has taken her by the elbow: it is Sandra, standing beside her. Wasn't she just onstage?

"Mrs. Burke?"

But Miriam cannot speak; she knows if she doesn't leave the room immediately she will be sick, or faint. The gymnasium seems like an enormous fishbowl, colors and shapes bending in the crooked, swirling light. At some impossible distance she sees

Arthur and Eliza dancing, like two figures swimming on the far side of a lake.

"I'm ill," she manages.

"I know. I'll help you."

A pair of metal safety doors, then the sudden white light of the hallway: guiding her by the elbow, Sandra leads her away, though Miriam is barely aware of any of this. All she knows is that the music is gone, sealed away behind her. Another door opens and she finds herself in a small room full of instruments; she is backstage, where the band keeps its supplies. Relief overwhelms her, like oxygen to the lungs. She realizes that she is sitting on a bench of some kind, and that Sandra has gone, but the moment she discovers this she looks up and sees that Sandra has returned, carrying her purse. She holds a paper cup of water before Miriam's face.

"Drink this," she says, and guides her hand around the cup.

Miriam lifts the water to her lips. It is cool but not cold, and she sips at it, thinking only of the water's taste, and her own pounding heart. The pain is gone, but in its wake it has deposited a kind of tingling numbness, scattered throughout her body like a luminous dust. *So this is what it will be like,* she thinks.

A few moments pass. She finishes the water, and Sandra takes the cup. "Do you need the bathroom?" Sandra has pulled a chair up, and is sitting directly in front of her.

"I don't think so."

"Do you want me to get Mr. Burke?"

Miriam shakes her head. "You've done more than enough. I just need to rest here a minute."

Sandra's eyes search her face. They are very blue—the blue of sapphires.

"He doesn't know," Sandra says then.

But before Miriam can say anything, Sandra goes on. "I didn't mean to surprise you. You haven't told Arthur, have you? Or O'Neil."

Miriam shakes her head. "No."

"And it's cancer? A kind of cancer."

Miriam nods, amazed beyond words. "Yes. I think so. I have a tumor in my breast. How did you—"

"It's all right." Sandra takes her hand. "I just do."

For a while they just sit there, their hands together. And Miriam is glad she has said it. Finally, she has used the words.

"I'll tell you how," Sandra says gently. "I don't know if it's the real reason, but I've always thought so. I was six years old, and I was diagnosed with non-Hodgkin's lymphoma. Do you know what that is?"

"I think so."

"Most people don't. I spent most of two years in the hospital. Little kids who get it nearly always die, but I didn't know that at the time. My parents sure weren't going to tell me. But I found it out, later. Chemo, radiation, things they'd never tried on anyone before. I had it all. And when it was over, I could always tell when someone was sick, even if they didn't know it yet. I guess I'd been around cancer patients so long, I could just read the signs."

"When did you know about me?"

"Well, when we first met, at the race, I thought it." Sandra tips one shoulder and frowns; Miriam can tell she has returned to the moment, to feel what it was like. "At dinner too. It was just an inkling. You'll probably laugh. Sometimes it's lights, or a sort of ringing sound. Sometimes it's just a feeling, like I'm remembering what it was like to be sick myself. I wasn't certain until I saw you just now, outside."

The understanding hits her all at once. "The hats," Miriam says.

"You've discovered my secret." Sandra smiles warmly, shrugging. "I just don't feel dressed without one."

The door opens then, washing the room with music and noise, and a heavyset boy steps inside. Like the other band members he is wearing a navy suit and a gold necktie, and his face is flushed with the exertion of playing. He stops when he sees the two of them.

"Christ, Sandy. Where have you been? We had to shuffle the playlist twice already. You were supposed to be off break ten minutes ago."

Sandra barely takes her eyes off Miriam. "Just a minute in here, all right, Joe? I'll be done soon. You can get along without me."

His face falls. "You don't have to be such a crank about it. We need sheet music for the third set, anyway." He kneels and rustles through a cardboard carton to find it, then leaves the two of them alone.

"We should probably get back," Miriam says.

"When you feel up to it." Sandra gestures toward the stage door. "They can fudge it for a while."

A question occurs to her. "Does O'Neil know about you?"

"About the cancer?" Sandra shakes her head. "I think he knows I was sick, but not the details. I'll tell him sooner or later. He thinks I'm just some kind of superachiever, and to tell you the truth, I don't want to spoil the illusion yet."

Her purse is at her feet; she remembers Sandra returning to get it. Miriam asks Sandra to bring her some more water, and Sandra leaves with the cup, reappearing almost at once. Miriam drinks it down—she hadn't realized she was so thirsty—and opens her purse to remove the small package with the glass trombone inside. She places it in Sandra's hands.

"It's just something small. I saw it today, and thought of you. But open it later. I don't want O'Neil to know just yet."

Sandra looks at the package in her palm. It is wrapped in thin white tissue paper, with a crinkly green bow. "I don't know what to say. Thank you, Mrs. Burke."

"You're welcome. And it's Mimi, okay?"

Sandra smiles. "Mimi, then."

They have risen to go when Miriam stops. "Sandra, this thing you can do." Miriam pauses, wondering what words to choose. "Can you tell if someone's going to be all right?"

Sandra doesn't answer. For a long moment she looks at Miriam, studying her, though her expression is nothing Miriam can read. Then she removes her hat, a dome of green felt, and places it on Miriam's head. The band is warm, and a little damp against her forehead.

"I'd say you will be," she declares, "if you go to the doctor."

Hours later, beneath the floodlights of the dormitory parking lot, they say their good-byes; Arthur and Miriam will be leaving in the morning, and won't see O'Neil and Sandra again. Miriam hugs each in turn, and watches as Arthur, awkwardly, does the same. As they are turning to go, Sandra hugs Miriam again, and whispers quickly in her ear, "I really believe it. Just remember what I said." O'Neil and Sandra are still standing in the parking lot when Miriam and Arthur drive away.

In the morning they awaken late to rumors of snow. They eat their breakfast and pack the car, and while Arthur is paying the bill, Miriam waits outside. The sky is gray, a northern gray; the air is very still. Around her the town and the campus are quiet, as if everyone is still asleep.

Arthur steps from the hotel. "I called O'Neil. I thought we might change plans and buy the two of them lunch."

"And?"

Arthur rubs his bare hands together in the cold. "He wasn't there. Or he wasn't answering. I left a message."

"It's just as well," Miriam says. In the pocket of her coat she carries Sandra's hat, folded, like a letter. "It's a long drive ahead. And they have things to do." She takes Arthur's hand. "It's time for Mom and Dad to let the kids be alone. Us too."

His face is incredulous. "You're okay with this, then?"

A new mood has filled her, a sense of lightness. "I think I was always okay," she says.

They drive away. Woods, houses, the limbs of the bare trees: Miriam watches the scenery from the passenger window, letting it all flow past, like pictures in an empty museum. Beside her in the quiet car Arthur drives with both hands on the wheel; with deft precision he negotiates each curve, each dip in the road ahead. She will tell him, she decides. She will tell him today, or else tomorrow, and he will be with her when she visits the surgeon on Tuesday, and then whatever happens, happens; but they will do it together, this last thing they have never done before, worrying together that one of them is finally dying.

They have driven just twenty miles when they see, up ahead, the low, barracks-like shape of a roadside motel, set against woods on a small rise above the highway. The sign hangs on a chain: Glade View Motor Court. Cable TV. Welcome Skiers! A dozen dismal rooms; they have passed it many times before, and each time she has imagined their interiors: the narrow, caved-in beds, the frayed shag carpeting reeking of old smoke, the floor-standing lamp that is also an ashtray. The idea arrives in her consciousness so fully formed it is like a memory of something that has already happened.

"Turn here," she says.

Arthur taps the brake. As the car coasts to the shoulder, he turns to her and raises an eyebrow in happy surprise.

"I'm not arguing. But, really?"

It is a little past noon. "Oh, just turn, love," she says.

November 12, 1979, Sunday afternoon. In room 106 of the Glade View Motor Court, Arthur and Miriam make love. They make love to one another in the icy room—the decor is just as bad as Miriam imagined—piling all the blankets they can find on top of themselves for warmth, and when it is over, they sleep—the happy, dreamless sleep of lovers.

It is after four when they awake. Dusk has fallen; through the paper-thin wall above their heads they hear the murmur of a television, and a man's voice saying, "Honey, watch this—you can see where the makeup stops on his neck. If that's a real gorilla, then I'm president of the United States." But they hear no reply; Miriam wonders if the occupant of the next room, whoever he is, is talking to himself. For a while they lie awake and listen, side by side but holding hands, though they hear nothing more from the other side of the wall; eventually the television goes off, and they hear the door of the next room open and close again. Outside in the parking lot a car engine roars to life.

Arthur rises to shower. Alone in the room, Miriam listens to hear if the man in the next room will return; when he doesn't, she flicks on the television, looking for the program he was watching, but can't find it. She watches a few minutes of a soccer game and then switches to a local station, where a woman in a canary-yellow pantsuit is giving the weather report, making broad, approximate gestures at a map of New England. Arthur is still showering; a slice of steam puffs under the bathroom door. She turns off the TV, settles back into the saggy bed, and then picks up the telephone from the nightstand. Kay answers on the second ring.

"Hi, sweetie."

"Mama?"

"It's me. We're in New Hampshire. We came up to visit your brother."

"I see. So, just how is the little squirt?"

"Not so little. He won his race. Well, not won. But he came in fourth. He's got a new girlfriend."

"So I've heard." Kay pauses. "Mama, where are you?"

"Where am I?"

"Your voice sounds . . . I don't know. Strange. Far away, maybe."

"Everything is fine, sweetheart. We stopped on the way home. I was just thinking about you, is all. How's Jack?"

"Jack, Jack. Let me see. Jack's at the library tonight, just like every other night. Jack is Jack, in other words. It looks like he may actually get that grant he applied for, by the way."

"The grant." Miriam searches her memory, coming up empty. She is suddenly so sleepy that at first she thinks her daughter is talking about somebody *named* Grant. "I'm sorry."

"It's not important, Mama. He applied for a university fellowship is all, so he doesn't have to teach while he finishes his dissertation. We talked about it a while ago, but I can see why you wouldn't remember." Then, "Do you really want to talk about Jack?"

"We could. He's your husband."

"So he is. This doesn't necessarily make him something to discuss, however. Mama? Is something going on there?"

Miriam touches her cheeks, and when her fingers come away glistening with moisture, she realizes she is crying.

"I think I'm just in a sad kind of mood. A winter mood. It's snowing here, I think. Or it's about to snow. I was just thinking about you."

"Well I was thinking about you, too, Mama. And you don't have to worry about me and Jack. He's really not so bad."

"Does he make you happy?" She is sorry the instant she has said it. "Forgive me. It's really none of my business."

"Of course it's your business, Mama. Why would you think that wasn't your business? And to answer your question, I guess I'd have to say that, on the whole, he has the *ability* to make me happy. I know a lot of women who don't get even that."

From the bathroom Miriam hears the groan of the pipes as Arthur shuts the shower off. "I think that's so. I was lucky with your father."

"Was?"

"Was what, honey?"

Kay hesitates. "You said 'was lucky.' Like you weren't lucky anymore."

"Did I? Well, that's wrong. Am, I mean." She nods her head against the pillow. "Am lucky."

A momentary silence falls, though not, to Miriam, an uncomfortable one. She listens to her daughter's breathing, even and clean, and her own, slower but somehow the same, mingling over the wires. In the glow of the lights from the parking lot outside, she imagines Kay in her cramped kitchen, sitting on a stool with the phone pressed to her ear, waiting to hear what she, Miriam, will next say.

"You know, I was thinking that I'd like to get Jack something special for Christmas this year. Can you let me know if there's something he'd like?"

"I will, Mama. That's sweet of you. I really will give it some thought."

"And not a book, though I know that's probably what he wants. Something more . . . I don't know. Personal."

"Okay, Mama."

"And for you, too, of course. If there's anything."

"There won't be, but thanks. Mama?"

"Yes, sweetie?" Her eyes are half closed.

"Is there something you're not telling me? Because the problem is, I have to go now. I really, really do. I have to pick up Jack at the library, and then we're meeting some friends for dinner. I was on my way out when you called."

"Oh." Miriam hears the disappointment in her voice. "Well, that's fine. We can talk later."

"If it was something I could change, I would. We haven't spoken in a while, and I'm really glad you called. But Jack's going to be waiting for me."

"It's really all right. You go get Jack."

"And everything's fine with you and Daddy?"

"Everything's fine, sweetheart."

"And the boyo's okay?"

She thinks of O'Neil standing in the dormitory parking lot, his arm around Sandra, as she and Arthur drove away. But the memory, she realizes, is not accurate. At the end they had stood together without touching.

"O'Neil's fine too. Don't you worry. You go get Jack, okay? He'll be waiting for you. Everything's all right. I love you, sweetheart."

"I love you, too, Mama."

And they hang up without saying good-bye.

Dusk in November, the last of the leaves pulled away; it is a little after five, and in the cities and towns of northern New England—in Rutland and Manchester, in Montpelier and Burlington, in Concord and St. Johnsbury and White River Junction and all the rest—the weathermen and air-traffic controllers see, on their radar screens, the same thing: the arrival of the first snowstorm of the season, a widening wedge of lights poking eastward from upstate New York and the Great Lakes. Their faith in their technology is absolute, a religion of professional habit, but they cannot help themselves; the eyes long to see what the mind already knows, and what science has predicted. They see the weather on the screen (there is something Christmassy about it, this expanding cone of light), and lift their gaze to the window, and the snow.

At a long wooden table in the college library, O'Neil takes no notice of the arriving storm; he has pushed his books and papers aside to place his head in the hollow of his folded arms, and is fast asleep, and dreaming. It is a simple, happy dream—a dream of springtime and a golden field in mountains—and O'Neil is both everywhere and nowhere in it. He is the mind of the dreamer and the dream itself, the sunshine and the dreamer of the sunshine, and his pleasure is intensified by a sense of recognition: though he does not know this and never will, it's a dream he's had for years. Beside him rest the leavings of his enterprise—his opened calculus text, a pad of paper on which he has scrawled the first equations of a problem set, his pitiless calculator, its batteries draining away—while all around in the high-ceilinged room, students are earnestly working, their minds trained like archers' arrows on tasks of great complexity. But nothing of this reaches him: not the scratch of their pens or the dry turning of their pages, not the buzz of the fluorescent lights or the muffled coughs and whispered conversations of a Sunday evening in a college library at midterm. Asleep, he soars alone through the vast interior space his mind has made—it seems not made of matter but light itself, to exist outside of time—and when at last he awakens, his dream of happiness exhausted, he raises his head from the table to the window to find his reflection looking back at him, and knows without seeing that beyond the darkened glass the sky has begun to issue snow.

Arthur, stepping from the motel room into autumn dusk, experiences the weather first as a kind of optical illusion; expecting neither snow nor darkness—the hour has escaped his attention— and disoriented from an afternoon in an unfamiliar place where he never planned to be, he sees stars instead, mixed with the cloud of his breath, and all the stars are falling. So persuasive is this vision that for a moment he is held captive by it, in mute awe of it. But then a lone car passes on the highway, traveling with an almost delicate slowness, and in the twin beams of its headlights Arthur sees the snow for what it is: the first, dry flakes of an approaching storm. He hears the soft sound of the car's tires on the road, and the metronomic rhythm of its wipers; as the car vanishes around the bend beyond the motel lot, he extends a single gloved hand past the edge of the concrete overhang and feels the barely de- tectable tap of crystals in his leathered palm, like a series of dis- embodied kisses. It is a strange and satisfying sensation—it seems both to encode this instance with a bright physicality, while also possessing all the familiar qualities of deep childhood recollec- tion, so that the moment is at once remembered and about to be remembered—and he knows what the next gesture would be, if he were a slightly different man; he would step beyond the over- hang, tip his head backward, close his eyes, and taste the snow on his tongue.

"Art? What's it doing out?"

Miriam's voice, coming from inside the room—the door is just ajar—nudges him from his reverie. Before answering he steps into the lot. On its packed gravel surface, and on the Peugeot's hood and windshield, a white dusting has taken hold. He tests for traction, shifting his weight without moving, and feels the soles of his loafers slide a little. It's hard to know how bad the driving will be. Probably not very bad to start, though they are headed west, into the heart of the storm.

"I think we'll be okay."

She joins him outside, wearing a sweater but no coat; her hair is wet from the shower. "The TV says six inches. More in New York." Her voice is noncommittal; she is merely presenting the evidence.

"We could stay the night here," he offers.

Miriam looks at the car, then back at Arthur. As always, when she doesn't know quite what she feels, or is presented with a choice that leads her no direction in particular, she pulls her eyes into a squint. "Is that what you want to do?"

The question hangs. And there is an answer, Arthur knows—something correct and patient that he should now say, that Miriam is waiting to hear and that it is his job to provide. To attempt this drive is foolishness. They already have a room. The Peugeot, an expensive disappointment, is not all it could be when the roads are slick. But he has already fallen in love with the idea, driving home through the snowy dark. He loves it because he can imagine it: the slow progress of the car, the sleepy stroke of the wipers, the whirl of flakes before the windshield, like water pushed from the prow, and the lights of the other cars on the highway, refracted in the snowy air; the dry wind of the heater and the hours of silence ahead. He imagines his wife asleep beside him, her body half turned in her seat and wrapped with the old blanket they keep in the car, a sweater or coat used to prop her head against the chilly window; he imagines arriving home in darkness, first into town, its streets quiet under all that new snow with no one about, not even the plows yet, and then the house itself. It is midnight, it is one, it is after two—who knows how long the drive will take? He will wait until the car is stopped and the engine is extinguished before he awakens her, to give her the present of their safe arrival. She stirs, rubbing her eyes. *Are we . . . ?* she asks. And, *How long was I . . . ?*

In front of their motel room he puts his arm around her waist and gives it a squeeze. "Come on," he says.

Their bags are already in the Peugeot; the only thing left to do is return the key. Arthur takes it to the office, where he finds the manager sitting behind the counter, smoking and watching a hockey game on a black-and-white television with aluminum foil crimped to the antenna. The picture is so bad, Arthur thinks, that watching it must be like listening to the radio. He places the key on the counter.

"We've decided to take off early," Arthur says, feeling that he should say something. "To get ahead of the weather."

The manager rises and accepts the key without comment, depositing it into a drawer under the counter. The carelessness of the gesture suggests to Arthur that it doesn't matter which key is which; perhaps they are all the same.

"I guess we'll be off now."

The manager, already back in his chair—green vinyl, with cigarette burns cut into its wooden arms—looks up, as if truly noticing Arthur for the first time.

"Right." He takes a long, distracted drag off his cigarette and taps it into a beanbag ashtray on the table beside him. "They say it could get bad."

"I was thinking that if we left right now, we could beat it."

The manager gives a thoughtful nod, then returns his gaze to the TV screen. "There's a theory," he says.

Leaving the lot for the highway, Arthur finds that the driving is surprisingly good. Already an inch has fallen, but the snow is dry, and the road lightly traveled; there has been no chance yet for the snow to melt and then refreeze as ice. He is mindful of the speedometer, keeping the car at just over forty miles per hour, but when he looks at it a moment later, he finds their speed has drifted upward to fifty. He taps the brakes; the wheels bite soundly.

"How is it?" Miriam asks with a yawn.

"Not awful." Arthur reaches over and touches her hand. "You want to sleep?"

She is halfway there. "For a while, maybe."

The highway from the motel heads due south, forming a lazy curve that traces the eastern foothills of the Green Mountains. Trees press close to the road; from time to time the forest opens on one side of the highway or the other, but it is too dark for Arthur to see anything, too slippery for him to permit himself anything more than a hasty sidelong glance. In the beams of his headlights the snow has thickened to a dense, whirling mass. A single car passes them in the oncoming lane, then another, then a third, all traveling with a conscientious slowness that neither suggests nor contains panic; it is not a night, yet, that makes people afraid. Arthur thinks about these other cars, where they have come from and where they may be headed; he thinks about Miriam, dozing now beside him, and his son and daughter, elsewhere, busy with their lives, and about the days when each of them was born; he thinks about Dora Auclaire, though as he does he realizes that he does not love her at all. He will never send his letter. He will destroy it, as soon as he can, and when next he sees her—on line at the grocery story, or at the clinic dropping off some papers—he will smile, perhaps say a harmless, genial word or two of greeting, and then go about his business in such a way that she knows, instantly, that all of it is over: the lunches, the looks, the promise, unfulfilled, of something more. He will never hold her hand again, nor imagine what it would be like to be alone with her. All of this he knows, but when he comes to a fork in the highway—the lone decision he must make between the college and the Massachusetts border—he completely fails to notice it, as he also fails to notice when he veers right instead of left. He doesn't notice the change in the highway number, the road's sudden, suggestive rise into the hills, or the sign that says, Scenic Route Ahead, its top edge dressed with a two-inch blade of snow. None of these. He will wash Dora Auclaire from his memory, as even now the silence of the car and the whirling cones of snow before him seem to wash away the very world, everything that has ever happened to him and everything that ever will—a dream of dreaming.

They have traveled just ten miles from the motel, but their journey is nearly done. The road veers sharply upward, descends into a hollow smothered by snowy trees, then rises again, ascending toward some unknown apex; at the top, as the car crests—the beams of his headlights vault into space—Arthur can see the sky again, a starless mass of stone, and then below him, the highway curving along a steep embankment. The dropoff is vast, a plunge into nothing; far below he detects an icy glint of river.

Perhaps he sees this. Perhaps, sleeping, he sees nothing at all.

Later, when O'Neil imagines the accident—in the days and weeks that follow, and then for years to come—he imagines that it occurs in silence, and that his parents' eyes are closed. Their eyes are closed like children asleep in a car at night, their faces and bodies in perfect, trusting repose, his father at the wheel, his mother beside him, and though it makes no sense to think it, he sees them holding hands—as O'Neil will one day hold his daughter's hand when a nightmare has awakened her, to tell her that he is there beside her, that in sleep we have nothing to fear. Silence, and his parents, and the snow: he inhabits this moment as if it were not imagined but remembered, with a vividness that seems to lodge in his bones, just as he feels, with his body, the moment when the car lifts on the ice and begins its long, languid arc toward the embankment. There is no guardrail, nothing for the car's front end to strike, to impede its progress or in any way change the nature of the scene, its dreamlike silence. The total, parabolic energy of their vehicle—thirty-five hundred pounds of diesel-powered French station wagon, traveling at or about the legal speed limit of fifty miles per hour—is suddenly, amazingly, tractionless. It is unbounded, set loose from the earth, and though jealous gravity will soon assert itself, whisking his parents to the valley floor at a velocity sufficient to snap the chassis in two, for this moment they are free; they are as free as ghosts, as comets, they are streaking across the heavens; Arthur and Miriam, together at last.

He was nineteen years old, happy. He did not know yet that it was possible for his life to change, and that once it changed, it would never change back. An hour would pass before his parents were found, and that is the hour O'Neil returns to, every day: the car in the river, the river in the valley, the valley gone under the snow.

ORPHANS

July 1983

O'NEIL BURKE WAS twenty-three years old, a college graduate who had traveled to Europe, but by the time his sister came to get him at the hospital in Stamford, six hours after the accident, he felt as if his life had stopped. It was eight o'clock when Kay arrived, still in her suit from a day of work, a slim leather case under her arm; the wide glass doors of the emergency room sighed open on their hinges, and there she was at last. She stood a moment in the doorway, searching the room with narrowed eyes, until she found him parked in his wheelchair by the sign-in desk, his left leg encased in plaster of Paris from knee to toe.

"God, look at you." Kay raked her fingers through his hair, clotted with knots of dried paint. She was a pretty woman who worked too hard—slender and brown haired like O'Neil, with a small nose and deep walnut eyes—and her tired face said: *Now this.* "Couldn't they have cleaned you up a little?"

"That was extra." O'Neil held up the magazine he had been reading, which was *Business Week*. In two hours, since the nurses had wheeled him back to the waiting area, he had read through the rack, everything from *Highlights for Children* to *Modern Maturity*. "Now," he said, directing her attention to the article, "it says here that what we are experiencing is not so much a recession strictly speaking, as a period of contraction before an expansion. Does this make any sense to you?"

"You'll have to ask Jack. O'Neil, what did they give you?"

He returned the magazine to the pile. "Some Demerol when I first got here. It made me throw up."

"It can do that. Listen, honey. I hate to ask, but do you have any insurance?"

"A technical question," O'Neil said, and paused for effect; the news was not good. "Technically, no."

Kay paid for everything with her Master Charge, then pushed O'Neil's wheelchair into the parking lot, where the orderly, a large black man named Donnelle, helped her drape O'Neil across the backseat of Kay's Volvo. The light in the parking lot was evening light—the day had disappeared—and insects throbbed in the trees.

"Thanks for everything, Donnelle." O'Neil leaned out the window so the two could shake hands; Donnelle met his hand with a firm grip.

"You mind that leg, now," Donnelle said.

When they had pulled out of the lot, Kay lifted her eyes at O'Neil through the rearview mirror. "Please don't pout, honey. I didn't even get the message until forty minutes ago. I came as soon as I could."

He had left messages for her everywhere: her office, the house, even the restaurant where she sometimes met Jack after work for dinner. "Oh, it's all right," O'Neil said after a moment. "Donnelle was good company."

"I can stop somewhere if you're hungry," Kay offered.

O'Neil shook his head. "There was a candy machine at the hospital. Also, they gave me some codeine, after the Demerol wore off."

In the front seat Kay sighed hopelessly. "What am I going to do with you?"

O'Neil tilted his head back and let the codeine wash over him like a warm, salty bath. He had more, twelve pills in all, in a little paper sack. "It's anybody's guess," he said.

They drove on, into the June evening. Under the spell of the codeine the headlights of the oncoming cars pulsed benevolently, and O'Neil watched them until his eyes fell closed. He began to dream, a loosely knitted patchwork of images from the past, but then his mind turned sharply to the moment of the accident: the noise below as the ladder popped loose, his roll down the roof and then the long fall through open air to the ground below. It had taken forever, and was over in an instant. The orthopedist who cast his leg had marveled at the quality of his injury—like a crack in porcelain, he said.

"Aw, fuck."

Again, Kay's eyes met his through the rearview mirror. "O'Neil?"

He shook his head to send the memory away. "It was a long way down," O'Neil said.

The accident occurred on a Wednesday, the third Wednesday in June. O'Neil had been painting houses for six weeks, since returning from eight months of backpacking around Europe. The company he worked for was called Professor Painter. The parent office was in Montreal, but Professor Painter had franchises all over the East Coast, and O'Neil worked for a branch that operated out of an apartment building in South Norwalk. O'Neil had no experience with this kind of work, but after he'd watched the training video, his boss, a Canadian named Joe, asked him if he'd like to be a foreman. What this meant was that O'Neil worked alone, though sometimes Joe sent other people to help. Usually they were college students, and most lasted only a few days before finding better, easier jobs.

The work was hard and paid just five dollars an hour, but

O'Neil liked it and took care to do it well. Painting a house was a large undertaking that required a certain amount of tactical thinking, but once O'Neil laid out his plans, his mind was free to go where it wanted. His months abroad had been a happy time, and that was where he spent his days, remembering the golden light of sunset on the Lido of Venice, or the sad, exciting spectacle of a bullfight in Barcelona. For many years he had been afraid of heights, but he discovered, to his surprise, that this fear had left him. Many days he drank his morning coffee or ate his lunch on top of the chimney or some other apex, his legs dangling in space. The houses where he worked were all located within a few miles of Long Island Sound, and over the crowns of the trees he could see the water, its soothing and imperturbable vastness, and on the clearest days, the island of Manhattan, a spiky smear etched into the southern horizon. People walking by on the sidewalk below would stop and wave, and O'Neil waved back, or lifted his coffee in a little toast.

When the accident occurred, O'Neil was working alone on the jobsite, a large Victorian in awful shape with handsome willows over a level yard that always seemed damp. The house, in an upscale neighborhood of old homes that had all been meticulously restored, was owned by a striking-looking woman in her mid-thirties with high, sculpted cheekbones and hair the color of onyx, and her husband, whom O'Neil had never laid eyes on. They had just moved in, or were preparing the house for sale—either way, their rooms were nearly bare. The couple had a child, a luminous baby boy named Henry who cried all day long, and O'Neil felt sorry for the woman, whose name was Patrice. She spent her days alone in her house with an inconsolable child and seemed to pass the hours in a state of suspension, waiting for her husband to return from wherever he was. O'Neil was curious about her, as he always was about the people whose houses he painted, though the fact that she was pretty, and seemed to like having him around, made him more interested than usual. Yet, as the weeks went by, he learned very little about Patrice. In all the time he spent there, no one had ever come to the house; sometimes she would drive off with Henry in her car, an old Mercedes with rust on the door panels, but these errands produced nothing more than groceries. It took him two weeks before he realized that he had never even heard her phone ring. What was she doing here, in this fancy neighborhood, in a house with no furniture? What did she do for money? Who were her friends? Most of his customers paid him no attention at all, but often Patrice would appear at the base of his ladder to ask him how the work was going, or else they would talk at the end of the day while he was cleaning out his brushes and trays. O'Neil looked forward to their conversations, as he believed she did too. Standing in her driveway he told her of his progress, or stories of his adventures in Europe— hitchhiking through the hills of Tuscany and the green valleys of the Rhine, waking at dawn on a ferry from Catania to Naples to find a purser rifling through his backpack, seeing Picasso's "Guernica" at the Prado in Madrid and weeping for an hour. O'Neil was not lonely, but when he told her these tales, he found they poured forth from him without effort, as if they were not things that had happened but living presences inside him, seeking release. But always on the drive home he would realize, with embarrassment, that he had done all the talking; she had told him nothing of herself.

The day of the accident, O'Neil was getting ready to take a ladder up to the porch roof to paint a pair of third-story gables when Patrice emerged from the side door, carrying a tray of lemonade. It was a hot, damp afternoon, the sky the color of old ivory, and the two of them sat at a picnic table in the yard to drink the lemonade. Henry was napping—*finally* napping, she said with

a wry smile, for the little boy slept rarely, and never for long—
and when she had seen him outside working, she'd thought: here
was a chance to bring him something cool to drink. Patrice was
wearing cutoff shorts and a loose man's dress shirt with the
sleeves rolled up, and as she spoke she placed her glass of iced
lemonade against her long neck, holding it there between sips.
How do you work in this heat? she asked him. She didn't mind the
winter—she had been raised in the cold—but sometimes in the
summer it was all she could do not to lose her mind entirely.
O'Neil wondered about the shirt, and the person it belonged to.
On her ring finger Patrice wore a plain gold wedding band, and a
large diamond that sparkled against her skin. These came from
somewhere, of course, but O'Neil had never seen her husband,
even though he usually worked at the house till six o'clock. In all
their conversations she had never mentioned him, not even in
passing.

He was about to ask her about this, deciding how he might do
so without seeming to pry, when the sound of Henry's crying
reached them from his bedroom window. Patrice, sighing with irritation, left him alone at the table; it did not seem she would be
back soon, so O'Neil returned to work, taking his ladder and
paint up to the porch roof. This was when he made an error in
judgment that was, in hindsight, completely obvious. The roof
was pitched ten degrees, and the standard practice was to nail a
pair of blocks into the roof joists to brace the legs of the ladder;
the company training video was absolutely clear on this fact. But
as O'Neil stood on the roof in the sweltering heat, his mind afloat
in the image of the glass of lemonade against Patrice's neck, this
extra step seemed like a technicality. *What the hell*, he decided, *I'll
just do it fast.* Without another thought he propped the ladder between the windows, kicked its base tight against the shingles,
scrambled up with his paint and brush, and had just enough time

to realize his mistake before the whole thing came down in a clattering chaos of paint and equipment. The porch roof broke his fall, and for one hopeful instant he believed he might stop there. But then he was in space again—a sensation so awful he knew he would carry it inside him all the days of his life—and the only thing left to do was see what happened next. A sound poured from his lungs, a wail of purest terror, and then he landed, hard, on his back, the ladder twisted up in his left leg like an enormous ski; in the sudden silence that followed, he both felt and heard a tiny crack of bone. For a few moments he lay there, amazed by everything, watching the paint he had spilled dripping from the gutter above his face, and then Patrice came running. "I'm sorry," she was saying, "I'm sorry, I'm sorry," and O'Neil wondered what she was apologizing for; the accident was, in every way, his fault. With damp rags she cleaned him up as best she could while Henry wailed on a blanket, and then she drove him to the hospital in her rusted Mercedes, watching from the doorway as O'Neil was wheeled into X ray, Henry still crying in her arms.

O'Neil had been living with Kay since he returned from Europe in late April, sleeping on a cot in a tiny room behind the kitchen that they use for storage, and paying her and Jack fifty dollars a week. The house, a one-story bungalow encased in aluminum siding, sat on a block that ended at a high cement wall and the freeway, and though the street seemed fine during the day—clean and neat in a neutral sort of way—at night a gloom descended, dogs began to bark, and groups of young men gathered on the corners. One early morning as he left for work, O'Neil discovered in his car an empty pack of cigarettes, and three butts in the ashtray. Otherwise, the car was untouched. No harm had been done, but O'Neil still worried about his sister, living in a neighborhood where strangers would smoke in your unlocked car when you weren't looking. The room where he slept was full of boxes with words written on them in black Magic Marker—*Dissertation Notes, Office Misc., Kitchen/Bath.* Early on, O'Neil had opened one box, marked *Wedding Presents* and found, inside, three brand-new waffle irons, still in their packages. The hidden bounty of these boxes amazed him, for O'Neil himself owned almost nothing. He had sold most of his belongings to pay for his trip and was still living out of the backpack he had carried with him to London and Paris, Lisbon and Rome.

Kay, who was five years older than O'Neil, was the director of a state agency that assisted teenage mothers, and Jack was an economist, doing his postdoc at a think tank in Stamford. When this was done, in a year or two, they would sell the house and move to wherever Jack found a tenure-track position. O'Neil hadn't a clue at all about Jack's job, which had something to do with labor, and Kay often joked that it would have rounded out his expertise nicely if he actually did some around the house. At such moments she appeared not to like her husband very much, but these glimpses were brief. O'Neil didn't feel one way or the other about Jack, who seemed to regard him with the generic masculine warmth of a fraternity brother. "How's the man?" he would ask O'Neil as they crossed in the hallway, or maneuvered past one another in the cramped kitchen. "What's the word, O'Neil?" One Friday, a few weeks after his return, O'Neil had come home late from a bar and heard Kay and Jack talking in low voices in the kitchen. He paused in the dark hallway to listen. Although he couldn't make out their words, he knew from their measured, parental tone that they were speaking about him. When would he move on? What would become of such a person as O'Neil?

Back from the hospital, Kay helped him to bed in his little room of boxes, and in the morning O'Neil awoke late to find that

Kay and Jack had already left for the day. Balancing on his crutches, O'Neil made coffee and took some more codeine and then paged Joe, who called him back in the early afternoon while O'Neil was watching a soap opera on the sofa, his cast propped on a stack of pillows.

"I just drove by the house," Joe said, and in the background O'Neil could hear the wash of traffic on the Post Road. "What the hell did you do to the roof?"

"I had an accident," O'Neil said.

"Those people are going to be royally pissed. Just get over there."

"Joe, I have a broken leg."

A pause followed, as O'Neil waited to hear what Joe would next say.

"Okay," Joe said, "I'm sorry. Tell me, how's your leg?"

O'Neil held the phone to his leg and rapped the plaster with his knuckles. "You can sign my cast, if you want," he said. "Also, you owe my sister fifteen hundred dollars for medical expenses."

"Jesus, O'Neil. Don't you have any insurance?"

On the television a couple began kissing with their eyes closed. "Why does everybody keep asking me that?" said O'Neil.

"Okay, okay. I have to tell them something. What's the woman's name? Patty?"

"Patrice. She drove me to the hospital."

"I always thought she was pretty good looking," Joe said, thinking aloud.

"Try telling her you're going to paint her house."

O'Neil passed the afternoon watching television and napping, and keeping off the leg, which had begun to hum with pain, like a low-bandwidth radio signal. He believed that Joe would call back eventually and try to settle the situation. He had never met anybody like Joe, who spoke about his native country with a rhapsodic patriotism that was like nothing O'Neil had experienced in his life. "People think Canada is cold," Joe liked to say, "but it's the warmth of the people that makes it special." O'Neil had serious questions about Joe's business practices—he underpaid all his workers so badly that almost no one stayed, and he seemed to be taking deposits on houses he couldn't paint in a million years—and yet O'Neil liked to think that his loyalty, doing an awful job nobody else wanted, would count for something in the end. But Joe did not call back, and as the afternoon wore on, it occurred to O'Neil that this silence might be permanent.

After dinner, when Kay and Jack had left him to catch an early movie, O'Neil put two pills in his shirt pocket and swung on his crutches out to the patio, a concrete slab attached to the back of the house that Kay and Jack had dressed up with plastic furniture and potted marigolds. O'Neil arranged himself in a chair and washed the pills down with a can of Coors, and waited for the codeine to kick in. The day was nearly gone, and the last of the light seemed to pour into the shadows like water down a drain. His body had always been highly responsive to medication of any sort, and this was true of the codeine, which made him feel like hammered tin. At times like this, O'Neil sometimes thought of Sandra, the last girl he had loved. They had broken up just a few months after his parents' accident—with so much on his mind, O'Neil had simply drifted away—and though they had managed to remain friends for the rest of their time at college, O'Neil often felt a stab of longing for her, and the way she had made him feel: more alive somehow, as if his life were an open door he had only to step through. The summer after graduation, Sandra had ridden her bicycle across the country, raising money for hunger relief; now she was in California, a medical student at Stanford planning a career in pediatric oncology, while O'Neil was painting houses and living in a storage room. He would have liked to call her, but what was there to say? On top of everything, Joe owed him two weeks' pay, and O'Neil had begun to wonder if he would ever see it, let alone the fifteen hundred for his broken leg. If his parents had still been around, he would have asked them what to do. For some time after they had died, when he was alone and feeling lost, O'Neil would speak to them, asking them questions about his life. Should I drop calculus? Should I buy a car? He has never told anyone about this, not even Kay, though secretly he believed she did the same thing.

Now, five years later on his sister's patio, O'Neil found that his memory of his parents, their incorporeal vividness, had receded. He could no longer hear their voices, or even imagine what they might say to him. When he closed his eyes he could still conjure their faces, but these images were static, like photographs. Sitting in the dark on Kay's patio, he understood that's just what they were—memories of pictures, nothing more. It wasn't just the codeine, O'Neil thought. They had left him alone.

The accident that killed their parents happened on a trip they had taken to visit O'Neil at college, the fall of his sophomore year. His parents had driven up for parents' weekend, and on the way home, in a snowstorm, their car went off the road and fell a hundred feet into a river gorge. All of this would have been clear enough—a skid on a wet road in failing light—if not for the fact that they had left the college at noon and crashed their car six hours later, on the wrong road entirely, having driven only thirty miles. Where had they spent the intervening hours? Their mother had telephoned Kay at four-thirty, but not said where she was. The stretch of road between the campus and the ravine where their car was found was empty: no towns at all, and no reason to stop. Sleeping in the college library, O'Neil had awakened at five to see, out the window, the first dry flakes falling; by midnight nearly a foot of snow was on the ground, and he had learned that his parents were dead. Identifying the bodies was a job that should have been O'Neil's—he was, after all, right there—but in the end he could not face this; he waited for Kay and Jack to drive up from New Haven and stood outside the police station in the snowy cold while they saw to this task. Then the three of them drove on to Glenn's Mills, the upstate New York town where O'Neil and his sister had grown up, to wait for the bodies to follow them for burial.

O'Neil arranged to take incompletes in all his courses and was planning to stay on at their parents' house until school started again in January, when Kay would return to New Haven and they would put the house up for sale. Though some might have thought this a morbid scene, a pair of orphans moping around the house, in fact the weeks following their parents' death passed quickly and became, for O'Neil, a time of strange and unexpected contentment. Unhappiness, he discovered, was an emotion distinct from grief, and he found it was possible both to miss his parents terribly—a loss so overwhelming he simply couldn't take it all in, like looking at a skyscraper up close—while also finding in the job of settling their affairs a satisfying orderliness. Accounts to be closed, bills to be paid, letters to be read and discarded, clothing to be boxed and carted off: he knew what he and Kay were doing—they were erasing their parents, removing the last evidence of their lives from the earth. It was, O'Neil knew, a way of saying good-bye, and yet with each trip to the Goodwill box behind the Price Chopper, each final phone call to a bank or loan company, he felt his parents becoming real to him in a way that they had never been in life. More than real: he felt them move inside him. Jack had returned to New Haven a few days after the funeral, and alone in the house, O'Neil and Kay slipped into a pattern that was, he realized, the same one his parents had kept, or nearly. The hours they ate and worked and slept, their habit of meeting in the living room in the evenings for a cup of tea—these were all things their parents had done, and on a night close to the end of their time together, O'Neil dreamed that he and Kay were married. It was a dream in which they were both the same and also different—they were at once their parents and themselves—and when he awoke in his old bedroom under the eaves, he felt not revulsion or shame but a fleeting certainty that he had been touched by the world of the spirits.

His discoveries were many—his father, for instance, owned nineteen blue shirts; his mother kept a needle and thread in her glove compartment; on a shelf in the laundry room, behind the boxes of detergent and fabric softener, someone had hidden a pack of Larks—and yet the actual circumstances of his parents' death, its strange location and hour, seemed unknowable. Then on a day just before Christmas, their father's Visa bill arrived, including a forty-two-dollar charge for a motel, the Glade View Motor Court, and the mystery was solved. The charge was dated the day they had died, November 12, and O'Neil recognized the name at once: the Glade View was a run-down motel set back from the highway, about an hour south of campus. Its curious existence, so far from anything, had always seemed so sordid and improbable that it had become a familiar landmark; O'Neil and his parents had joked about it often, to fill the final minutes of their long drives together to the college. This was where they had spent the last afternoon of their lives together. O'Neil felt no embarrassment learning this—far worse had been the discovery, in his mother's dressing table, of her diaphragm, and beneath it a faded pamphlet on "natural birth spacing." And yet it was still troubling, like opening a door to find, behind it, another door just like it. O'Neil and Kay sat on the sofa, passing the bill back and forth between them, reading it over and over and shaking their heads. A motel. They had visited O'Neil at college, then stopped on the way home at a seedy roadside motor court, and, leaving, had turned themselves around in the storm. It was almost funny; it made, O'Neil realized, no sense to him at all. Did they do this all the time? What other secrets were they taking with them? And suddenly he realized how little he truly knew about his parents. The bills and blue shirts were nothing. A new sadness touched him, and at once he knew it was the one he had waited for. No more or less: it was the simple wish that he could have become a man before they died.

On Friday evening, with no word from Joe, O'Neil asked Kay and Jack to drive him to Patrice's house to pick up his car, an ancient Buick he had bought out of the classifieds the week he'd returned from Europe. He hoped that the painting had proceeded without him, but when they arrived at her house the scene he found was one of abandonment, as if time had frozen at the moment of his accident. His ladder still lay in the yard behind the yew bushes, and beside it a nearly empty can of hardened paint. Though he hadn't thought of this before, he had spilled most of a gallon on the porch roof, which was now a total loss—it would have to be reshingled, and this, O'Neil knew, would cost Joe more money.

Patrice answered the door before he could knock, holding Henry on her hip. Henry was wearing only a diaper, his eyes were glassy from a day of tears, and Patrice wore the stunned and hopeless look of someone who hadn't slept in days. O'Neil had taken the last of the codeine that afternoon, and looking at Patrice, this thought made him feel unworthy.

She tipped her head toward his cast. "Does it hurt?"

"You're the first person to ask me that," O'Neil replied. "It did, thank you, for a while."

She moved her hand through the air toward him, stopping just shy of his face. "There's paint in your hair," Patrice said.

The three of them made their way to the front yard, to get a better look at the roof. From where they stood, O'Neil could see a broad splash, marking the spot where he had first made impact, and below it a wide ribbon of paint that traced his course down the sloping roof to the ground below.

"I feel just terrible about this," O'Neil said. "This is completely my fault. Also, I never thanked you for driving me to the hospital."

Patrice looked sweetly at Henry, who smiled back into her face. "What else could we do, Henry?" she said. "Leave this poor man in the yard?"

She helped O'Neil cover his crew kit with a tarp and store the rest of the equipment, in case it rained. She seemed to have no expectation at all for when the work on her house would resume, and O'Neil didn't know what to say about this. Probably it wouldn't.

"What will you do?" she asked him, when the time had come to go.

"It's hard to say. I'm thinking maybe law school."

She smiled at this answer. "I meant about your hair, O'Neil."

Then, for just a moment, they exchanged a deep regard. Patrice's eyelashes, O'Neil saw, were long and thick and, though she wore no mascara, seemed braided. Such a small thing, but that was what he saw. His mind took hold of this image, pushing aside all other thoughts, and he imagined what her eyelashes would feel like, brushing against his cheek. He thought it would be nice to kiss her—more than nice. But sad too, and in a way he had not felt before. They held one another's gaze a second more, and then Patrice looked past him to the Volvo parked at the curb, where Kay and Jack were reading the newspaper.

"Who's that now?" she said. "You've brought someone."

O'Neil followed her eyes to the car. "That's my sister and her husband. They're Kay and Jack."

Patrice turned with her hip so Henry could see and lifted his little arm to help him wave. "I'm really sorry about your leg, O'Neil," she said. "It's not the same without you around here."

They said their good-byes, and Jack took O'Neil home in the Buick, with Kay following in the Volvo. As they turned the corner onto Post Road, O'Neil lifted his eyes to find Jack looking at him through the rearview mirror.

"Nice-looking woman," Jack said, and winked knowingly. "What do you say, O'Neil? Maybe I should take up house painting."

O'Neil said nothing. This was when he realized he'd never seen Patrice's husband because she didn't have one. His assumption that this man existed was just that—an assumption. Or perhaps Joe had led him to believe this. Either way, there was no such person. It was just Patrice and Henry, and their big empty house that no one was painting for them.

O'Neil tried to wash the paint from his hair, but it was no use, and the next week he finally asked Kay to cut it. Using a pair of sewing scissors from the kitchen junk drawer, Kay snipped off most of his hair, while O'Neil sat wrapped in a plastic tablecloth and Jack swept up the trimmings with a whisk broom. The good news was that Joe had finally called O'Neil back, and after dinner he picked him up in the company van and drove him to a bar in Port Chester where they used to go after work. The bar was called the Moosehead, and was owned by some Canadians who, like Joe, seemed imprisoned in a sentimental exile. A Canadian flag hung over the bar, there were maps of Canada and travel photos of Canadian destinations on the paneled walls, and if they stayed long enough, O'Neil knew, the bartender would ring a bell and lead everyone in a chorus of "O Canada."

"About the money," Joe said regretfully, after they had taken a table. He had a weight lifter's body, square and solid, and a blond moustache that he liked to stroke with thumb and forefinger. "We may have a tiny problem there."

"Don't tell me that," O'Neil said.

"The situation is," Joe continued, "the status of the company is a little tenuous at the moment. Technically, I have no employees at all, if we don't count you. You might say that, as of last week, we are no longer an official branch of Professor Painter."

"You have no insurance."

Joe wagged a finger over their glasses. "Let me get the tab for these beers."

"Is this how they do things in Canada? Pay you in beer?"

Joe left the table to select a song on the jukebox and returned with a bowl of nuts. "Oh, don't be mad," he said. "Hey, this is you and me. Am I missing something here? We'll absolutely work this out."

"Somebody has to finish that house," O'Neil offered.

"Right," Joe replied, chewing a mouthful of nuts. "That's completely right. And I'll do it myself, if I have to. I'm just saying we might not have explored all our options at this point."

"Joe, she's totally alone over there," O'Neil said.

"See?" Joe nodded hopefully. "There's something."

In the parking lot they settled on three thousand dollars: fifteen hundred for O'Neil's trip to the hospital, another thousand for back wages, and five hundred dollars compensation for his pain and suffering. O'Neil doubted he would ever see this money, but two days later Joe appeared at the house with a check, and a letter for O'Neil to sign. The letter said, in essence, that he was no longer an employee of Professor Painter, Inc., and that he held both Joe and the parent company harmless of any responsibility for his accident. O'Neil wondered if such a letter was legal—in the purest sense it was a form of extortion—but he was glad to get any money at all, and signing the letter seemed the only way to make this happen. The check did not bounce, and O'Neil gave Kay the fifteen hundred in cash one night after dinner.

Kay looked the bills over. "I hope he didn't make you sign anything," she said.

The next day, a Sunday, was the Fourth of July, and the three of them drove to the beach in Old Greenwich, to barbecue and watch the fireworks over the Sound. The shells were to be launched from a barge anchored offshore, and after they had eaten their chicken and drunk their wine they positioned lawn chairs at the shoreline to watch the display. The evening was clear; darkness came on with the swift evenness of a curtain falling. As stars appeared above the still water, the first cannon boomed, and the people cheered as the shell leapt heavenward to release its package of tendriled light.

"What is the magic of fireworks?" Jack said to O'Neil. Kay and Jack were holding hands, and O'Neil understood this remark as a way to include him, although Jack also appeared genuinely moved; his face glowed with the wine, and his eyes were moist in the reflected light of the display. "Is it the way they're here one moment and gone the next? Are we just remembering other times?"

Before O'Neil could answer, Kay leaned over to her husband and kissed him. "Sweetie," she said, and squeezed his face, "you're wasted."

Back home Jack went off to bed, and Kay joined O'Neil in the kitchen.

"I'm sorry about that," she said sadly, and took a place across from him at the table. "Jack can't hold his liquor at all."

"He was right, though," O'Neil said. "I *was* remembering."

Kay thought a moment. "I miss them too."

She left then and returned moments later with an envelope,

which she placed on the table in front of O'Neil. He knew, even before he looked at it, that it was something their parents had left behind. Their father was—had been—a lawyer, and on the outside of the envelope was his name and the address of his office, embossed in heavy black ink, and then the name of the person the letter was meant for, a woman named Dora Auclaire. O'Neil saw that one end of the envelope had been opened with a single, neat stroke of a knife. He slid the letter out, and as he unfolded the heavy paper he felt his heart grow large. The letter was written in his father's hand, a single sentence long. *Dear Dora*, it said, *It would have been nice for me too.* He had signed it, *Love, Art.*

"I'm sorry, O'Neil. I thought it was probably time you saw this."

"God Almighty." He put the letter down, though at once he picked it up again. "How did you find it?"

"It wasn't hidden, if that's what you're thinking. It was just sitting there in the top drawer of his desk. I found it just a couple of days after the accident when I was looking for the lease on his office. I guess I shouldn't have opened it, but there was no address, and I thought it might be important."

O'Neil read the letter again, its one taut sentence of yearning. Dora Auclaire: He searched his memory for this woman, but came up with nothing. "Jesus Christ, Kay."

"I know, honey. It's not good news."

O'Neil sighed, uncertain what to say or think. "Any idea who she was?"

"He did some legal work for her, I do know that. A will, some real estate stuff." Kay shrugged. "It wasn't really my business to look."

"I can't believe Dad was screwing around." O'Neil shook his head; he was suddenly cold. "I mean, they went to a *motel*."

Kay took his hand. "He never mailed it, O'Neil. And the letter doesn't prove anything. There's a lot we'll never know about them."

O'Neil looked at the floor. "Can't know, you mean."

"Don't, can't. It's all the same." She paused; he felt her eyes on his face. "They were just people, O'Neil."

"How can you say that?" He pulled his hand away, though he was instantly sorry for doing this. "They were our parents."

Kay rose and lit the stove for tea. When her back was turned he closed his eyes, and tried to remember them, his parents. For some time he had longed to hear their voices again. But he could not imagine his father saying these words.

Kay returned to the table and pulled her chair close to O'Neil's. "Honey, I'm sorry. Really, I am. But I think it's time we talk about you doing something with yourself."

"I thought I was."

Kay frowned. "Painting houses for this con man?"

"Oh, Joe's not so bad."

"Joe's a liar, and a thief. What about law school? You've talked about law school."

"I think that was just something to say."

"Okay. No law school." Kay sighed maternally. "How about teaching? You're good with kids."

"Have you ever even seen me with kids? I don't think I even know any."

For a while they sat in silence. The kettle whistled, and Kay left the table to pour the tea, which smelled like lemon and roses. She placed a cup on the table in front of O'Neil, then leaned over to put her arms around his shoulders and kiss the top of his head.

"They had their lives, O'Neil. Go have yours. That's what I'm saying to you."

"You're kicking me out."

"I love you, boyo." She pulled away to fix him with an even

gaze. "And, yes. When the leg's better, off you go into your life. And off I go into mine."

When Kay left him, O'Neil sat alone at the table, drinking his tea. No one had called him by that name in many, many years. He remembered the day he had graduated from college and the moment, stepping from the dais with his diploma in his fist, when he had lifted his eyes to search for Kay. A sea of sunlit faces, and then he had found her, waving to him. Of all the people in the crowd, Kay was the one who belonged to him, and he had never loved her so much as he did at that moment, the way a drowning man would love a life ring. What would he do without her now, in the life she was sending him to? The letter still lay on the kitchen table, beside the salt and pepper shakers; he read it once more. *Dear Dora. Love, Art.* What did you do with something like that? It was a riddle, as the motel bill had been a riddle, and he knew he had no hope of solving either one; that was the point that Kay was making. It was not beyond imagining that she had saved the letter for a day such as this one, believing it would do the trick. O'Neil finished his tea, knowing what he was about to do but still taking the time to envision it, so that later he would know if the image he had made in his mind was the correct one. It was. He rose on his crutches, took the letter to the stove, and when he dipped it into the blue flame of the burner, the paper caught so quickly he was still holding it when it disappeared.

There was one thing left to do. The next afternoon O'Neil dressed in clean shorts and a polo shirt and hitchhiked the five miles to Patrice's house. The crew kit still sat in the driveway with a tarp over it, and the yard was quiet under the mild shade of the willows. O'Neil had tried to page Joe for a couple of days, but he'd heard no reply, and it seemed likely that he was already back in the Canada he loved.

Patrice let him in and led him to the kitchen, where she sat at the table to resume spooning cereal into Henry's mouth. Grains were caught in the little boy's hair and eyebrows. "How's the leg?"

"Not so bad," O'Neil said. "I'm afraid I have some news. I don't think anybody's going to be painting your house."

Henry picked up his cup and began to bang it on the tray of his high chair. Patrice scooped more cereal from the nearly empty bowl, and as she brought the spoon to the little boy's mouth, O'Neil saw her pause to wipe a tear from her eyes with the back of her hand.

"I'm truly sorry," O'Neil said.

"I have to say I shouldn't be surprised." She lifted her tired face toward him. "I'm not very good at reading the signals. Any chance of finding him?"

"None at all. I'd say we've both been had." O'Neil shifted on his crutches. "How much did you pay him?"

She sighed miserably. "Oh, four thousand dollars." Patrice put her palms to her eyes, then opened them like doors to look at Henry. "What a goddamn idiot your mother is. Say, hello, idiot."

Standing at the counter, O'Neil wrote the check. He would have gladly written it for more, but fifteen hundred dollars was all he had. In any event, it would probably cover the repairs to the roof. He had wondered all morning if he would write the check when the time came, but the moment it did, he found it was easy, and made him feel lighter than anything had in a long time.

Patrice stored the check in a drawer. "I won't cash this, you know," she said.

"It's my hope that you will."

They kissed, then, for the first time—a kiss that O'Neil realized he had been imagining for weeks, a kiss of tender longing. He touched her face, still damp with tears; he tasted these as he kissed her, their salty essence, and when they parted O'Neil saw that Henry had fallen asleep in his high chair. Patrice freed the little boy from the belt that held him in place and led O'Neil back through her empty house, waiting at the top of the stairs with Henry in her arms while O'Neil hobbled up on his crutches. He stood at the door to Henry's nursery, waiting for the cascade of tears that would bring everything to a crashing halt, but this never came; a moment later Patrice crept from the room, holding one finger over her lips, and took O'Neil down the carpeted hall to a large room with nothing in it but drapes, a mattress, and an alarm clock on the bare floor beside it. The clock, O'Neil saw, was blinking 12:00 A.M.—not the correct hour at all. O'Neil lay on his back while Patrice helped him remove his shorts over the bulky cast, and this fact, which might have seemed strange, did not. With everything else—the kiss in the kitchen, Henry's plunge into sleep, the blinking alarm clock, and the sunshine enfolded in the curtains—it seemed to belong to several periods of his life at once, as if they had stepped together outside the flow of time. She removed her skirt and blouse and placed them, folded, in a bureau drawer. The light was behind her, where she stood. She folded O'Neil's shorts and put these aside as well. Then she returned to where he lay and all thought left him.

When the sun had moved from the windows Henry called from his crib, and they dressed and fed him juice and slices of apple in the kitchen before taking him out to the hammock in the yard. It was afternoon, an afternoon in July. Together they lay and rocked, the long branches of the willows enclosing them like a tent.

"Would you like to hold him?" Patrice asked.

O'Neil did, so much it surprised him. Patrice helped him lift the little boy from the space between them and onto O'Neil's stomach. Henry was clutching a stuffed cube with bells inside and handles on the corners, and O'Neil pulled on these, to make the chimes ring. Henry frowned, but did not cry. O'Neil watched the boy bob up and down on his chest, listening to the bells, a sound that seemed to come from under them and all around.

"I forgot to tell you," Patrice said. "I like what you did with your hair."

"My sister cut it for me."

Patrice took a strand of it in her fingers, narrowing her dark eyes to examine it. "Well, she did a good job. I cut hair for a while, and this isn't at all bad."

He knew nothing about her: the jobs she'd had, the places she'd lived, why she was alone. Henry's body was warm and damp, and his breath had the dry, pasty smell of papier-mâché. O'Neil wondered what the little boy might make of him, this man with them in the hammock. He understood then that Henry's father was dead, or gone so far away that it was all the same. There was no knowing, or need to know.

"I think I like the house this way," Patrice said. With one bare toe on the ground she moved the hammock to and fro. "I think I'll leave it half painted to remember you by."

"This is just the one time, then," O'Neil said sadly.

Patrice took his hand in hers.

"For the record," O'Neil said, "I wish it weren't."

Patrice nodded thoughtfully. "You will find her," she declared.

"Her."

"Her. Yes." Her voice was pale; she seemed to have left him behind, in memory. And yet she was smiling at him. "The one you are meant for."

O'Neil said nothing. There was no reason to think it; and yet it seemed so. A few minutes passed, and Patrice squeezed his hand again. "You will."

O'Neil rose. "I believe you," he said. Then he kissed each of them good-bye, and swung on his crutches toward home.

LIGHTNESS

March 1985

SHE THOUGHT OF IT AS *the lightness;* that was the name she gave it. The first time it happened, Mary was a little girl, alone. This took place in her bedroom in the apartment on Naomi Street in North Minneapolis, in a time before her sister, Cheryl, was born. Mary remembered nothing else about this place, for they lived there less than a year; the building was owned by a relative, and her father managed it, collecting rents and maintaining the apartments and grounds, while going to college at night. This was a difficult period for her parents, a time of small children and no money, and, as Mary later learned, her parents had nearly divorced. Her father would tell her about this on a trip they would take together to San Francisco, the year before Mary herself was married. Though the tale was meant to be cautionary—marriage is a long haul, he told her, like carrying a sofa up a flight of stairs and trying to wedge it through a narrow doorway—Mary also understood that the story was a happy one: her parents had, after all, stayed together, and by the end of that year her mother was pregnant again. She told him then about the hummingbird, her only memory of that year. They were standing together on the fantail of a ferryboat, crossing the choppy bay. A hummingbird, her father said, laughing and shaking his head in the wind. All that arguing, and what you remember is a hummingbird. My God, we thought we'd scarred you for life.

This was how she remembered it: yellow sunlight and the high, purple smell of the lilacs; her own tiny body, and the feel of a hummingbird's wings beating inside her. Their apartment was on the ground floor; beneath Mary's bedroom window was a lilac bush. On a summer afternoon, Mary was kneeling on her bed to look out the window when the bird appeared, darting between the blossoms on a blur of wings. Never had she seen such a bird. It seemed not to fly but to float—its long beak and inexplicable aeronautics made her think it might be a kind of insect—and yet whenever it moved, it seemed to disappear, reemerging at some adjacent spot of air as if it had not traveled through space but around it. Pure pleasure filled her, watching this wonderful new thing at her window, when suddenly she wasn't watching: they were one and the same, Mary and the hummingbird and the lilac bush, and all the dense bright heat of the summer afternoon. She felt herself suspended; she seemed, like the hummingbird, to be both in one place and also everywhere, her consciousness joined to another, far larger than her own. The sensation was new to her—she had no words for it—and yet it did not frighten her; she wanted to close her eyes to make it last. She did, and thought: *Who's there? Who's there?* But when she opened her eyes she found no one; even the bird was gone.

The second time she was at a friend's birthday party; Mary was nine, or ten. Hats, balloons, games that seemed childish but were still fun: The girl whose party it was, Simone, had invited no boys, or else they simply had not come. It was February, a Saturday afternoon in Minnesota, and the house, a rambler in the same subdivision where Mary lived, was a modest variation of her own. The party was held in the basement, a low-ceilinged room with brown paneling and shag carpet the color of moss. Mary's mother kept a bag of presents in the coat closet for birthday parties, and Mary had selected Spirograph, which now embarrassed her: all the other presents were better, more grown-up. Bonnie Bell Lip Smacker, a bottle of Love's Baby Soft, a poster of David Cassidy, a neon-purple Hula Hoop—the last a child's toy but also something older girls did, girls who had hips and waists and could keep the thing spinning for hours. What could she have been thinking with the Spirograph? Still Simone had thanked her, pausing dutifully to open the package and insert the pen into the gears, drawing a single fleur-de-lis before putting it to the side. Spirograph, Simone said, smiling. Cool. I haven't used this for years.

They sang "Happy Birthday" and ate the pink-frosted cake, and when Simone's mother had left them in the basement, one of the girls, Simone's older cousin Rose, showed them how to practice kissing with a pillow. They taped the poster of David Cassidy on the wall, and took turns kissing this as well, tilting their faces as they knew they were supposed to; you had to be careful, Rose instructed, not to go straight in, or you would bump noses. When this was done Rose took one of the empty pop-bottles and placed it, on its side, on the coffee table. The girls all sat around the table while Rose explained the rules and gave the bottle a lazy spin.

Mary watched as the bottle turned on the wood—it seemed to go around forever—and then it came to rest, pointing at Mary like a finger. All the girls laughed, though Mary knew this wasn't personal: they were simply relieved that the bottle had pointed at someone else.

Mary curled her hair behind her ears. "Sure," she heard herself say, "I'll kiss you."

"Remember what I said about the noses," Rose warned.

It happened so quickly it was nothing. Mary had never been kissed on the lips before—her parents did not do this—and she leaned across the table, letting her eyes fall closed and trying to think of David Cassidy, and kissed Rose. *So this is kissing,* she thought. A pause fell over the room—Mary felt this silence, as she was also aware of the taste of pink cake-frosting and watermelon Lip Smackers—and when their faces parted Mary realized that with this kiss the game had ended. The bottle was a dare, meant to be accepted only once; because Mary had done this, the others were absolved.

"When you kiss a boy," Rose said confidently, "you'll want to use your tongue."

Mary said nothing; this did not seem true. Use it how? Around them the girls laughed again; they had no idea either.

"You'll see," Rose said.

It was later, on the car ride home, that she felt it. Darkness was falling; the snow, in great piles beside the roadway and the houses, had turned a pale and lifeless gray. At her waist Mary was holding the small party favor that each of the girls had gotten, a jewelry-making kit wrapped in cellophane, and her father was smoking, tapping the ashes from his cigarette through a slender crack in his window. How was the party? he wanted to know. Did she have fun with her friends? What was that there, honey, that little thing on her lap? Was it a prize that she had won? The moment was common, and yet everything about it had begun to feel strange to Mary. More than strange: The smell of her father's cigarette and the close heat of the car, the slipperiness of cold vinyl beneath her jeans, the remembered taste of Rose's kiss—all of it was both less than real and somehow more, as if she were dissolving into sensation itself, like a lozenge on the tongue. A warm weightlessness flooded her, neither pleasant nor unpleasant, and she wondered if she had responded to her father's questions, though it seemed so; her father was beside her, nodding and puffing away. Mary closed her eyes. In school they had been warned about drugs, and all the girls had read *Go Ask Alice*, both thrilled and frightened by this story of a girl so like them who had sailed away as easily as a balloon cut from its string. *Daddy,* she wanted to say, *Daddy, something is happening,* but these words did not come. A new awareness filled her, a sense that someone was very near, inside her even, a presence without form or substance yet somehow known to her; she felt her lips move to speak its name but as she did, it vanished altogether, and when she opened her eyes she found only the lights of her own house looking back at her, glowing to greet her in the winter twilight. Her house. Simone's party. The car in the drive. Just like that she was back from wherever she had gone.

"Honey-bunny?" Her father was looking at her. "The garage?"

The transmitter sat on the seat beside her. Opening the door was a badge of honor, the desideratum of a thousand squabbles between Mary and her older brother, Mark, and sister, Cheryl. Usually Mark was the victor—like all boys he had a way of getting what he wanted. Now, alone with her father, the privilege was Mary's, uncontested, and yet it no longer interested her. Opening the garage door: so what? She pressed the button with her thumb; the door hauled itself open, washing the snowy yard with light.

"You seemed to go off into your own world there, kiddo," her father chirped, pulling in.

But Mary was not alone; she knew that now. She was not, and would never be, alone.

The memory of what she'd felt in the car did not fade, and Mary waited for this feeling to visit her again. This did not take place until many years later, a year that began in the town of Twig.

She was twenty-two; on the hill above the town stood the college where Mary had graduated in June. She'd had friends and boyfriends, sung in the choir, failed one course (economics: a mistake), and passed the rest with A's and B's. At graduation the bishop of Oslo had delivered the keynote address, speaking through an interpreter before boarding a helicopter that lifted him into a June sky of flawless blue. His advice was sensible—walk modestly, cherish your families, obey the laws of man and God— but as his helicopter sailed away, washing the graduates' upturned faces with the beating air of its blades, Mary understood, with a jolt, that she'd made a terrible mistake. How would she do any of this? While her friends had interviewed for jobs and filled out their applications to graduate school, Mary had spent the winter of her senior year writing a long paper on Baudelaire and taking walks through the snowy sanctuary of trees and prairie grasses behind the campus. She had majored in French, because it was easy and beautiful, but it had prepared her for nothing, and now, behind the mask of her sunglasses, her robe still fluttering from the wind of the helicopter, she felt her face warm with the shame of this discovery. After the ceremony she drove north with friends to a rented cabin on an icy lake where they spent a week drinking beer and waterskiing, but she no longer felt herself to be a part of them; when the week was over, and these same friends drove off to Chicago or Minneapolis or even Los Angeles to begin their lives, Mary returned to the town of Twig.

The bar where she worked was called the Norway, and she shared an apartment over a shoe store with two boys, Curtis and Russell. They had been roommates at the college, where they'd graduated a year before. They did not seem to like one another very much, though Mary had come to understand this was common with men who lived together and were also friends. Curtis sometimes tended bar at the Norway and spent his afternoons before a small easel in the corner of the apartment, smoking and painting. He was small, with dark hair, pale skin, and a sharp chin, and his paintings, Mary thought, were like him—still lifes of fruit or fish, rendered with painful, photographic exactness, on canvases precisely one foot square. Russell had red hair, which he wore in a thick ponytail, and a beard; he was a large man, with a broad chest and powerful arms, and he reminded Mary of a portrait she had seen of the Viking warrior Leif Eriksson, though the similarity stopped there. Russell's girlfriend, Laurie, lived in Des Moines, and in the evenings he wrote her long letters in his bedroom, listening to records or the radio, and then at 4:00 A.M. he went to his job at the bakery, making rolls and cakes. He was applying to Ph.D. programs in Renaissance literature, and the plan was that he would go to school somewhere that Laurie, who was a librarian, could also find a job. Unless Russell had just showered, flour could usually be found somewhere on his person—his beard, his shoes—and sometimes he would return from work so caked that he looked like an actor from a Kabuki play.

Mary liked Russell more, and Mary believed he liked her too. But there was Laurie to think of—his devotion to her, and the almost stately happiness this gave him, were the same qualities that both attracted Mary and made anything between them impossible—so it was Curtis she ended up with. This began one warm night at the end of fall, and on Thanksgiving weekend they drove north in Mary's old Citation to Curtis's parents' house in Duluth, a gloomy Tudor on a bluff above the sullen bulk of Lake Superior. Curtis's father was a judge who liked to hunt, and at Thanksgiving dinner his mother served a goose that he had shot in the wetlands behind the house, while his younger brothers kicked at one another under the table and the wind off the lake rattled the windows of the dining room. Mary and Curtis had been seeing one another just two weeks, and yet they seemed to regard her as a permanent and promising addition to his life. What did she think of Curtis's paintings? they wanted to know. They were beautiful, yes, but wouldn't it make more sense for him to pursue something more grounded, such as law or business, while painting as a hobby? And Mary: did she plan to go on working at that bar? What else was in store for a bright young lady like herself? Mary's family was very quiet—her memories of childhood were like a movie without sound—and by the time the goose was cleared away, she was exhausted and had barely eaten anything. Curtis's younger brothers fought over who would get to bring her dessert—an enormous tart topped with sail-like wedges of chocolate—and when dinner was over they left the table to play basketball in the driveway while Mary and Curtis took a walk along the bluff in the dwindling light.

"I'm sorry about that," Curtis said. "I think my parents really like you, though."

Beneath the pines they stopped to kiss, listening to the thunk of the basketball. Curtis's face was soft—he had no beard at all—and when he kissed her, Mary often thought of things that seemed arbitrary: the gray undersides of spring rain clouds, a cat licking its paws, sheet music with notations penciled in the margins. This time she thought of a raisin, squashed on the steps of her grandmother's porch by the weight of a tiny tennis shoe. At just that moment it began to snow.

"Well, here comes the winter," Mary said. "You know, you should probably tell them not to like me too much."

On the drive south to Twig they decided to stop at Mary's parents' house in a suburb northwest of Minneapolis. In the five years since she had left home for college, her parents had prospered—her father sold advertising for a Christian country-and-western radio station that had gone national, while her mother owned a card and gift shop called Thinking of You—and each time she returned home, Mary was met by the sight of some new major purchase: a pool table, wrought-iron patio furniture, a big-screen television. This unlikely bounty in her parents' lives was painful to Mary; she was glad they finally had the things they wanted, but it was also true that she had borrowed most of the money to pay for college, and was now facing student loan payments the size of a house mortgage.

No one was home, but a new pop-up camper sat in the driveway, and Mary and Curtis used the crank to open the camper's compartment and fiddled with the miniature appliances before driving on to Mary's mother's store. The store, in a downtrodden shopping center surrounded by aging subdivisions, should not have succeeded, but in fact Mary's mother, Gretchen, did quite nicely. Early on she had latched on to a new line of china figurines called Cu-tee-pies—dewy-eyed children in occasional costumes, some holding puppies or rabbits or other small animals—and had wangled an exclusive from the distributor, gambling on the chance that they would become collector's items, which was exactly what had happened. In the window of her shop hung a banner that read YOUR CU-TEE-PIE HEADQUARTERS, and behind the register Gretchen kept a locked case of retired Cu-tee-pies, some selling for as much as a hundred dollars. For graduation she had given Mary a figurine wearing a cap and gown with the words *Congratulations Princess!* engraved in gold letters on its china base. She suggested that Mary might want to put it somewhere safe, such as a deposit box at the bank, in anticipation of the day when it would be worth a great deal of money: "a *great* deal," she said knowingly. But Mary had no place like that, and now it sat on her kitchen table, beside the salt and pepper shakers.

It was the Monday after Thanksgiving, and the small store bustled with holiday shoppers. Mary's father, Lars, had taken the day off to help and was wrapping Cu-tee-pies in tissue paper at a table set up in the back. Mary and Curtis sat down to help him.

"Mary says you're a painter," Lars said to Curtis.

"He's had a show," Mary offered.

Lars waved a piece of tape from his fingers. "Is there money in a thing like that?" he asked Curtis.

"There can be," Curtis said. "But not usually, no."

Mary's father shook his head sadly and held up a Cu-tee-pie waiting to be wrapped, a little girl in an elf costume clutching a daisy.

"Guess how much my wife makes on this thing," Lars said. "Don't guess, I'll tell you. Thirty bucks retail, and fifteen of it goes right into the till."

"Those are excellent margins," Curtis observed.

"It's a racket, if you ask me. Listen," Lars said, and lowered his voice, "I'd like to help out. Let me buy one of your paintings."

"You really don't need to do that, Dad," Mary protested. "You haven't even seen them. They might not be the sort of thing you like."

Lars shrugged amiably. "Just pick the one that you think I'd like best."

"We saw the camper," Mary said neutrally.

"Oh, that," Lars said, and cleared his throat. "We got it out of the *Pennysaver*. Your mother has ideas about going out West. When we'll have the time I just don't know."

Mary's mother returned with Chinese food from the restaurant next door. Like her husband, Gretchen was very tall, and looked much younger than she actually was. She wore her hair in a long loose ponytail that fell down her back, and this afternoon was dressed in a denim skirt and a sweatshirt embroidered with teddy bears. Mary adored her mother with a hopeless affection, like an unrequited crush. She understood this feeling was common in middle children, as Mary was, but there was also a story. Mary's mother had spent her first ten years of life in an orphanage in Grand Forks, North Dakota, run by the Sisters of Mercy. Though Gretchen was the first to say that it hadn't been a bad place at all, the experience of growing up in an institution—of eating, bathing, and sleeping in large groups presided over by kindly old women who meant well but did not always remember her name— had left her with a view of childhood that was sentimental and general. She seemed to draw little distinction between Mary and her older brother and younger sister—often she mistook one for the other, and once had driven Mary to a guitar lesson that was, in fact, her brother Mark's—and nothing could dissuade her from the opinion that her children, who had clothes to wear, food to eat, and a house to live in, were perfectly contented at all times. As she grew, Mary came to see that her mother was merely replicating the impersonal, well-intentioned affections of the nuns who had raised her. But still she longed for more; she longed to be known.

Gretchen served them noodles in brown sauce on paper plates. "So," she began cheerfully, "am I to understand you two are no longer roommates?"

"We are roommates," Mary said.

"A mechanical question," Gretchen went on. "How do you date someone you live with? I've tried to imagine how this works."

"I just bought one of Curtis's paintings," Lars said, changing the subject.

Gretchen looked up, as if the painting were there to see. "Really? Which one?"

"I don't know yet," Lars said, and waved his chopsticks around. "It's a surprise."

They ate their lunch, then opened their fortune cookies and read them aloud. Mary's read, simply, "You will come into money," and in the parking lot, Gretchen gave her a fifty she had taken from the register.

The bill was soft in Mary's hand. "Doesn't it confuse the books, just pulling money from the register like that?"

"The books, the books," Gretchen said wearily. "I am the books." She hugged Mary close, then Mary and Curtis together. "Be happy together, children."

By the time they returned to Twig, darkness had fallen, and the sky over the alleyway behind the shoe store was thick with stars. Mary dressed for work in black pants and one of Curtis's white dress shirts, and put on her heavy coat to walk the three chilly blocks to the Norway. The insides were dim and smoky, and the tables were crowded with students from the college, back from their Thanksgiving holiday and now optimistically drunk. Mary's favorite customer was a man named Phil, a rail-thin alcoholic with a walrus moustache yellowed from smoking, who got by on small checks from the state. Phil lived in a tiny clapboard house by the grain elevator, and his only companions were his cats, whom he had named after different places in Vietnam: Saigon, Da Nang, Haiphong. Each night, Phil came in and put seven dollars on the bar, and drank till the money was gone: a total of six beers at a dollar a can—Pabst Blue Ribbon, or Grain Belt—and a dollar tip for Mary. This was very little, considering how much time he spent at the bar, but Mary didn't mind, and if Phil was still sober he sometimes helped her clean up, telling her stories about his cats, or about the war in Southeast Asia, in which he had not fought.

Mary said hello to Phil, took an apron and serving tray from behind the bar, and went to a table of four boys who had just come in.

"Anybody here even close to twenty-one?"

Grumbling, the boys produced a variety of documents. Most had been falsified in one way or another, but the unwritten rule of the Norway was that an honest try got you one drink. Then Mary looked at the last card.

"What's this?" said Mary. "It's a library card."

"The age is right there," the boy explained.

Some dates had been typed, poorly, on the bottom of the card.

"So it is," Mary said.

"I'll have my usual," the boy said. "A whiskey sour."

Mary flipped the card onto the table. *"Au revoir, mon enfant, "* she said. "Begone, junior."

The boy returned his library card to his wallet. "Fine. Give me a Coke if that's how you're going to be."

"I will if you ask me nicely," Mary said.

The boy rolled his eyes, and his friends snickered. "Mother, may I have a Coke?"

Mary paused and cocked her hip. "You may," she said.

Later in the evening, Mary took her coffee break at the bar with Phil, who was just finishing up his fourth Blue Ribbon.

"How's Curtis?" Phil said. It was Curtis, in fact, who had banned Phil's cats from the bar. Whenever Phil asked this question, the bitterness of the experience was in his voice.

"Not so bad. He just sold a painting," Mary said.

Phil shook his head and smoked. "Truthfully, I sometimes wonder if that boy's good enough for you."

Mary helped herself to one of his cigarettes. "It's not like we're getting married, Phil."

"I'll tell you something I heard." Phil glanced over his shoulder and lowered his voice to a gravelly whisper. "You know that college? On the hill? Kids there are so rich they'll throw away the keys of a brand-new Mercedes. Just pitch them in the trash."

"I don't think that's true," Mary said.

Phil frowned into the broad mirror above the bar. "I watched my buddies die, and for what?"

"I went there, Phil," she said.

Phil nodded gravely. "So you know," he said.

*

In January the temperature fell, as it always did, and the snow piled up in enormous mounds around the town of Twig. Distances seemed to grow longer in the cold, and at night the stars shone hard and pure, like chips of ice, as Mary made her way through the silent streets between her apartment and the Norway. At the end of the month Mary came down with something that felt like the flu; she was tired all the time, and when she wasn't sick to her stomach, her mouth was filled with the taste of metal. Curtis and Russell took care of her, bringing her glasses of ginger ale in bed, or bowls of heated broth. Mary joked that it was nice to see the two of them getting along, though they did not seem to get, or enjoy, this joke.

Her stomach began to feel better, but the feeling of lassitude did not depart—it seemed to have settled in her bones—and when her period did not come, Mary knew what had happened. The directions on the package said that she should wait until morning to take the test, that the concentration of hormones in her urine would be highest at first waking. But the hours that she kept, working late at the bar and seeing just a few hours of sunlight each day, made this seem like advice for some other woman. She took the test alone in the apartment at two in the afternoon, neither expecting nor receiving a different result than the one she got, then dressed and went to work at the Norway.

She wondered what she would do. She could not say that she loved Curtis, but even if she had, this love would be nothing to trust. In any event, she could not see Curtis as a father. She was afraid, but also felt, strangely, that this fear would guide her, that it would help her choose. In college she had known girls to whom the same thing had happened, and the ones who paid the highest price were those who seemed not to care. They went away for a day or two, an interruption no greater than a trip to the dentist to have wisdom teeth removed—many, in fact, claimed this very alibi—then returned to their lives as if nothing had happened; but a month or so later, just when the crisis seemed over, they would find themselves barricaded in their dorm rooms, unable to sleep or eat or even dress, weeping uncontrollably or else feeling nothing at all. Mary would see one of the resident advisors knocking quietly on the door, and then asking questions—is everything all right with so-and-so?—and the next thing anyone knew, the room would be empty, the mattress turned over and propped against the wall, and that would be the end of it.

On the day after the test Mary awoke in an empty bed, and knew that the worst of the sickness had passed. Curtis had taken the Citation to Minneapolis to show some of his paintings to a dealer who bought artwork for model homes in housing developments, and Mary spent the afternoon cleaning the apartment before visiting Russell at the bakery. The air of the bakery was moist and sweet, and under the long banks of fluorescent lights Russell was moving trays of bread dough, molded into loaves, in and out of the oven. Mary watched him, still in her heavy coat.

"What will you do?" he asked.

"What does anyone do?"

They took pint cartons of milk from the refrigerator and sat at a stainless-steel table in the back, eating heart-shaped Valentine cookies sprinkled with purple sugar that stuck to their fingers.

"I can speak to Curtis." Russell took a long drink of milk to wash down a cookie and brushed crumbs from his red beard. "The word I'm thinking of is 'responsibilities.' "

Mary found this hard to envision. "You two don't even like each other," she said.

Russell thought about this and tossed his empty carton in a trash pail full of tiny snippets of dough. "That could work in my favor." He paused and looked at Mary. "Either way, you know, you should probably be talking to him."

Russell was waiting to hear from graduate schools, and they

discussed his prospects. His first choice was the University of Iowa, but Laurie opposed this plan, having had enough of Iowa.

"The thing is," Russell said, shaking his head, "I can't even really explain why I want to get a Ph.D. anymore. What's so important about Elizabethan courtesy manuals? Why do I love the things that no one cares about?"

"That's always the question," Mary agreed.

Russell's grandfather was also a baker, in a small town in the Iron Range. "I once asked him, 'How did you know—really know—that you wanted to do this with your life?' "

"What did he say?"

Russell climbed off his stool and wiped his hands on his apron. " 'The old baker died.' "

Twig was famous for very little, but in 1874, in the dead of winter, the Jesse James gang had held up the town bank. Unlike his well-known defeat at the town of Northfield in the summer of 1876, the James gang had strolled into Twig Savings and Loan and made off with the money easily, plunging the town into a financial abyss that had nearly erased it from the map of time. It was an odd event to celebrate, but every year on the anniversary of the robbery the Lions Club staged a reenactment on Main Street, and in the evening there were fireworks over the baseball diamond.

That night Mary and Russell went to the fireworks together, and when the last ashes had scattered over the snowy baseball field, Mary left him to begin her shift at the Norway. She finished at midnight and sat down with Phil, who was wearing a lopsided cowboy hat, as he always did for "Jesse Fest." It was one of Phil's greatest disappointments that the Lions Club had never asked him to play the role of the great bandit himself. On the bartop in front of him was a single bullet, and he picked it up and pointed it at Mary, who raised her arms in mock alarm.

"Don't shoot, Jesse," Mary said.

Phil returned the bullet to the bartop and thoughtfully smoothed out his moustache with thumb and forefinger. "It's the wrong caliber, anyway. Have a look at this." He searched his shirt pockets and produced a photocopied wanted poster of Jesse James, which he held beside his face.

"Now, what am I seeing?"

"I got it at the library," Phil explained. "When I saw it, I, too, was surprised at the degree of likeness."

Mary studied the picture another moment. "There's always next year," she said.

"Not the way I hear it." Phil dejectedly folded the poster back up. "You think they haven't seen this already? I am persona non grata in this town."

Mary got Phil his last beer and got one for herself.

"You shouldn't drink," Phil said to her.

Mary poured her beer down the sink and got a Coke instead. "God. Who told you?"

"You shouldn't, you know. Or smoke." Phil lit one himself and crumpled the empty pack.

Mary sat down beside him again and waved the thick air away. "It's the same, just being in here. I'm serious. Did you talk to Russell?"

Phil frowned. "Who's Russell?"

"So you didn't talk to him."

"I always wanted a son." Phil sighed, his eyes pooling with tears. "Now it's too late."

Mary pointed at his beer. "I've lost track. How many is that?"

"It's all right," Phil said, and rose stiffly to go. "I'm done for tonight."

She helped him with his coat, a denim jacket so filthy it seemed weighed down by dirt. He had the cowboy hat but no scarf, and she took her own and wrapped it around his lanky neck, tucking the ends into the jacket. "Straight home, all right? It's cold. Call when you get there."

Mary left the bar and returned under a full moon to the apartment over the shoe store. Curtis was working at his easel in her old bedroom, and Russell was asleep. She couldn't explain how Phil had known—although, in hindsight, she recognized that this might not have been so; his words were ambiguous. Mary made cocoa for herself and Curtis and told him her news.

Curtis sat beside her on the sofa and put his arms around her. "A baby," he said happily; and yet he did not look at her as he said this. "How did it happen?"

"I think in the usual way," Mary said.

"We were careful, were we not?"

"There's careful and there's careful," Mary said.

They agreed that they would wait a week to see how they felt. That night, in bed with Curtis, Mary thought about Phil. He hadn't called, but she had not really expected him to. She saw him walking home through moonlight to the run-down house he shared with his cats, across a field of snow as blue as radioactive milk. She saw him lying down in the snow, and then the wind began to push snow over his body, until only the tips of his shoes were showing, but they were her mother's shoes, and it was her mother under the snow. Then she woke up and realized she had dreamt this.

Curtis said that he wanted to marry. His desire did not seem completely sincere, but under the circumstances Mary wondered how it could have been. In any event, it seemed to Mary that they should at least try. It surprised them both how easy this was to do—no blood tests, just a few papers to sign. Curtis made the necessary phone calls, and on a Tuesday they drove to city hall in Minneapolis and got in line. After, Mary planned to call her parents, and then the two of them would drive back to Twig; she would work in the bar that night, and Curtis would get back to painting.

Curtis dressed in a dark suit-coat and jeans, and Mary wore the blue wool dress she had worn beneath her choir robe in college. She had no flowers, though many of the other women in the waiting room were clutching small bouquets at their waists. Each couple had a number, and every few minutes a clerk with a clipboard would appear through a door behind the desk to call the next couple in to take their vows.

"This is crazy," Curtis said.

"It isn't exactly what I planned for my life either," Mary said. She was holding their number, thirty-six. The couple they had just called was number thirty-two. "On the other hand, it seems I've planned very little."

Curtis looked like he was about to cry.

"I can't," he said helplessly. "Not to either one of us."

Mary took his hand, threading their fingers together. "I know," she said.

They left the building and returned to the car. "Don't do it," Curtis said, his knuckles white on the wheel.

"Don't?"

Curtis took a deep breath. "I don't . . . believe in it," he said.

"No one does," Mary said.

They drove out of the city and stopped at an Ember's for lunch. Her circumstances made it difficult for Mary to know what to order; already the hunger had begun, a force like possession, and yet she now knew this would come to nothing.

"I'll go with you," Curtis said finally.

"Who's asking?" Mary said.

The clinic was in St. Paul—a small white house on a residential street with baby strollers left on the porches and brightly colored plastic toys strewn in the yards. Mary parked her car and walked around the block twice before stepping onto the porch. Inside, a dozen women sat on plastic chairs. Some were very young, and had brought their mothers with them. Seeing these women, Mary wished she could have, too, but of course this was impossible— her mother was, after all, adopted, and under different circumstances, might not have been born at all. Mary gave her name at the desk.

"Where are the demonstrators?" she asked. On a stool by the front door Mary had seen a pile of leaflets, weighted down with a stone.

The woman looked at the clock on the wall, then back at Mary. She was spooning yogurt from a cup and had tucked a pencil behind one ear. "I think he usually goes to lunch at one o'clock."

Someone, a nurse or doctor, examined Mary and told her to come back in two weeks. This seemed like a long time, but Mary didn't see how she was in a position to argue. Outside, a single demonstrator patrolled the sidewalk, a bald man wearing a sandwich board and mittens. One eye looked at her, while the other did not; the second one was glass.

"This isn't the answer," he pleaded.

"Fuck you," Mary said.

Spring came early to Twig, and the next two weeks brought storm after storm to the little town. Mary moved back into her old bedroom, with its window looking out over the street above the shoe store and its sign, a single boot with an upswept toe, creaking in the spring wind. It was clear that things were over with Curtis—that, when the time came, they would not emerge together on the far side—but in these two weeks of wind and rain, they became a couple again, in a way they had never been before. They were tender and affectionate with one another, and when she came home each night from the Norway, Curtis made her something to eat and then said good-night to her at the door of her bedroom, as if they lived in different towns.

On the eleventh day, a Saturday, Mary returned from the Laundromat and found Curtis sitting on the sofa, clutching his eye. She thought he might be crying, but when he pulled his hand away she saw the green-and-purple bruise, and the cut along the ridge of his cheekbone, a line of blood dried black. The eye itself was uninjured.

She sat beside him and touched his cheek with the tips of her fingers. "What happened?"

"Russell did it," Curtis said.

Mary tried to imagine this but couldn't. She wrapped some ice cubes in a warm dish towel from the laundry basket and held it to his eye. "I didn't know he knew how to hit. Where was this? Outside somewhere? Or here in the apartment?"

Russell had hit him with his radio. Mary folded the laundry while Curtis iced his eye. Their things were still mixed together, and she sorted them into separate piles of neatly folded clothes on the old trunk they used as a coffee table. She had always done it this way, but as these piles accumulated, they became something more.

"I thought I'd go back home," Curtis said.

"That's probably best," Mary heard herself say. "I'm sorry, but could you please do it now?"

In the morning he was gone, and two days later Mary drove herself to the clinic. How terrible, she thought, to be twenty-two, and already have the worst thing of her life to remember. Then she imagined a strongbox, like a small safe, and she took this idea and placed it in the box. Afterward, she rested an hour on a cot, drank the juice and nibbled the cookies they gave her, and then got back into the Citation. They had told her not to drive after the abortion, but no one actually checked on this, and she drove halfway to Twig before she stopped to vomit in a field of broken corn.

She managed to drive the rest of the way home, climb the stairs to the apartment, and collapse on the couch. They had told her not to take aspirin—it thinned the blood—but that was all she had, so she took two and wrapped herself in a blanket. She drifted in and out of an unhappy sleep. Late in the afternoon Russell came home from the bakery, his hair and hands dusted with flour. She hadn't told him that today was the day, and now she saw she should have. He brought her a tray of tea and cinnamon toast, and sat on the couch near her feet.

"I'm sorry, that's all I know how to make."

"It's perfect," Mary said, chewing her toast. "I didn't know how hungry I was."

Russell looked at the floor with desolate eyes. "Oh, he's an asshole."

"I don't know if he is."

That evening a gusty wind tossed the bare branches about. Mary lay on the sofa and listened to the storm approach. It seemed at first to be very far away, and then was suddenly upon them. At the same moment that the sky turned yellow, they heard the tornado sirens; the heavens opened, and hail began to pelt the windows, a sound like pennies falling.

"Check the TV," Mary said from the couch.

"There's no time." Russell lifted her off the sofa and carried her in his arms down the stairs. A green haze had descended over the street, and the wind had ceased, freezing the scene in its abandonment—a bad sign, as Mary knew. Hailstones were scattered over the sidewalk, some as large as marbles, mixed with old leaves and twigs that the wind had torn from the trees. Cars were parked at haphazard angles; their drivers had dashed inside.

"What now, my hero?" said Mary.

He carried her around the building to the gravel alleyway, down a flight of concrete steps, and into the dim basement. There Russell placed her, still wrapped in her blanket, on the floor by the water heater. The wind resumed, the lights went out, the heavens shook with thunder. Russell lay beside her on the damp floor and kissed her.

"Your beard tickles," Mary said.

The tornado touched down a mile away, near a highway overpass. It skimmed along an empty oat field, fingering a deep rut in the damp soil, searching here and there, then found a farmhouse, and blew it to pieces.

She had lied to Phil; she had a little money, after all. Years before, an uncle had left her ten thousand dollars in his will. She had met him just a few times, and Mary remembered him only vaguely—a pale, perspiring man, who smelled like peppermint and sat on her parents' patio in the sunshine drinking glasses of iced tea. He was a butcher in California, but did not seem like one. Her parents had put the money in a savings account, earning a dribble of interest, but even so, it had grown to a little over fourteen thousand dollars in the six years since Uncle George had died.

She left Twig in the summer. Curtis had come back to get the rest of his things; Russell had moved back to his parents' in Bloomington and, in the fall, was starting graduate school at the University of Illinois. The day before her departure she held a yard sale on the sidewalk outside the shoe store, and by evening all that remained were some stained kitchen pots, an asparagus fern, Russell's broken radio, the Cu-tee-pie her mother had given her for graduation, and a card table of paperback books. In waning light Phil helped her carry the pots and the asparagus fern and the radio to the Dumpster behind the Norway, and with a fat

Magic Marker she wrote a sign for the table of books: FREE, TAKE WHAT YOU LIKE. THE TABLE TOO. She left it where it was and awoke that night in her empty room to the sound of rain, fanning over the pages of her books.

She drove north the next morning, a hot, wet Sunday in July, beneath a sky the color of milk. The air conditioner in the Citation was broken, and she drove with a damp kerchief around her head, listening as the Minneapolis stations came in clearer with each passing mile. She had thought about leaving the Cutee-pie behind, but she had had enough of that, and it sat on the seat beside her. In Bloomington she stopped at Russell's parents' house and signed the title of the car over to him.

"I should pay you something," he said, opening his wallet. They were standing in the driveway in front of the house. He had been mowing the lawn, and wet grass clippings clung to the weave of his shirt.

She brushed some grass away. "You already have," she said.

She accepted a dollar, and the next afternoon Russell drove her from her parents' house to the airport in the Citation. He had not kissed her since the evening of the storm. She knew that he would want to, but also that he wouldn't know if this was the right thing to do or not. It was. In the busy loading zone, her suitcases piled at their feet, they kissed each other, taking their time. Then she carried her things inside and boarded her plane and flew away, through the summer night to Rome.

In the fall she wrote him a letter. She was in Florence, where she had been since September. She lived near Santa Croce, sharing an apartment with her cousin, who was a student at the same school where Mary was taking courses: a seminar on Dante, Italian language and culture, figure drawing. From her apartment, in the old servants' quarters of a great palazzo, she could see through the buildings the dirty Arno, and below her the small piazza where sunlight pooled on the cobblestones and old men gathered to listen to soccer games on the radio. She had a boyfriend, an American she'd met walking in the gardens behind Pitti Palace, where she had gone with a sketchbook to draw. He'd approached her where she stood, looking at a sign displaying a map of the gardens and park, and asked in a halting Italian that made her laugh: *"Dove siamo?" Dove siamo:* Where are we? He was blond and tanned, and had a broad, happy smile, and didn't look at all like Curtis, nor remind her of him. He loved to talk, to tell stories about himself and the places he'd been. He had been out of college a year, worked in San Francisco as a carpenter, and was now traveling with friends. She never got to meet them. The two of them talked on a shady bench in the park, and when it grew dark he caught a bus back to the hostel to retrieve his backpack, and stayed; and though she did not make love to him then, she soon did, and knew that she was cured. She was twenty-three years old, an American girl in Europe making love to a boy from Ohio who was funny and kind and had no plans for her at all; he would find an apartment, a job teaching English, they would travel together to Rome, to Venice for *carnivale,* to Greece when the weather grew warm; she was cured, her heart was cured. *Dear Russell,* she wrote,

> *Thank you for your letter, and congratulations to you and Laurie. Your news makes me happy, and if I am back in the summer, I will come to your wedding.*
>
> *It is just a few months later, but already those days in Twig seem like a distant memory. Is it the same for you? The mail is slow here, and the phone is impossible, so I have heard almost nothing from home; so perhaps that's the reason. But I also know that our year there was like no other—it was like a year*

outside of time—and I'm glad we were together, to know that it happened.

She wrote this in a coffee bar, late on an October afternoon. She told him about her roommate, and about her classes and friends, and the way the trains were always on strike and it was always warm; she wrote him of her life. When she was done she sealed it without reading it, bought a brightly colored stamp from the young woman behind the counter, and slid it into the postbox by the phone. On the busy street the sun fell over her, and for a moment she stood still, tasting autumn sunshine. She closed her eyes, hiked her bag up high on her shoulder, and that was when she felt it, one last time: the lightness. It blossomed inside her and widened, like the rings on a pond, suffusing every thought, and she knew what it was, that it was a child. Then it was a second, and then a third, so that she knew that in her life she would have three, two girls and a boy. Motorbikes sped past, laughing students, tiny weaving cars; but their voices, their eyes—all seemed far, far away. She knew that people had stopped and gathered around her; someone had taken her by the elbow, in case she might fall. She stood on the street, on the old stones of Florence, her eyes closed, one hand touching her chest where her heart was, and felt the spirits of each one of her children, not rising but falling; they came from above. Then a fourth passed through her—different than the others, for it was a presence of great hesitancy, both there and not there—and she knew who this was, too. *Good-bye*, she thought, *good-bye*, and she turned from everyone and hurried down the street of the ancient city so they would not see her weeping.

GROOM

May 1991

THE MORNING HE IS to be married, O'Neil Burke—thirty, orphaned, a teacher of ninth- and eleventh-grade English—awakens first at 3:00 A.M. to laughter and the bright crash of glass on pavement, again at 5:00 when the sun is rising, and once more at 8:00, when he lifts his head from the pillow, moist with the sweat of his hangover and uneasy dreams, and looks out the window by his bed in the old hotel. Two floors below he can see the parking lot, his friends' cars, the sweeping lawn, splendidly green; beyond that the stand of hemlock and white pine ascending the steep hill. By his own car someone has dropped a beer bottle, and he remembers the sound of it breaking, and his friend Connor's voice, cheerfully drunk, barking, "God-*damn!*" The air is still and moist, the sun warm for a morning in late May this far north, and the windows of the cars are glazed with Vermont's heavy dew. O'Neil hears the slap of a screen door, and while he watches, a woman exits the rear of the hotel and crosses the lot to her car, a new sedan that is probably rented. It is Simone, one of Mary's friends from high school; O'Neil hadn't met her until the night before, at the party in the hotel bar. She has already dressed for the wedding, in high sling-back heels, a pale green dress open at the shoulders, and a wide straw hat with a silk flower and red ribbon, forked at the back and trailing in the swing of her rich blond hair. The hat, O'Neil thinks, looks good on her, though it wouldn't look as good on most women, and because she is wearing high heels, her trip across the uneven pavement of the lot takes some time, as if she knows someone is watching. When she reaches the car she keys the trunk and removes a large white package done up with a bow, the same red as the ribbon of her hat. Holding the package, she lifts her face and sees O'Neil watching her from his second-story window, and waves. Or, perhaps it isn't O'Neil she has seen, just a shape through the screen. Embarrassed, O'Neil returns the wave.

His mind does not dwell on this, but turns to the weather, on which everything depends. While he has watched Simone cross the lot, the clouds seem to have thickened, congealing overhead in a portentous way. The wedding is scheduled for noon, in the meadow high above his sister's house, five miles away. The meadow is reachable only by a narrow path; if it rains, even a quick shower, the path may become too muddy for their guests, or worse, it may wash out. In any event, the meadow will be soaked. O'Neil begins to worry, and so he rises, hurriedly washes his face and brushes his teeth, and puts on running clothes to go up the hill behind the hotel to have a look. It was clear, he remembers, when he first woke up, but now he doesn't know what it's going to do.

O'Neil is sitting on the bed, pulling up his socks, when there is a sharp knock on the door and Stephen, the best man, pokes his head into the room. His hair is wet, and his cheeks are smooth from shaving; he looks remarkably alert, O'Neil thinks, for someone who drank nearly all night, especially the sour, heavy beer made in the hotel's microbrewery. It was good beer, O'Neil remembers, but not the sort of thing to drink too much of.

"I can't believe it," Stephen says. He sits down heavily on the empty bed next to O'Neil's. "You're going running? Go back to bed."

"Is that what you're wearing for the wedding?" Stephen is dressed in jeans, old sandals held together with electrician's tape, and a T-shirt that reads "I Am a Womanmade Product." O'Neil frowns, remembering Simone, her slow progress across the parking lot, like a model on a runway.

"Relax, will you? This thing is hours away. Have a beer. You want a beer?"

"I'm running up the hill." O'Neil has begun to lace his shoes, one-hundred-dollar Nikes with molded orthotic inserts to balance his wobbly knees. Climbing a steep hill seems a good way to begin the day of his marriage, a suitable purification, but as he leans over to tie the laces a watery dizziness fills his head and the energy that launched him from bed departs, leaving him exhausted and frightened. He has to take a deep breath, then another. Then the feeling passes; he is fine.

"I don't know about this weather," he manages. "What's it doing out?"

"Little of this, little of that." Stephen fishes in the pocket of his jeans for a cigarette, which he lights and leaves in the corner of his mouth, his right eye squinting artfully above the trail of smoke. "I hate to tell you, but Mary warned me you might try to bolt"—he gestures broadly at O'Neil, now dressed to run—"and you're not going anywhere."

"So come with me. It's not far. How late were you up, anyway? I heard you for a while out there."

"Don't know." Stephen shrugs. "Two or so. Connor's still asleep." He looks at the end of his cigarette and frowns acidly. "You know, this really tastes *bad*." He crosses the room to find an ashtray and crushes it out. "All right," he agrees. "I'll meet you out front. This should be a lot of laughs for you. I can't run at all."

Outside, O'Neil sees he was right about the weather. The breeze has picked up, and heavy clouds have gathered from the west and south, over the hill that stands behind the inn. At his car he kicks aside the broken glass, steps back, and places one foot on the bumper to stretch out the calf. His lower back is tight, but the leg stretches out fine, and he holds the position for ten seconds, feeling the muscle grow warm and pliable before he changes to the other leg. He does his hams, his quads, each exercise bringing him closer to the moment when he will feel that he has moved into his body, and his day can begin. He is sitting on the grass, his knees apart and the soles of his shoes perfectly aligned, when the screen door slaps and Stephen trots into the yard. He has changed to jogging clothes: cutoff shorts and a fresh T-shirt, sleeveless this time, with the emblem of a cruise line printed across the front. On his feet he wears black high-tops with plastic orange basketballs embedded in the tongues. The leather actually looks buttery, O'Neil thinks.

"Don't you have any other sneakers?" O'Neil nods glumly at Stephen's feet. "Those will give you shin splints, believe me."

Stephen has begun, mockingly, to do jumping jacks, slapping his hands in the air over his head and counting numbers at random: "Six, fourteen, a hundred and eight." Then he drops to the ground and does five snappy push-ups, wheezes hard, and collapses on the moist grass. "You know," he moans, "the problem is I love to smoke. I mean, I truly love it. It would break my heart to quit."

It is nine when they set off together down the drive, O'Neil holding back a little to let Stephen set the pace. O'Neil doesn't quite know where he's going, but he thinks there must be a way up the hill, something with an obvious name: Top of the World Road or Bella Vista Lane. From there he should be able to get a good look at what's headed in their direction. The wedding is three hours away, and though a tent has been erected in his sister's yard as a backup, it is important to both O'Neil and Mary to be married outside. They came up with the idea months ago, when there was still an inch of gray snow in Philadelphia and spring seemed a long way off. On the invitations, they wrote no address, only "The Meadow, Hanford, Vermont," and shaded the paper with pastels: a stroke of green for the earth, blue and pink and bits of brown to hold the sky above it. It was a fun night, coloring the invitations at the dining room table of their small apartment, and O'Neil and Mary finished a bottle of wine while they worked, as they had done when they were first together and nervous with one another. But this was different. They were making wedding invitations.

O'Neil and Stephen run for a while in silence, under heavy trees that obstruct their view of the sky and the weather it contains. They are circling the hill, O'Neil knows, skirting its base, but there doesn't seem to be any way up. Beside him, Stephen breathes heavily, and once in a while O'Neil pulls back to let his friend catch up. Stephen is holding his arms too high—as if he were carrying a pile of wood, when they should be closer to his waist to open the chest—and he is running on his toes, which scuff noisily when he lands. This will hasten the shin splints his heavy sneakers have already guaranteed, but O'Neil decides not to say anything. After about a mile they pass a big house with a barn and two speckled horses grazing on the front lawn; a dirt road veers to the right, along the edge of the property. A bent sign at the roadside reads, Skyline Drive, and beneath that, a warning: Minimum Maintenance Road. Someone has shot three holes in the sign, their edges haloed with rust. Beyond, the road turns again to the right and ascends into the trees.

"No way," Stephen says. He stops and bends at the waist to brace himself on his knees. For a second O'Neil thinks his friend is about to throw up. Stephen gives his head a horsy shake and spits hard onto the gravel.

"Just don't think about the hill." O'Neil's legs feel thick and sore, and he knows that if he stops moving his courage will leave him.

"It's these shoes," Stephen says. "I can't *believe* you let me wear these fucking shoes." He spits again and collapses on the ground, bracing his back against the thin signpost. He waves O'Neil on, his eyes already closed. "Here is where my job ends," he says.

O'Neil doesn't respond, and starts up the hill alone. He guesses it's a mile at most to the top, but he runs easily in case the distance has deceived him. It surprises him, how bad he feels. Though he has slept only six hours and that not well, he hasn't run for three days, and usually his body stores the energy. Today he feels as if he's never run at all; his side aches, his fingers tingle with a strange coldness, and he cannot find the correct rhythm— legs, arms, lungs, the body's musical sentence in three-quarter time—to match the hill that rises under him, carrying him up into the woods. The road is sloppy from late spring runoff, and O'Neil hears the soft gurgle of a nearby creek, winding its mossy way down the hillside. He passes a small house, then a second, larger one, with a gracious wraparound porch and a hammock slung in the yard, and he wonders how it would be to live up here as his sister does, to raise a family in this country of tall trees and long winters; for a moment he imagines that such a life is what he would like to have someday, believing it but also hoping that turning the idea around in his head will carve a space his jangling body can slide into. When it doesn't, he thinks about Mary, who is awake by now and dressing for the wedding in her room with her friends, and about the children they may someday have, the kind of work they will do, and the houses they will live in. He thinks about a book he read years ago—a book he loved and had forgotten—about a boy who lives alone in the forests of Maine and befriends the trees and animals. He thinks about his sister, who will stand with him at the altar, her husband and sons; he remembers his parents, how he misses them on this, his wedding day.

O'Neil has climbed for ten minutes when the road levels and gives onto a grassy clearing with a view to the north and behind him, higher up, a field in which a herd of sheep dreamily graze. O'Neil stops and stands with his back to the field, resting his hand on a smoothly weathered fence post. Below him he can see his hotel and the town of Southwich, its grid of streets and houses and shops, and his heart expands at the sight of this happy and attractive place that exists for no reason. To the west he finds the main road where it follows the lake, a shimmering expanse two miles away, and beyond it the great sullen peaks of the Adirondacks, now socked in heavy haze. Again O'Neil looks east, toward his sister's house, and counts seven lines of clouds drifting almost imperceptibly toward him in the lazy air. Far off, a curtain of rain falls into the hills.

It is here, alone with the town laid out below him, that O'Neil allows himself to think about his parents and remember the accident that killed them twelve years ago. This is why he has come. He does not believe in heaven, or the existence of consciousness after death, but he knows that his awareness of them is never far, like a ghost that travels beside him, always at the edge of his vision; and that when he wishes to feel close to them, as he does today, he can bring this awareness into focus, briefly, in a picture. He closes his eyes and lets his mind range. The image he selects is from his sister's wedding, a year before the accident: his father in his tuxedo, standing on a chair to toast the gathering; his mother laughing, her head thrown back in release, her face opening with pleasure at the wit of the toast O'Neil can no longer hear. *There is my father*, he thinks, *my father, toasting. There is my mother in her blue dress.* He holds the picture in his mind as long as he can, until the colors blend and shift, the signal breaks up like a radio station gone out of range, and what remains is only a spidery light that dances against the interior of his closed eyes and the memory that they are dead. Then he says a prayer against the rain and heads down the hill.

Stephen is asleep at the bottom, and together they walk back to the hotel. By the time they return it is after ten. Mary's parents are finishing breakfast in the dining room, and before O'Neil can hurry up the stairs they see him and wave him over. They are dressed for the wedding, and O'Neil, in his damp T-shirt and shorts, stands awkwardly by their table and eats a cinnamon roll while they talk about the weather. If it *looks* like rain, Gretchen wants to know, will they still hike up to the meadow? She hopes he'll say no—Mary's family has been a little uncomfortable with the plan all along—but he says he's not sure; he'll have to talk to Mary. Probably, he says, if it looks like rain but isn't actually raining, they will go ahead with it.

O'Neil finishes his roll, takes another off the table to eat later in his room, and excuses himself to meet his friends and dress. He has nearly crossed the lobby when the manager stops him and hands him the phone: his sister.

"What about the weather?" she asks.

O'Neil rubs his eyes. He is exhausted by the question, and doesn't want to make any more decisions. Guests are beginning to come downstairs. He really needs to go get ready. He tells his sister he doesn't know.

"Well, it's raining over here. It *was* raining, anyway. I don't see how the old folks are going to make it up the path." There is a scratching noise on the line, and O'Neil's sister's voice drifts away. "Stop it, Noah. Here, play with this." Then she returns. "O'Neil? Sorry, he's fussing. The caterer is here too. I think she wants to talk to you about the chairs. If it's raining we'll need to put some under the tent."

"That's all right." O'Neil thinks for a minute. What is it he needs? He looks up to see their friends, Russell and Laurie and their young son, Adam, coming down the stairs, the three of them wearing rubber boots and Russell swinging a folded umbrella like a putter. They laugh when they see him still in his running shorts with his wedding an hour away, as if this is typical in some way, which O'Neil knows is certainly true. He is late for almost everything: the last one dressed, the last car in the drive, the last to turn in his grades; except for Stephen, he is the last to marry. "Listen, Kay," he says.

"Jack, can you do something with him, *please?*" There is a shuffle as Kay hands his youngest nephew off. "What's that, hon?"

"I'm stumped. I can't think anymore. I'm not even dressed." O'Neil knows she understands what he is really asking; just to let things slide until he gets there, and if there's anything left to decide, he'll do it then, or let the momentum of the day force the last pieces into place. "I think I need some ad hoc parenting here," O'Neil says.

"Steady, kid," Kay says. Several moments pass. More guests are coming down the stairs, waving to him and shaking their heads at his dishevelment, and O'Neil wants to leave the lobby very badly.

"Okay, how about this," Kay says at last. "No comment on the weather, the caterer can do whatever she wants with the chairs, and anybody who wants to mess with the groom has to go through me. All right?"

Relief washes over him. "I love you. I mean, you're my only living relative, but even so."

"Ditto. Don't go bugging Mary. I know that's what you want

to do, but that bad-luck stuff is nothing to fool with. Jack didn't see me, and so far so good."

O'Neil hangs up, asks the hotel manager please not to give him any more calls, and heads to the kitchen to see if he can scare up a tray of tea and rolls for Mary. His plan is to place it beside her door, knock, and quickly retreat. He believes he has forgotten something, some detail like the caterer's chairs, but he cannot recall what it might be, and he is just as glad to bring Mary some breakfast and let things take care of themselves. The kitchen is empty, but O'Neil looks around and finds Alice, the woman who tended bar the night before, reading the newspaper in the crowded pantry. Breakfast is over, she says, but she is sure she can put something together.

"So, are you nervous?" she asks, pouring Mary's tea. She has a pleasant face, with the soft, butterscotchy tan of someone who spends a great deal of time outdoors in all weather. Her blond hair is tied in a thick Teutonic braid that falls the length of her back, the end just touching the top of her jeans. "You don't look nervous." She laughs, showing the lines of her eyes. It is a laugh that says that she, too, is married, that it happens to everyone.

"I don't know," O'Neil says. "I think maybe I'm just getting used to it."

"Well, don't be." She hands him the tray. On it she has placed, beside the basket of muffins and the mug of tea, a thin glass vase holding a single yellow rose. She wipes her hands on her apron. "Take my word for it. It's the happiest day of your life. You'll see."

"Is it?" O'Neil, holding the tray against his stomach and looking at the rose, feels a tightness in his cheeks and suddenly knows he is about to fall apart. He cannot account for this, because as far as he knows he isn't nervous, or sad, or even especially happy, though what he feels seems related to happiness. It is as if he is suddenly inside his own emotions, so far inside them that he may have neglected to breathe, and he rests the tray on the counter and inhales deeply through his nose. He notices Alice has left the room. Then she returns, dragging a wooden chair from the pantry.

"Here," she says, and slides the chair under him. "You rest a minute."

O'Neil does as she says, and Alice hands him Mary's tea. He takes a small sip, letting the cup hang under his face to feel the sweet steam on his cheeks. The cup is like a warm, smooth stone in his hand, and he realizes he is shivering.

"The same thing happened to my husband. It's all right. You can stay in here as long as you need. Your family is probably driving you crazy."

"Maybe I shouldn't have gone running," O'Neil says. "I hardly slept at all."

"You're just tired." Alice is crouched on her heels in front of O'Neil, looking into his face. Behind O'Neil the kitchen door swings open and without averting her glance Alice says, "Just a minute in here," and the door swings closed again. "When's the ceremony? Noon?" O'Neil nods. "Well, then, in a couple of hours it will all be over, and the two of you will be together. That's the nicest part, I think."

"This is the day you always remember," O'Neil says, inexplicably.

Alice smiles and takes his free hand. Hers, like the cup, is smooth and warm, and covered with flour dust. "That's right," she says.

"My parents aren't here," O'Neil explains. "They died a long time ago. Maybe that's what's bothering me."

"I wouldn't be at all surprised," Alice says. "That's very hard, at a time like this. You must be missing them."

"I have my sister, though," O'Neil says. "She was in the bar last night, with her husband. We're getting married at her house."

"Well, that's something. That's a lot."

"And Mary, of course. I have her."

"So that's your family," Alice says. She gives O'Neil's hand an encouraging shake. "Sounds like a nice one. That's all a family is, in my experience, is people who look after you."

For a while they stay like this, their hands knitted together, O'Neil drinking the tea. His shivering has stopped, and what he feels now is a languorous contentment that rises from his feet to his legs and chest and arms, and he knows that he could just as easily go to sleep as do anything at all. He would like to go to sleep with Alice watching him, there in the warm kitchen where she works.

"I truly appreciate this," O'Neil says. "I'm in your debt."

"It's nothing." Alice shrugs, the long rope of her hair swinging. *"De nada."*

O'Neil rises and takes the tray. He has finished the tea, but the muffins are still there in a wicker basket covered with a blue napkin. The clock above the stove says that it is just past eleven, and guests will be arriving at the house now. Probably Mary is already there. He puts his hand over the napkin, feeling the radiant moistness of the muffins rising through the cloth, and then Alice lifts her face to him and kisses his cheek. It is the nicest thing he has ever felt in his life, and he instantly wants to tell Mary all about it.

"For the groom," she says.

Upstairs, his friends are waiting for him: Stephen, wearing his blue suit, and Connor, dressed improbably in seersucker and a pink bow tie. It is a surprising scene; both men, lying on the twin beds of O'Neil's room, are fast asleep, their hands folded at their waists like pharaohs. The room is dark behind closed shades.

Stephen's eyes open when O'Neil sits beside him on the bed. He nods hopefully at the tray on O'Neil's lap. "Breakfast?"

O'Neil hands him the basket of muffins. "Did Mary leave yet?"

Stephen bites into a muffin and nods. "A few minutes ago. I saw them from the window." He reaches across the space between the beds and lightly slaps Connor's shoulder. "All hands on deck. Our boy is here."

"What time is it?" Connor is instantly awake. He has driven up alone from Boston because his wife, an intern at the same hospital where he is a surgical resident, couldn't get time off from work. "There you are," he says to O'Neil. "So?"

"I don't know," O'Neil says. "It's late."

"That's the beauty of it." Connor brushes a hand over his coarse hair and grins. His hangover, O'Neil knows, is probably terrible. "No groom, no wedding."

O'Neil takes a beer from the cooler and heads to the bathroom to shower. The pressure is wonderfully strong, and he takes his time, letting the hot needles run over him, thinking only of the weather, how he hopes it won't rain, and of his good, loyal friends in the next room. He has known them since high school, seventeen years; soon he will know them longer than he knew his own parents. When he is done he wraps himself with a rough towel and stands in front of the mirror and drinks the beer, which tastes good to him as it always does after a run. He fills the basin to shave, but when he takes the razor in his hand he sees that he is shaking; not shivering, as before, but his hand won't be still. He finishes the beer and opens the door. Stephen is standing at the window now, smoking a cigarette, and Connor is sitting in the room's one upholstered chair. For an instant they seem not to notice him. Then Stephen turns and smiles.

"How's it going in there, tiger?"

"Not so good." O'Neil holds out his quavering hand to demonstrate. "You were right. I don't think I can shave."

"Ah." Stephen nods. "Connor? This is your department, am I right?"

Connor moves swiftly to the ice chest and removes another Ballantine, wiping the glass on a towel. He hands it to O'Neil. "As your doctor, I advise you to drink this. Now, then—" Connor pulls the desk chair into the bathroom and O'Neil sits, sipping his second beer, which he knows he shouldn't have. Connor spreads the cream on O'Neil's cheeks, then moves behind him and gently takes O'Neil's chin in his hands. His face close to O'Neil's, he begins to shave him, his eyes following the path of the razor.

"Are you sure you know how to do this?"

"No."

O'Neil closes his eyes and lets himself feel the scrape of the blade over his chin, where he usually cuts himself. In his ear, Connor's breathing is a thin whistle, and smells a little of beer. O'Neil can't believe how late he is, but there doesn't seem to be anything he can do to hurry himself up.

"There you go, champ."

O'Neil looks at his reflection in the mirror, Connor standing beside him with the razor in his hand. He rubs his hands over his cheeks and neck, the firm point of his Adam's apple.

"Nice," he says.

"I can do the rest too," Connor offers, rinsing the blade. "I had to do that in medical school."

"I'm feeling a little queasy," O'Neil says. He looks up at his friend, in his hilarious seersucker suit. "How about an appendectomy?"

"Only," Connor says, "if you promise to hold very, *very* still."

Stephen has laid out O'Neil's clothes on the bed, and while he dresses, Connor and Stephen drink the rest of the beer and talk about Connor's wedding, which was the summer before, up in Montreal.

"You're really lucky," Connor says. He is hunched over in his chair, absently swinging his empty beer between his knees. "A wedding should be small. I look at the pictures now and think, Did I really go to that party? Though you should see them." He rolls his eyes and clucks his tongue happily. "Like something from a magazine."

At the mirror O'Neil struggles with his tie. It's new, with bright swirls of yellow and blue to set off the threads of his suit, and he can't seem to get the lengths right. He ties it first with a Windsor, then with a double Windsor, and each time the skinny end comes out too long. Then, without thinking, he somehow gets it right; he yanks the ends and a tight dimple appears below the knot. He slides into his jacket, shaking his shoulders to pull loose the shape. He is looking at his reflection, taking it in, when suddenly he remembers: the boutonniere. He was supposed to pick it up that morning at the florist's across from the hotel. But there is no time now. He takes the rose from Alice's tray, squeezes off the stem with his fingernail, and pushes it through the button-hole of his lapel.

O'Neil turns from the mirror to tell his friends he's ready, and finds them standing at the far window, their broad backs toward him. His eyes follow their gaze; it is Simone, once again crossing the lot to her car. O'Neil's first thought is that he isn't so late after all, that not all the guests have left. But then this thought is pushed aside, he sees Simone through his friends' eyes, and he knows he is looking at a beautiful woman, maybe the most beautiful woman he has ever seen in his life, crossing the lot below them. Her steps

are slow, graceful, without calculation; she seems almost to float. O'Neil is filled with a reverent awe, traveling the length of his body like a beam of light.

"Unbe*liev*able," Stephen says.

"They're different from us." Connor, his hands buried in his pockets, shakes his head in amazement. "It's really very simple. I speak not as a married man but as a scientist."

The three men watch while she opens the driver's door, removes her hat, and, balanced on her slender heels, lowers herself sideways onto the driver's seat, her legs dangling out of the car so that she can smooth the front of her dress. She pulls the door shut behind her, places the hat on the seat beside her, and arches her back to examine herself in the rearview mirror, pushing a hand through her long hair. The engine purrs to life and she backs out of the drive.

Still they do not move. The silence of the room falls over them. It is as if they have seen an apparition, a sign, as if they have dreamed the same dream together. Then his friends see that he is ready, they gather their things, and they take O'Neil to his wedding.

It is twelve-fifteen by the time they arrive at the house, and O'Neil's sister meets him at the door. It rained a while back, she tells him, after they spoke on the phone; just a shower, but the path is too muddy to go up the hill.

"I know," O'Neil says. "Where's Mrs. Cavanaugh? I'll talk to her."

O'Neil enters the crowded house to look for the minister and finds her in the den, taking a last look at her notes for the homily. She is wearing a thick wool sweater under her vestment, and O'Neil hugs her, embarrassing both of them, because he has never hugged her before. "I think we're going to do it under the tent," he tells her. "If that's okay. Plan B."

They agree to start in about ten minutes, and O'Neil excuses himself to find Mary. But out in the living room he realizes it's hopeless; Mary is upstairs with her friends, and he knows that if she wanted to see him she would be downstairs now. His gaze travels the packed room. Somehow, everyone seems to know that the wedding is moments away, and O'Neil realizes that, just as he had wished, all the last decisions have been made for him, that his late arrival was expected and understood, as much a part of the fabric of the day as food and vows and the problem of the weather. There is nothing more to do now, nothing to arrange. He sees a photographer gliding through the crowd, and notices for the first time that the room is filled with flowers; he hears, drifting from the lawn outside, the sound of a fiddle, playing a waltz that he and Mary chose a month before, though he does not remember choosing it, just as he does not remember hiring the photographer or ordering the flowers; none of these. Stephen hands him a glass of water, and he drinks it down in one gulp, asks for another, and drinks that down too. *It is May twenty-ninth,* O'Neil thinks. *I am thirty years old. The woman I will marry is upstairs.* These simple facts seem suddenly to hold his whole life, and he is glad for it, right down to his bones. They have saved him, though he did not know he had to be saved. And something he heard earlier in the day comes back to him: *Then, you and she will be together. That's the nicest part, I think.*

His sister is beside him. "See?" she says. "It's not so hard."

"So this is what it's like."

"That's right, hon." Kay smiles at him and takes his arm. "This is what it's like."

She leads him outside. The guests have followed them out to the lawn, and O'Neil sees that chairs have been put under the tent with an aisle for them to pass through, and that the sky is low and gray. He sees that two chairs are empty, where his parents would be, and he remembers what it was like to love them, as, with his sister and Stephen, he follows Erin Cavanaugh to the front of the tent. He turns and as he turns the day drops away and his vision takes in the whole company—Mary's parents and siblings, the people they work with and have gone to school with, their friends and their children—and in his heart he marries each one of them, for he knows that this is the one sacrament, the one blessing in his life; and then they, too, depart his consciousness, leaving only Mary, who stands at the far end of the tent. Slowly she approaches, her hair wreathed in the deep silence of flowers; then she is there. Mary. He takes her hand, and then, as if they themselves had willed it—as if such acts of love were possible—a soft wind shakes the tent, the air descends, and gently, it begins to rain.

MAMMALS

April 1992

THEY WERE NOT gamblers, but the resort had a small casino, and that was where they spent the first two days. Kay and Jack: the trip was a reward for two hard years, the rough waters they had crossed together, and though they had imagined it as time together as a family, empty days lounging in the stolen sunshine, they had barely stepped outdoors. They left to eat and sleep and check on Mia and the boys, but always they returned—both winning and losing, yet always winning a little more—and by the morning of the third day, after a twelve-hour run when they had not gone to bed at all, they were ahead four thousand dollars, enough to pay for the week-long trip.

It was Kay who decided to stop. Ten A.M.: she'd just won three hands in a row—another sixty dollars—when an overdue exhaustion washed over her, a sense of absolute completeness, like the last bite of a meal. She understood at once that she was done.

"You know, I think I've had it," she said.

Jack nodded, but kept his eyes on the table. His cheeks and chin were dusted with stubble the color of ash. He signaled to the dealer, a young black man with dreadlocks and a fine, copper-colored nose, that he was in. Expressionless, the young man dealt the cards: a ten, and an eight on top. The dealer drew a deuce. Jack waved a flat hand over his cards to say that he would hold where he was. His bets were small, ten or twenty dollars, but many times just five. He gambled carefully but also with a be-mused wonder, like a man puzzling over a problem that seemed to work no matter what he did. He was an economist, but his work was very theoretical; when it came to actual dollars, he had no head at all. It was Kay who balanced the checkbook and paid the bills and kept the ship on course. She watched as Jack won again.

"Jack? Are you listening? Let's cash in."

He kissed her quickly on the forehead. "Go get some sleep if you want."

The idea made her yawn. Four thousand dollars: not a fortune, she thought, but certainly a reason to be cautious. She had friends from college who had real money now: the bankers and lawyers who were just making partner, the doctors whose loans were fi-nally paid off, even a novelist whose books did well. She read their news in the alumni bulletin and felt a stab of envy. To such people, she knew, four thousand dollars would seem like nothing at all. And yet it had taken Kay and Jack most of a year to set aside that sum, stealing a few hundred dollars here and there from his salary at the college.

Now the same amount sat before them on the table, neat rows of blue and red chips with the name of the resort etched at the center—a windfall that had cost them nothing. What was it about these chips that made them so pleasant to the touch? As tired as she was, still she longed to hold them in her hands.

"Seriously, Jack. How can this last?"

"I don't know how it's lasted this long." He placed his bet on the table, and the dealer laid out fresh cards. "See? Twenty-one." It was: a king and an ace, she saw. The dealer paid out.

She was too exhausted to press. "Come soon, then."

Alone, she stepped from the casino, into the blazing light and building heat of the morning. The air smelled of flowers and the sea. The resort was like a compound, encircled by high fencing that made a U around one side of the bay and a beach of perfect white sand. The brochure had mentioned the casino almost in passing—it was just one more diversion, like the tennis courts and scuba lessons and limbo contests on the patio after dinner—and the two of them had joked about it. What kind of idiot would go to the Caribbean and fritter the time away playing cards in a dark room? But now the trip was half over, and they'd barely done anything else.

Their condo was empty, the beds rumpled and unmade. Searching from the windows, Kay found the boys down on the wide empty beach, and Mia, reading a book, her long, blond form stretched out in one of the lawn chairs that the resort staff put out each morning. Sam was eight, Noah five. She wondered if they felt neglected, but knew this wasn't so: Sam wanted only to do as he wished, and Noah wanted nothing. It had been the hardest thing, to realize that she could only offer him comfort, that she would never really know him at all—that to be with Noah was, in some sense, to be alone.

She showered, dressed in a bathing suit—modest, matronly, one of those awful things with a skirt, but that was all they sold to women like her, women who were supposed to be *older*—and examined herself in the mirror. Thirty-six years old: her hair, a rich chestnut, had begun, here and there, to gray. She had never been a small woman, but now, after the boys, there was a wideness to her hips that was, she understood, a permanent rearrangement of the bones. And yet, looking at her reflection, she knew she was still, somehow, pretty. Her features were delicate and expressive; her legs were sturdy and lean, roped with muscle from the long walks she took now each day; her eyes and teeth were bright. The year of her illness—that awful year, they called it—had made her skin seem thinner somehow, almost translucent. Now, eight months later, her strength had returned, like wind filling a sail. The suit, with its high neckline, betrayed nothing.

The boys were making sandcastles, splashing in and out of the waves with buckets. They had no impulse to accumulate: all they built they destroyed at once, even Noah, who followed his brother's lead in everything.

Sam took her hand and pulled. "Mia says we can go sailing if you say okay."

"Did she?" The resort kept a fleet of rickety day-sailers on the beach. She tousled Sam's hair, stiff with salt and sunshine. "After lunch, we'll see," she said.

"We want to go sailing *now*," Sam declared. "Mia said she'll take us."

She knelt before the two of them. Their bodies were thin, absolutely without fat, and after three days in the sun, as brown as new pennies. Sam was tall for his age and hazel eyed, all knees and elbows and sharp angles, like his father; Noah, under a thatch of brown hair, had a wide, chunky face that on a different boy, one who smiled and laughed, would have been a constant barometer of his feelings. But his smiles, when they came, seemed like accidents. One eye, his left, did not look straight at her but just slightly away, a degree of misalignment that only someone close to him would notice. The condition was known as Brown's syndrome, and was sometimes associated with autism. It was Noah's eye, looking up at them from his cradle, that had first alerted them that something was wrong.

"Daddy's made enough money to pay for the trip," she told them. "What do you think of that?"

The littler boy wrinkled his brow and tipped his face to look at her. "Playing cards?"

"That's right, playing cards. Grown-up cards. Mommy made some money too."

"Can we buy a boat?" Sam asked.

"It's not enough for that."

"I found a jellyfish," Noah announced. His world was a series of encounters with animals of all kinds; almost nothing else interested him. After a series of unhappy experiences with stray cats and wounded birds, they had tried to domesticate this compulsion with a menagerie of small pets: fish, turtles, a pair of lop-eared rabbits named Dopey and Doc. He seemed closer to these creatures than to any actual person, caring for them with complete devotion, and yet when they died, he seemed not to notice.

"Where was that?"

He pointed purposefully. "Over there. On the sand."

"It was a *dead* jellyfish," Sam said, scowling with boredom. "Big deal."

Noah's eyelids fell closed, like twin windowshades coming down. "Jellyfish. Any of various marine co-el-enter-ates of a soft, gelatinous structure, esp. one with an umbrellalike body and long trailing tentacles; medusa. Two. Inf. A person without strong resolve or stamina." He pronounced the abbreviations exactly as he had seen them written in the dictionary. His face as he spoke was a perfect, emotionless blank.

"That's wonderful, honey. Did Mia show that to you?"

The little boy frowned mysteriously. "It *was* dead," he confirmed.

Up all night gambling, yet here she was, being a mother. For a while she helped Noah chase minnows in the shallows with his net, then moved a chair next to Mia's, under the shade of a wide umbrella.

"How is the cards?"

Kay lay back in her chair. Just a few minutes with the boys had drained her; she knew right away that she would be asleep within moments. "We were doing pretty well when I left. I think we're on a hot streak." She sighed and turned to look at Mia. "You don't mind? I know it wasn't what we planned."

Mia shrugged. From the wicker bag on the sand beside her chair she removed a hairbrush and, squinting into the light, stroked the underside of her long ponytail. "The boys are being good. Have the fun."

"Well, their mother isn't. Their mother is fried."

Mia paused. "Fried?"

"Tired," Kay explained, and closed her eyes.

She dreamed of being a girl, playing poker with her father in the kitchen, a dream that was also a memory: she had actually done this, years ago. One pair, two pair, three of a kind, straight: at the kitchen table, her matchsticks piled neatly before her, she calculated her bets according to a sheet of paper that listed the order of hands. It was notebook paper, folded and folded again, worn to the softness of chamois cloth from years of travel in her mother's purse. Her parents played with friends; her mother was lucky, her father explained, but claimed to forget which hand was which. The light of the kitchen was winter light, cool and angular; Kay was eleven years old. Her father taught her to bluff, how to build the pot slowly when the cards were good, when to fold and be gone. Don't fall in love with a hand, he warned her; even a good hand could lose. Wear a lucky color, but don't count on it. Music played on the tinny speaker of the kitchen radio; she was wearing a nightgown, but was not cold, and her father was alive. He shuffled the cards to deal. *Five-card draw,* he said. Suicide kings and one-eyed jacks were wild. He showed her the cards, the jack with his averted gaze, the king with a sword in his head. *Daddy?* she said. *Daddy, I married Jack. That's good,* he said. *I know you did. I was there, remember? I've always liked Jack.*

The light grew brighter and brighter and brighter still, the music louder and louder, and then she awoke to sunshine and heat, and remembered where she was. She had slept two hours; the boys and Mia were nowhere to be seen. Just a few hundred yards off the beach a cruise ship had sailed into view—deck after deck piled high above the water, an impossible vision, like a floating wedding cake. The grinding of the anchor, lowered on its chain, had awakened her, and something else: somewhere, a ragtime band was playing.

She found the boys at the snack bar, eating grilled cheese sandwiches and French fries off paper plates. Mia sat across from them, holding her book up with one hand, like an old painting of a woman reading in a park. *Jane Eyre,* a copy from the library, its plain covers wrapped in crinkling cellophane; she read voraciously but without discrimination, everything from pulp romances to *The New Yorker* to Sam's books on baseball.

Kay sat down between the boys and helped herself to one of Sam's fries. "Has Jack come out yet?"

"The professor said to tell you he is still winning." Mia tucked a long marker in the pages of her book and closed the covers. "He did not want to disturb you."

The fries were greasy and covered with salt: delicious. "How's the book?"

Mia frowned. "Very sad. But I think it is helping with my English."

"I haven't read that since college. I haven't really read *anything* since the boys."

Mia shrugged and gave a neutral smile. "The professor thought I would like it."

Kay ordered a club sandwich and iced tea, but the boys were too fidgety to wait, and she ate alone while Mia took them back to the condo to watch a movie on cable. Noah was not too old to take a nap, but she knew that Sam would keep him up. In any event, it

JUSTIN CRONIN

was enough just to get them out of the sun for a while. It was their first vacation since she'd been sick, their first real vacation ever, not counting trips to friends' houses or Jack's parents' in St. Louis—why not let them do as they liked?

She paid for lunch with the number of their condo, and returned to the casino. Jack was sitting at the bar, eating a hamburger. He told her he was up fifteen.

It took her a moment. "Fifteen *thousand?*"

"There are people in here who'd think that was nothing." He bit into a pickle and wiped his hands. Sixteen hours at the table; he didn't look tired at all. "See that room back there? Poker, the real stuff. I saw a guy lose twenty big ones on a single hand."

Big ones—he'd never talked this way. "They don't live on a college teacher's salary. Jesus, Jack. Fifteen thousand dollars." So much money, out of nowhere. She couldn't believe it. "We can pay off all the cards, and the van too."

"Don't forget Uncle Sam."

"Okay, just the van, then." She laughed at herself. "*Just* the van. What am I saying?"

She stayed with him while he finished lunch, telling stories about the hands he had played and won, and then walked with him back to the blackjack table.

"Is this such a good idea? Playing more?"

He thought for a moment and nodded. "I think I'm all right," he said. The dealer had changed; this time it was a young woman with cornrows, just a year or two older than Mia. She broke the seal on a fresh deck.

"Actually, I haven't had this much fun in a long time. I feel like I could play all day. What are the boys up to?"

"They want to go sailing. Mia made a promise, I'm afraid."

He rubbed a hand over his face. She knew how much he

wanted to play, to ride this lucky streak. "You want to sit in a few hands? I can take them."

"No, play if you want. Just be sensible. When you're too tired, quit." She kissed him one more time and squeezed his hand. The van was two years old; they'd bought it just before she'd gotten sick, after the old Volvo his parents had given them had finally died. How many payments left? All gone in a stroke, the slate wiped clean. "Fifteen thousand dollars, Jack. I can't believe it. We can really use this luck."

His hand found her waist, and he pulled her toward him. "This puts me sort of in the mood," he said into her ear.

She accepted the embrace but then pried herself loose, suddenly embarrassed. She wrinkled her nose. "You need a shower," she laughed.

The cruise ship was still anchored off the beach. A gate had been lowered at the bow, and a fleet of inflatable dinghies ferried passengers back and forth from the beach across the blue, blue waters of the bay. The sun was so hot it made her shiver.

She signed the rental agreement perfunctorily, barely bothering to read what it said. She hadn't sailed for years, not since she was a girl at camp, but thought she would remember how. In any event, there was almost no wind. A young man wearing tennis whites and a huge wristwatch helped her rig, while Mia put Noah into a life jacket. *Windward, leeward, tack, gibe:* the words were all still there, unused for decades, like old bicycles hanging from the rafters of a cold garage.

"You know how to do it?" Stitched on his shirt pocket was his name, Thomas. His accent was southern; he had just graduated from college, she supposed, and was taking a year off to fool around in the sunshine.

"I think so." She looked the boat over and nodded uneasily. "Well, the truth is it's been a while."

He smiled encouragingly at her. Besides taking care of the boats, he was also the diving instructor, he'd explained. "It'll come back to you." He directed her gaze across the water at an outcropping of dark stones, marked with a steel tower. "Just don't go past those rocks. Nothing dangerous, it's just open sea after that."

Kay and the boys arranged themselves in the boat, and Mia and Thomas helped them push off. The crunch of sand along the hull, and then they were afloat; in the stern Kay pulled the little cord that dropped the rudder into place.

"Bon voyage!" Mia called from the beach. "Happy sailing!"

A mild breeze lifted them into the bay. Kay negotiated the tiller and mainsheet, clamping the line in her teeth as she adjusted the sail, then tying it fast to its cleat. She peeked quickly over her shoulder; the beach streamed away.

"So this is sailing," she said to the boys. "What do you think?"

"Will we see any dolphins?" Noah asked.

"I don't know, honey." Tiller, mainsheet, rudder, centerboard. What had she gotten them into? She breathed deeply, steadying herself. "There'll be lots of fish to look at."

"Dolphins are mammals that live in the sea," the boy intoned. "They nurse their young, and breathe air, like humans. Dolphins can stay submerged, under the water, for five minutes or longer, and have been known to dive as deep as eight hundred feet."

"That's right, honey. Did you read that in a book?"

"*Creatures of the Deep.*" It was a gift from the boy's uncle, Kay's brother, O'Neil. Noah had carried it with him on the plane.

"God," Sam groaned. "You are *so* weird."

"Your brother is not weird," Kay corrected. "He's different."

Sam rolled his eyes. "God, you are *so* different."

They skimmed past the cruise ship, its stern high above them, and the name, *Windward Princess,* painted in black. A vortex of churning water trailed behind it, holding it in place. Once beyond it Kay set the boat to tack, pointing close to the wind, and explained to the boys what would happen.

"Hard a-*lee!*"

The boom swung above their heads, catching with a firm snap as the sail filled once more with air. A clean tack; she felt a swell of pride. They were running parallel to the beach now, in the shadow of the ship, which stood between them and the shore. On the decks above people were watching them, leaning out over the rails. Some of them waved.

"Go closer," Sam pleaded.

She pointed the bow tight to the wind; the boat heeled in reply. It was all coming came back to her, the play of the wind and the sail and the hull, how all of it was connected by unseen lines of force. The boys scrambled up beside her as she pulled the mainsheet taught. Above them the side of the great ship loomed, a wall of white steel a hundred feet high. One of the inflatable dinghies zoomed past, and they banged into the chop, spray flying over them like jewels of water.

"Hold on tight, guys!"

They rounded the bow, emerging into a pocket of still air and a view of the beach. Mia was still standing where they had left her, talking to the boy who had helped her rig. Boys, Kay thought—of course she would want to. She'd given her the rest of the afternoon off to talk with boys.

"Who's that?" Noah asked; he spoke too loudly, uncertain how far to raise his voice over the sound of the water sliding under the hull.

She let out the mainsheet and refastened it in its cleat. "His name is Thomas."

"Is he Mia's friend too?"

She looked again. The boy stood at her side confidently, his hands in his pockets. Mia seemed to be laughing; with one hand she reached up and did something with her hair, setting it loose over her shoulders to catch the light. The image caught Kay short, not with alarm but with wonder, the purest amazement at time's passage. It was as if, at this distance, she could see something she had been unable to discern before. When had it happened? She thought of the skinny girl who had come to them two years before, nervous and tall and poorly dressed, her English halting and full of strange phrases: "Were you born in the hallway?" she asked, incredulously, when the boys had done something careless; or, to urge them on, "Give the iron." Too ill to pay attention, Kay hadn't noticed the change. Lying on the sofa after her infusions, or in bed with a basin on the worst days, it was all she could manage to feel a helpless gratitude that somebody was there to help, to love and encourage the boys when she could not. Now she was well again, and Mia was reading *Jane Eyre* and flirting with a college boy on the beach. Her skinny body and bad clothes were gone. She wore a black bikini and a white cotton T-shirt cropped to show off her slender waist and all the rest, and as Kay watched, Mia touched her hair again, and then, with a slowness that betrayed her thinking, lifted one bare foot and dragged her toe through the sand. When had she learned to do this, to hold a boy's interest with the smallest gesture? He would ask her, if he hadn't already: *Do you have friends in Vermont? Do you like the cold, does it remind you of Denmark? Do you like these people, the family you work for? When do you get off work?*

She drew her gaze away. "Of course they're friends," she told the boys. "You don't want Mia to have friends besides you?"

"Daddy is her friend," Noah said. "But it's a secret."

The boat stopped suddenly. *What the hell . . . ?* She pushed the tiller this way and that; they were held fast. Too close to the beach, she had run them aground. The lurch of the hull had sent the boys spilling forward. Later, she would remember this moment as almost comical: Kay with her boys alone at sea, the news that was not news, quite, breaking over her at a moment when she was simply too busy to think about it.

"Oh, damn," she said, and heard the anger in her voice. *"Damn, damn, damn."*

Sam's face lit up with delight. "Are we sinking?"

"No, of course not. We just hit the bottom, that's all."

Noah began to wail. "We're sinking! I don't want to!"

"Sam, help your brother," she said crossly, pulling in the mainsheet to find the wind. On the beach, suddenly, Mia and Thomas were nowhere to be seen. *Daddy is her friend. . . .* She shook her head sharply to return her mind to the boat. "Can't you see my hands are full? He doesn't understand."

"We're sinking!" Noah repeated. The little boy had begun to cry.

Sam glowered across the boat at his brother. "No, we're not, stupid."

"Sam, *enough.*" She paused a moment to calm herself. "Everything's fine. We're perfectly safe. The beach is right there."

Slowly the boat pivoted on its centerboard, pointing into the wind. *The centerboard,* Kay thought. She reached forward to find the lever that lifted it into its pocket. She did, and they were free, slipping stern-first away from the beach. When they were clear she put the centerboard back down and pointed the boat once again toward open water.

"Come here, both of you."

The boys moved to the stern beside her. "Here, Noah. Take the tiller. Feel it? See how it moves the boat?"

With Kay's hand on his he moved the rudder back and forth; but his heart, she could tell, was not in it.

"I didn't mean to say it," Noah said. He looked at her plaintively, his eyes windowpaned with tears.

"It's all right, honey." With her free arm she hugged his thin shoulders. "You're not in trouble."

She gave each boy a turn steering the boat. So, there it was, and Noah knew. Had she? And did Sam? His silence said he did.

"We'll make a pact. Everything we do and say out here is just for us. Not for Daddy, or Mia, or anybody. Agreed?"

"Like pirates," Noah said, his voice gone far away again, to safety. "Argh, avast, blow the man down."

"That's it. Like pirates on the high seas. Sam?"

Beside her the older boy looked away.

"Sam?"

"If it's a secret, you're not supposed to tell."

When they returned, Jack was in the shower. His news was good—he was ahead eighteen thousand dollars. He was going to take a nap, he said, and have dinner with them, and then return to the casino to play.

"You just don't screw around with luck like this," he said. He spoke to her through the frosted mirror as he shaved. In the room behind them the boys were dealing hands of go-fish on the carpet. "I'm going to pay off the house before I'm through. I tell you, I'm on a roll."

"What's a roll, Daddy?" Sam asked.

"It's when you can't lose. And don't eavesdrop. You liked the sailing, boys?"

"Noah got scared."

"Be nice to your brother," Jack said. "Would that kill you?"

"Can we buy a boat?"

He dried his face with a towel and winked at Kay. "What kind do you want?"

"A white one." Sam held out his arms. "With a big motor."

"Ah." He nodded gravely. "I'll have to play a lot more cards for that." He turned from the mirror to face Kay. "Seriously," he said quietly, "the minute it goes south, I'm out of there. You know that, right?"

"Well." Then, "Should I worry?"

"C'mon, Kay. Eighteen thousand bucks." He frowned, searching her face. "You have to trust me on this. After everything we've been through, I think that would cheer you up."

She wanted to laugh, but stopped herself. Was it possible, she thought, that she had actually known? How could she not have known? Another person had stepped into the circle. And yet here she was, with her husband and boys, in the Caribbean, Jack shaving, the boys playing cards, all of it exactly the same as if Noah had said nothing at all.

"I'm not complaining about the money, Jack," she heard herself say. "I just think we should spend some time together."

"And we will, I promise. I absolutely promise. I've just got to ride this thing out."

Kay did not reply; Jack sat on the edge of the bed to wriggle into his shorts. "I was thinking. Maybe we should give Mia something extra, considering all the time we've been away."

A gift, she thought: a lover's gift. She pushed the thought away. "Is that really necessary? She's getting a nice vacation on top of what we pay her," Kay said.

"She said she wants to go home in the summer. Maybe we could spring for the ticket. I don't see why we shouldn't spread the luck around a bit." He rose, and clapped his hands. "Okay, boys, outside. Daddy's hitting the hay."

He slept three hours, while Kay minded the boys on the beach.

Mia had the rest of the afternoon off; she would join them for dinner, and then stay with the boys during the evening, so Kay and Jack would be free to do as they liked. It was, she knew, what made the trip all possible, having Mia along to help. Without Mia there would have been no trip at all. Why was she not angrier than she was? The air was calm, the sky a richly saturated blue above the quiet bay. The cruise ship had vanished without a trace. She watched the boys swimming and digging in the sand, but her thoughts were far away, back in the year of her illness. So sick: it was as if she had gone to some distant country, far away from all of them. It wasn't the surgery she had minded most of all—all the books and movies had this wrong; the breast was trying to kill her, she wanted it gone—but the hair on her pillow when she awoke each morning, long strands of it marking the place where her head had been, and the whiteness of her scalp as it emerged, first in a crown at the top, then all around. She tried not to let the boys see. *I am falling away,* she thought. *I am being disassembled in the smallest parts.* She had sores in her mouth, on her tongue, down the back of her throat. Always, the final taste of blood. The days between rounds of chemo passed in a haze of exhaustion and worry. She took pills to sleep, pills to cheer her up, pills to help her keep her food down or stop the diarrhea that sent her dashing to the toilet. And always there was Mia: shuttling Sam to school or Noah to his therapist, unpacking groceries in the kitchen or negotiating with the boys over naps or treats, bringing Kay a glass of water or a mug of tea on those days when that was all she could keep down. She heard, from her room, the sound of Mia's voice, mixing with Jack's and the boys'; one day she sat at the top of the stairs and simply listened. The four of them were playing Parcheesi, or trying to; Noah would not sit still, kept moving his piece at random, and yet, somehow, the game had proceeded, Mia cajoling the boys and letting Noah cheat a little, Jack saying,

"See? Watch what Mia does. Do what Mia tells you, boys." She listened for an hour, and knew what she was hearing: the sound of a family, though one she was not part of. The cancer had traveled to twelve nodes in arm and chest. N12, the chart said. It was not the best situation, they told her. In a college town there could be no secrets, or so she'd thought. The house filled up with friends and colleagues, her bedroom bloomed with scarves and hats, the freezer burst with casseroles. One day, at the end of a month when the bills had piled up, she walked to the end of the driveway to the mailbox and found, tucked in an envelope, five hundred dollars in cash.

But then it was over; she was still young, and her strength returned quickly. She walked each morning, ate the proper foods, gave up the stolen cigarettes at parties. Her hair came in; one day she left the house without a hat and didn't realize until she was already downtown and saw her reflection in a store window. At Sam's hockey games, or in line at the grocery store, or in the back of the church after services, a sea of amazed and happy eyes met hers. *Look at you!* they all said. *You're looking so well!* Healthy, normal people: how did they do it? She marveled at their innocence, their easy greed for life. She had friends who rock-climbed, drove without seat belts, who hadn't had so much as a checkup in years. What could they be thinking? She had stepped back into the world, but not completely; she was an imposter, half ghost, a spy from the shadows. She carried her new health through the crowds like a crystal chalice, and every three months she returned to the far side of the river, that awful ward of the dying: more blood drawn, chest X rays, tumor markers. In August, a year after the surgery, she had a full-body CAT scan—dreadful, a ride in a coffin, her ears pounding with a sound like sheets of metal pushed through a sawblade. It was when the doctor reported the results, smiling for the first time at the good news, that she knew that everyone had expected her to die. Beside her, Jack had broken down and wept.

A waiter came by; she asked for iced tea, then changed her order to wine, though she knew she would only taste it. The boys were building mud castles on the wet plain left behind by the receding evening tide. The waiter returned, bearing her single glass on a tray. After such a year, here she was, holding a glass of wine on a beach a thousand miles away from the April mud of Vermont. She sipped the wine, its cold sweetness like golden light on her tongue. Sunshine, her body strong, Sam and Noah happy again, or at least not afraid: what else was there to wish for? When she was very sick, she had tried to imagine a day like this one, to hold it in her mind. So perhaps that was the reason: all of it felt like a gift.

"Come here, boys."

They came to where she was sitting. Their bare chests were streaked with wet sand. She hugged them together.

Noah touched her face. "Mama, why are you crying?"

She hadn't noticed. She wiped a tear away with her thumb. "I'm just happy to see you. Sometimes grown-ups cry because they're happy."

Sam frowned skeptically; she thought he was going to ask about his father. "You're not sick again, are you?"

She hugged them again. "Not at all," she said.

When they returned to the condo, Jack was snoring away. His arm lay over his eyes. Thirteen years of marriage: her mind circled this thought, feeling only a mild surprise at the swift passage of time. In the adjoining room she bathed the boys, dressed them in clean shorts and T-shirts, and took them to the restaurant to wait for their father. It was the early seating for dinner; most of the other guests had children with them, even babies. At the table next to theirs a young mother spooned food into a little girl's mouth from a tiny jar. A quick, heady thrill passed through her, remembering the years when the boys were small: Sam's tiny mouth as he reached for his bottle, the smell and heat of Noah's skin, like warm bread and cinnamon. So delicious, even to be near them; there were days, she had joked, when she could have eaten them whole. One wasn't supposed to feel this way anymore— having children was a sideline, a concession to biology one made in the midst of other things—and yet it was the only true desire she'd ever possessed.

"When's Daddy coming?" Sam asked.

She opened their menus. "He'll be along. Why don't we order?"

She ordered hamburgers for the boys, filet for Jack, swordfish for herself. She had given Jack a nudge before they'd left for the restaurant, and she worried that he'd fallen back asleep. But just as their food arrived, he appeared in the doorway of the restaurant.

"Sorry." He seated himself next to the boys. Beside Noah and Sam she saw how pale his arms and face were. "How was the beach, boys? Did you miss me?" He tousled Noah's hair. "How's our zoologist? See any fish?"

The little boy shrugged and chewed. "Minnows."

Jack looked around. "Where's Mia?"

"I gave her the rest of the afternoon off," Kay said. "I think she met someone."

Jack salted his steak and said nothing.

"A boy her age," Kay explained. "He works with the boats."

"His name is Thomas," Noah said.

Jack frowned. "She should be careful," he said.

The waiter came to the table, and Jack ordered a beer, and Cokes for the boys; they were each allowed one soft drink with dinner. "I'm just saying we might be liable. If anything happens. You get off the grounds, it's a different world down here."

"He seemed very nice," Kay said. "You wanted her to have some fun, remember?"

They finished their dinner. Outside on the patio a steel band was setting up to play. As they were leaving, Mia arrived, half running, wearing a sundress, her hair gleaming and wet from the shower. The boys took her each by a hand.

"We went to a castle," she told them breathlessly. "On motorbikes! Just like in Denmark. It was very fun."

"We finished dinner," Kay said. "But go get something and charge it to the room."

"It's fine," Mia said, smiling. "I've eaten already."

"Can we go to the castle?" Sam wanted to know.

"Maybe tomorrow," Kay said.

"Why is it always maybe?" Sam stuck out his lower lip the way he had done since he was a baby. "Just say yes."

Mia tugged at his hand. "Listen to your mother, Sam," she said firmly. "If she says maybe, then it is maybe for you."

At a metal table they listened to the band while the sun went down over the darkening bay. Kay could tell that Jack was antsy to get back to the casino. She left them on the patio and went into the information desk in the lobby, a large open room with plants and flowers everywhere. Was there a castle nearby? she asked. Something *like* a castle? The attendant took a brochure from a dispenser behind his chair and unfolded it on the counter. Glossy photos of a ruined stone structure with ramparts high above the sea; piles of cannonballs and people waving; a map with the castle's location on a solitary promontory marked by a red star: It was actually an eighteenth-century Spanish fort, the attendant explained. They could rent mopeds, he said, though the roads were narrow and steep. A van could take them, too, for thirty dollars.

She made a reservation for the van for 9:00 A.M., before the sun would get too hot, tucked the brochure in the pocket of her dress, and returned to the patio. The brochure said that the fort's high vantage point made it a good spot for whale watching; it was this that had made her decision. She wanted to give Noah a whale.

The band had stopped playing by the time she returned; the table was empty. Down by the water's edge she saw the boys and Mia. The last of the light was about to go. She took off her shoes and joined them. The sand around and under her feet still hummed with the heat of the day.

"You missed it," Sam said cheerfully, and arched his back so he was walking on his hands and feet together. "Mia taught me to limbo."

"How low can you go? How low can you go?" Noah recited. His face and voice were bland; the music was in his head, she knew, a perfect recording without a trace of feeling, except perhaps a mild curiosity. She smiled at him as he clapped his hands joylessly.

"We came down to look for dolphins," Mia explained.

She looked at Mia. "Did Jack go back to the casino?"

"The professor said to tell you to meet him there," she replied.

"I see." What else was there to say? But she found herself glad; she had time yet. Let him gamble. "Perhaps later," Kay said.

They strolled the length of the beach, Noah dawdling to pick up shells left bare by the tide. Behind them the ambient sounds of the resort grew faint. They made their way to the end, where the sand stopped and a chain-link fence topped with razor ribbon sealed the edge of the property. She had seen it before, in daylight, and thought nothing of it; now, in the darkness, it gleamed forbiddingly. Beyond it stood a run-down house, the stucco peeling away. A skinny dog was chained in the front yard, chewing at something in the dirt. On the porch steps a light suddenly blazed: a match, and then, from the shadows, the scent of marijuana. She heard a man's deep laugh, and then a pair of voices talking, words she could not understand. Without warning fear sliced through her. How sturdy was the fence? Had they been seen?

She stepped back, calling to her children in a harsh whisper. "Come away from there, boys."

Sam held fast to the fence, plainly interested. Here was something new. "I want to see—"

"*Now.*"

They retraced their steps back toward the resort, a blazing oasis of light and music, and by the time they had returned to the condo, her nervousness was gone. The air had taken on a floral sweetness; above them the palm fronds rustled, a sound like girls in taffeta skirts descending a flight of stairs. The steel band had resumed playing on the patio. For the adults the night was just beginning, but for the children it was over; the boys were completely drained by the day, even Sam, who snuck a thumb into his mouth as he stood before the toilet to pee. She tucked them in and told them no nonsense, and joined Mia on the porch.

She was wearing a sweater around her shoulders, and held her purse. "I was wondering," Mia began, "if you don't want to play cards tonight—"

"Go, go," Kay said. "Take the rest of the evening off."

She hesitated, but her face was delighted. "Thomas says there is a party, for the staff. I can be back in time to watch the boys if you change your mind."

Kay waved her away. "You've done enough," she said.

She sat in a rocker on the porch and waited for Jack. She supposed that his not returning was a good sign; it meant he was still winning. A gauze of stars hung low above the bay, and a gentle wind blew. At eleven she went inside and dressed for bed, but sleep would not come; sometime later she felt the pressure of the air in the room change and heard the door open. She rose and went to the hall. Mia was putting her purse on the table.

"Oh!" she said, startled. She put a hand over her heart. "You frightened me."

"I'm sorry. I thought it might be Jack."

"It is very late. I didn't mean to wake you."

"I wasn't sleeping." She paused a moment and regarded Mia, the girl before her. She didn't quite know what she was looking for. Mia was barefoot, and her feet were sandy; more sand was on her throat, in her hair, the pure white sand one found just above the high-tide line, as fine as powder.

"Kay?"

"It's nothing. It's all right." She tried to smile. "Did you have a good time?"

"It was just a party." She shrugged. "American boys can be so . . . what is the word? They want things."

"Needy."

"Yes, they need us. Even the little ones!" Mia laughed. "You can see it in Sam. He's going to be quite the lady's man, I think."

"Like his father."

Mia said nothing; her face showed nothing.

"When we get back, I'm going to release you," Kay said. "You can stay a month, and we'll pay for the ticket home."

Again, Mia's face showed no emotion. She looked at the ceiling, then back at Kay. "I don't know what to say. Perhaps that is for the best."

"It's going to be hard for the boys. You'll have to help me make it easier for them. They're my first concern. I'm not going to tell them until we get back to Vermont."

Mia nodded. "Of course."

"I don't see the situation as in any way your fault, Mia. You've been a great help to me, and to this family. I want you to know that."

Mia nodded and crossed her arms. Her eyes swelled with tears, though her face was firm. She swallowed once, then exhaled sharply through her nose. "But still, I am fired."

"Yes. I'm sorry to say it, but yes."

After Mia had gone to her room, Kay dressed in a skirt and blouse and sandals, brushed her hair, and looked in on the boys once more. They were asleep in a jumble, the sheets of the double bed they shared twisted around them in the heat. She watched them breathe and sleep, as she had done for hundreds of hours since each had been born, then wrote them a note to tell them where she was, and left it on the table where they could see it.

She was two months pregnant. She had figured it out that morning, or begun to, when she had awakened on the beach and heard the band playing on the ship. She had skipped her period again, but she hadn't taken this absence seriously, not until she'd heard the music. She knew there was no such band; the sound was coming from inside her. Crazy, but that was how she'd known with Sam and Noah. She tried to imagine this new baby, hoping for a girl, but all she could see was a tiny face pressed to her remaining breast, a child who would never know there had ever been two.

Carrying her shoes, she walked across the sand to the casino. She found Jack at the table, and knew at once that he had lost it, lost it all. The eighteen thousand was gone, and more; he was down three grand. It was poker that had done it. Bored with blackjack, he had decided to sit in a few hands, and lost it all fast. For two hours he had tried to recoup his losses at the blackjack table, and watched more dribble away. He'd hardly slept the night since they'd arrived, three days ago. His eyes were wild and desperate.

"Help me," he said.

"Goddamn it, Jack." She took him to a quiet corner. "How much cash do we have left?"

"Three thousand." He put his face in his hands and began to weep. "Kay, I'm sorry, I'm sorry."

She computed rapidly. Three days left; they could get by on a thousand if they had to, two to play it safe. The rooms were paid for. How much had they charged for meals, the boat, the trip to the fort to give a whale to Noah? She took his wallet from him, heavy and warm from his pocket.

"We'll talk later," she commanded. "Go back and sleep now."

The casino was quiet; only a few tables were running. She cashed five hundred dollars in travelers checks and took her place at one, stacking her chips on the green felt before her. A waitress approached her and she asked for a glass of water, no ice. It was 2:00 A.M.; she had a van to catch at nine. Seven hours to win back three thousand dollars. She rolled up her sleeves.

"Ma'am?"

She met the dealer's eye. Others were waiting for her bet before the cards could be dealt. In a moment the game would begin again, but still she paused. In the condo her babies were sleeping; all around she felt the blueness of the sea. It was all real, it was this world and no other, and she was in it. She pulled a fifty-dollar chip from the pile.

"Deal," she said.

GHOSTS OF WINTER

January 1995

MARY AND O'NEIL: they were like any couple. She, just thirty, her figure slender, her beauty pale and Nordic, not striking but sensible; he, two years older, with large, soft hands and a web of creases just taking hold at the corners of his eyes. Homeowners, voters, employees; the provisional adulthood of their twenties was over. They were both teachers, work they told themselves was honorable, though it was, in reality, a career each had chosen by accident, a temporary arrangement made permanent when bolder plans drifted away. Their house, in an older suburb outside Philadelphia, was trying to bankrupt them; the wiring was bad, a spring rainstorm sent them scurrying with kitchen pots, there was lead paint everywhere, chiseled with cracks fat enough to wedge a dime into. Its history was obscure. Prying away a piece of rotten window trim, O'Neil had discovered a Christmas card, dated 1879, with these words, written in schoolmarmish hand so precisely shaped that O'Neil first thought they were typed: "You mention the knife which arouses my curiosity as to whether you received the calendar. I should be much obliged to you to advise me in this regard. I received for Xmas anything and everything from stiff-backed handkerchief to coil-spring ear laps." They passed their weekends in dust masks and tool belts and old clothes spattered with paint—blue for the bedroom, linen for the living room and hall, a buttery yellow for the guest room that seemed cheerful in the store but turned out to be a bad mistake, the color of electrified lemons—and on Monday mornings emerged from the front doorway to begin another week of teaching, crescents of paint under their battered fingernails, their shoulders bent below the weight of textbooks so fattened with underlines they seemed to have been left out in the rain. In the evening, half watching a television program or listening to music, they graded tests and essays on the sofa, breaking the silence of their earnest work only to ask small questions of each other, or solicit an opinion: Would you like tea? Could I borrow your Hi-Liter? Now, does this sentence make any sense at *all*? Sometimes, beneath a blanket they had brought from upstairs, their still faces grazed by the glow of the television, they fell asleep right there, slipping into an unconsciousness that was somehow deeper for having occurred by accident, and awakened hours later to the flow of images on the television screen—a gangster loading a pistol, a woman in a leotard pumping a ski machine, a flight of birds above a grassy field—that they had swept into their dreams.

And yet, there was something uncertain about them. It was hard to say why. Their love was eclectic and sensual—O'Neil, for instance, sometimes placed his nose against Mary's cheek simply to smell her skin, or bathed in the water she had just used—and their lovemaking surprised them with its ease. So many years of nervousness; why had no one told them that sex was meant to be funny, and that they could say the things they wanted to and ask for what they liked? They were happy, it was true; they had reached a point of happiness in their lives, a place of rest after a journey of some difficulty, and they frequently marveled at this fact: how, of all the people in the world, and all the lives they might have led, they had somehow found this one together. O'Neil had been raised in upstate New York, Mary in Minnesota. How unlikely was it that they would have ever met at all? They had told the story many times, retracing their steps from the private school where they'd come to work (French for Mary, English for O'Neil), through a maze of time and space to the snowy towns of their youth. They recounted it all with pleasure, chiming in to finish one another's sentences or highlight some detail to keep the telling fresh, but didn't this simple exercise, good natured though it was, testify to the fragility of their good fortune? O'Neil's parents had died when he was in college, killed in a car wreck; Mary's family was far away, a race of chilly Germans on the plains. Wouldn't such people regard any human attachment, the possibility of happiness itself, with skepticism? So perhaps that was it; perhaps it was their very happiness that made them afraid.

For a while the challenges of their house distracted them, its insatiable appetite for their labors. They pleased themselves by working hard, and then, later, with the idea that the house was haunted. The notion delighted them at once, even as they knew it was foolish; but once the idea arose—it was Mary, over dinner, who first suggested it—evidence bounded into view. There was, of course, the Christmas card O'Neil had found. (Coil-spring ear laps? What unfinished business with the knife?) And there was no question that the house at times hinted at some benign inhabitation. Lights blazed and dimmed; ceiling fans reversed themselves of their own volition; doors swung open and closed without warning, pushed by unaccountable drafts. Hidden lines of connectedness seemed to snake through the structure; they had discovered, for example, that the toilet lid in the second-floor bath would sometimes slam when they turned on the kitchen disposal. In the basement—an inhospitable, gravelike hole where they stored old boxes and did the laundry, with crumbling plaster walls and miles of sketchy wiring stapled to the joists—pockets of frigid air lingered, and once, mysteriously, the washing machine had overflowed. Later, O'Neil found a tube sock stuck in the basin drain, and certainly it was possible that it had found its way there by accident, but wasn't it also true that this occurrence, like all the others, bore the qualities of a prank?

Then, in December, on a night after Christmas in the third year of their marriage, Mary awoke from a troubled sleep and realized that for some time she had been listening to the sound of footsteps. Strangely, she felt no alarm; she had been anticipating this, or something like it. She lifted the covers and stepped gingerly into the cold hall, where the apparition waited. It was a young woman—she appeared to be draped in a cloud of stars—and her blond hair was done curiously: not in some elaborate style of the past, but cut unevenly at the ends, as if by pinking shears. On her slender body she wore a smooth white smock that fell to her ankles; her feet were bare. "We got your card," Mary said, thinking this would be a good icebreaker, but the woman—just a girl, Mary realized—gave no reply. A wardrobe stood at the end of the hall, where Mary and O'Neil kept old clothing that no longer fit but, for one reason or another, couldn't be parted with. The girl smiled at Mary and stepped into the wardrobe, sealing the door behind her.

Then O'Neil was at her side. "What are you doing?"

"It's a girl," Mary whispered. "She's in there."

O'Neil returned to the bedroom and reappeared with the tennis racquet he kept under his side of the bed, an old Jack Kramer he had bought at a yard sale for a quarter.

"I don't think she's here to play tennis," Mary said.

O'Neil stepped back and cocked his racquet, though Mary could tell he was doing this only to humor her. "Open it when I say," O'Neil commanded.

Mary sighed with irritation and opened the door. Of course there was no one; Mary had already figured this out. O'Neil poked the head of his racquet through the row of hanging coats and dresses. "Yoo-hoo," he said.

"She was in there."

"You were dreaming," O'Neil said. "You were asleep, sweetie."

"She has fled the scorn of the unbeliever," Mary said.

He yawned and kissed her on the forehead. "Perhaps that's so."

"I saw what I saw," Mary said.

Under the covers of their bed Mary, sleepless, gazed up into the darkness. She knew that O'Neil was probably right—as a girl she had been a sleepwalker of some renown, once letting herself into the neighbors' house to make a peanut-butter-and-jelly sandwich at their kitchen table—and yet she felt that her experience in the hallway could not be explained away so easily. The details were striking, as was her memory of them. The girl had smiled; she wore a smock; she had an awful haircut. It was puzzling but not frightening, and Mary lay awake for some time, replaying the images in her head. Then, as she watched, a twinkling, reflected light began to dance on the ceiling above her face. This, too, seemed a part of the night's enchantments—it seemed to be the light of angels—but then Mary rose and went to the window and saw that it had begun to snow; the falling flakes had tripped the motion sensors over the back door, bathing the yard with cones of snowy light.

By the next morning a foot of snow had fallen, and a cold wind blew. School was still closed for Christmas break, and Mary and O'Neil passed the day baking pointlessly enormous batches of tollhouse cookies and watching movies on cable television. Late in the afternoon, when the storm had ended, they bundled up and walked the streets of their neighborhood. They moved heavily through the deep snow, holding one another up as they stumbled onward. Everything was quiet; the scene they beheld was one of glasslike stillness, a diorama of a snowy town. In their neighbors' yards lay the abandoned evidence of the day's amusements: snow forts, snowmen, sleds and saucers scattered everywhere. But now it was too cold, and all the children had gone inside. At a distance they heard the plows lumbering through the neighborhood streets, the chains on the tires ringing.

Back at the house they removed their wet coats and blue jeans, and O'Neil made tea. In boxers and socks he carried their mugs into the living room, where Mary waited on the sofa, a blanket drawn up to her chin.

"I want a baby," Mary declared.

O'Neil put the tea on the table. His glasses were fogged, and he drew them to the tip of his nose and lifted his eyes to her face. "Right now? The stores are closed."

"I mean I want to make one."

O'Neil grinned, enjoying himself, as she'd expected he would. "I thought we'd have spaghetti."

"Fine, make fun," Mary said, and removed the blanket to show him that she, too, was wearing only her underwear. "We have work to do."

A baby: of course that was what they would want. They had discussed this before, when they had first begun to talk of marriage. They had agreed that children were a part of their future—it was, in fact, one of the things that had attracted them to one another, this willingness to let such things happen in due course—and that they would know when the time was right.

Now the moment was upon them, and they set to the task at once—that very night, there on the sofa while their tea grew cold. After, they made the spaghetti O'Neil had promised, and talked at the kitchen table about the child they wished to have. They decided that they would like to have a girl, and that she would be named Nora, Emily, or Zoë. She would both be and look like Mary, though they also hoped she would draw certain qualities from O'Neil: his even temperament, his comfort talking to strangers, his easy athleticism and knack for tools. Her life would be interesting and prosperous, and they skipped around inside it as if they were perusing a magazine, reading an article here and there, returning to the table of contents to find another subject of interest. She would choose law or medicine, they agreed, though she would also harbor a lifelong passion for literature, and perhaps find time to take a Ph.D.—to finish the same degree that Mary had abandoned. They would take her often to the city, to expose her to music and theater and art, but in later life she would live in a cottage by the sea. They had never talked like this before, with such certainty about what they wanted for their lives, and by the time they went to bed, it seemed impossible to think that Mary wasn't pregnant already.

But she wasn't: not that month, and not the next one or the next, and by the time spring came, they had begun to worry. Mary had been pregnant once before—years in the past, a painful story she did not like to revisit—and from that experience she had carted away one belief: getting pregnant was easy. "Like falling off a log onto a man," she said. The irony, now, was obvious, but it was hard to complain. So many years of thwarting their own biology, of rubber diaphragms dusted with cornstarch and sleek condoms in their foil pouches—they could hardly expect, now, to conceive on demand, like people ordering dinner in a restaurant. Mary kept track of her cycle, taking her temperature each morning before she rose and recording the information on a sheet of blue-lined graph paper she left by the bed. But by fall, when school resumed—after a summer of making love in bed, on the sofa, in a friend's beach house in Cape May, on a picnic table in the Poconos, swinging in a hammock in the yard on Mary's birthday—they agreed that something wasn't working the way it should.

Their insurance plan allowed them to begin fertility counseling in November. The doctor who saw them was a young woman, very precise, with pencil-gray streaks in her long black hair.

"My prediction?" The doctor looked over their chart and shrugged at what she saw. "Pregnancy is just around the corner. You only need to give it time."

"We've given it a year," Mary said.

"And what a year I'm sure it's been. Sometimes, however, it can take longer." She dropped her eyes again to the chart. "Thirty-two years old. A history of irregular menstruation. Your period comes and goes like the March wind." She closed the folder conclusively and waved a hand over it. "Have you tried wine?"

Mary leaned forward. "I'm sorry?"

The doctor settled back into her chair. "A glass of wine can ease the tension."

"I am not tense," said Mary.

"Aren't there tests?" O'Neil asked. "Shouldn't you be examining my sperm?"

The doctor yawned and glanced at her watch. "Pardon me. But no. It's not something we do at this point. Have you ever looked at sperm under a microscope? It's like the hordes at Mecca."

That night they did as the doctor suggested and split a bottle of Chardonnay. It cost eleven dollars, was as sugary as a candy bar, and by the time they were finished they were both tipsy and babbling like toddlers. Struggling out of his jeans, O'Neil stumbled on the corner of the bedroom rug and watched as one of the finial posts on the bed frame rose toward his face, slowly and then quickly, like the bow of an ocean liner bursting from a bank of fog. In her robe Mary led him to the bathroom, sat him down on the toilet, and held a Ziploc bag of ice cubes to his nose.

"There's always adoption," O'Neil said through his thickening nose.

"We're too old," Mary said hopelessly, and began to cry. "Who would adopt us?"

In early January they returned to the doctor, who once again did nothing even remotely medical, apart from taking Mary's temperature. Her questions seemed arbitrary. Did they sleep with the windows open or closed? Did they bathe, or take showers? Was O'Neil still jogging in the cold? The doctor listened to their answers, nodding and clicking her pen. Perhaps, she concluded, they might take a trip together, to take their minds off getting pregnant.

"I've found there's something about a hotel that can be helpful for couples with this problem," she said.

"This problem?" Mary repeated.

"Try one with movies in the rooms," the doctor said.

It seemed silly; nevertheless, they decided to do it. All they had was the weekend, so they planned to drive north to see the town where O'Neil had grown up. In all their time together Mary had never actually been to Glenn's Mills. The drive to upstate New York from Philadelphia took five hours, the last of these on country highways through scenes of such heartbreaking rural poverty that all they could do was marvel. But Glenn's Mills itself had obviously been discovered. In winter twilight, fidgety from so many hours in the car, they drove down the town's main street, past boutiques and antique shops, tearooms and craft studios. Though Christmas was long gone, pine boughs still hung from the streetlamps, which were ornately Victorian, like something from the set of a play. They half expected to see men out walking in capes and top hats, but most of the people on the street were wrapped in heavy parkas with scarves pulled up to their chins, hurrying somewhere, their heads tipped against the cold.

"None of this was here when I was a kid," O'Neil explained. They glided past an herbal shop called the Witchery, then a corner Mobil station with a sign in the window that said: We Have Cappuccino!

O'Neil waved a sorry hand. "Who drinks all this espresso? This was always a boiled-coffee kind of town."

At the Mobil station they bought turkey sandwiches, taco chips, and a six-pack of beer, and found their motel. It was clean and new, two stories tall, and bathed in a fluorescent glow. They ate their picnic on the bed, then put on their pajamas and climbed beneath the stiff covers. A folded card waited on the nightstand with the names of the movies they could order in their room. The usual fare, and then they came to the ones they were looking for: *Up and Coming, Hot Housewives,* and *Pillow Talk II: Debutantes After Dark.*

O'Neil voted for the third. "I liked the original. Is Doris Day in this one?"

Mary shook her head and continued to read. " 'The sexy adventures of a rich girl in Europe.' It stars somebody named Chandra Loveman, though I don't suppose that's her real name." She wrinkled her nose and peered at O'Neil with her head tipped to one side. "It doesn't seem like enough to go on, really."

"I'm not familiar with Ms. Loveman's oeuvre," O'Neil said, "but I would be willing to learn."

They picked the first movie, because Mary, who had done graduate work in poststructuralism, liked the pun in the title. The movie was very dark, and there was a great deal of moaning in the shadows, and a soundtrack that pulsed tumescently whenever the sexy parts came along, which was nearly all the time. The plot was thin, but actually more than either of them had expected. A beautiful young man, orphaned by a tornado that destroys his family's farm, moves from Iowa to California to find work in the movie industry. No sooner does he step off the bus than he is beset by unscrupulous female casting agents and producers, all seeking his favors. They are determined to corrupt him, but he outsmarts them; his past is gone, his gentle life in Iowa smashed by the four winds, and what is there for him now, but to give himself wholly to his gifts? It was all straight out of Balzac, and vaguely interesting, but the story would never last for very long, and then the music would resume, and the moaning. Sometimes the camera zoomed in so close that neither of them could tell what they were seeing.

"I'm not trying to be uncooperative," Mary said after some time had passed, "but I have to say, this isn't doing very much for me at all. What is that? Is that somebody's leg?" She waved her beer at the screen. "Honestly, I haven't a guess."

"We could see what else is on."

Mary traded her empty beer for a fresh one from the small icechest beside the bed. Under the blankets she was wearing a flannel nightgown and woolen socks. "It's your six dollars," she said.

They scanned through the other channels and selected a nature show about a family of bobcats. The mother had a pair of cubs; she taught them to hunt, and play in the dust. She brushed them clean with her long tongue.

Mary turned toward O'Neil in the dark room. The screen flickered blue across the small round lenses of his eyeglasses.

"You know, in this light there's something about you. It's very appealing somehow."

"Is this the beer talking?" O'Neil asked.

Mary kissed his nose and settled down beside him. "I like this show much better."

"Those are cute kittens," O'Neil agreed.

For a while they watched without talking. The kittens grew; finally the day came when it was time for them to strike out on their own. Mary watched as the mother cat led them away from the den, on some pretense, then kept on walking. The show ended with the mother cat, on a rocky outcrop, looking over the arid valley where she had left her children behind.

"It must be hard for you to be here," Mary said into O'Neil's chest. "I don't know why I didn't think of it before."

"I'm all right," O'Neil said, but in the dark, almost invisibly, she knew him to be weeping.

The next morning, cold and clear, they put on heavy coats and boots and walked around town while O'Neil pointed out the sights: the pharmacy where he had once shoplifted baseball cards, his father's old law office on Main Street and the library where his mother had worked, the blue clapboard house where his sister, Kay, had taken piano lessons from a woman named "Mrs. Horsehead." Whether this was her actual name, or a nickname made up by her students to be cruel, O'Neil could not recall. At a pottery gallery they looked at vases without buying any, and when the morning seemed over, they had lunch at a diner behind the town hall, called the Coffee Stop. The insides of the Coffee Stop were dim and smoky—it seemed to be an oasis of what the town once was—and the booths and counter stools were packed with large men in flannel work shirts whose dirty hands and nicotine-stained faces bespoke a life of ceaseless toil. Mary bought a copy of the local paper to read over her grilled cheese sandwich, and that was when she saw the article. She read it in its entirety, then passed O'Neil the paper, folded back to show the photo of the house—a large white four-square with black shutters that she recognized at once as O'Neil's, from other photos she had seen. Even the paint job was the same.

"Boyhood home gets rave review," she said.

O'Neil's parents' house had been turned into a restaurant, called Le Café. Beside the picture of the house there was a second photo of the restaurant's owner, smiling and shaking hands with a woman O'Neil had gone to high school with, who was now the mayor of the town. The owner, who was also the chef, was a tall man, handsome and bald, with a neatly trimmed goatee. He had trained at Cordon Bleu, it said, "in Paris, France." "It has always been my dream to open a country inn," he told the reporter, "to return the finest cuisine to its source, such as one finds in the hills of Tuscany or Provence." Before moving to Glenn's Mills he had owned a successful restaurant in Manhattan.

O'Neil looked the article over then put the newspaper aside. "Unbelievable. A fucking restaurant."

"I'm sure it's a shock."

"This place in Manhattan. How successful could it have been, if he ended up here?"

Mary dipped her grilled cheese into a small pool of ketchup. "What kind of food do they serve?"

O'Neil searched the article again. "It doesn't say, not in so many words. Seriously, how would anyone around here know the difference?"

The waitress, an old woman in a ruffled apron, came to their booth and refilled their coffee cups. O'Neil looked out the window at the snowy town.

"There ought to be a law against this sort of thing," he remarked. "It's like a desecration."

Mary looked at her sandwich. "I do see your point. On the other hand, I would like to see your old house. And we could use a good meal."

Mary stayed at the table while O'Neil went to call about a reservation. The waitress brought her the pie she had ordered—

cherry, with a dollop of vanilla ice cream—and she decided not to wait for O'Neil to return to begin eating. The cherries, she could tell, were canned, but the crust was excellent—light and buttery and still warm from the microwave.

O'Neil returned, shaking his head. "They couldn't take us until eight-thirty," he said. He sat across from her, frowning. "I remember when everybody around here was in bed by then, if they weren't beating their wives. That was always a problem in these parts."

"Oh, idle threats," Mary said, forking the last of the pie into her mouth.

After lunch they returned to their hotel, watched the second of the three movies, napped through the afternoon, and awoke to the disorienting early darkness of a winter evening. O'Neil went to get more beer while Mary showered, and returned to find her lying on the bed wrapped in a thick towel, reading from the Bible she had found in the bedside drawer. Her hair was wet and thick, and she had scrubbed her face so hard it looked dusty.

"Now here's something," she said, and began to read aloud from the Bible, squinting without her glasses at the tiny print. Her eyesight was very poor, and yet she often read this way. " 'When a man hath taken a new wife, he shall not go out to war, neither shall he be charged with any business; but he shall be free at home one year, and shall cheer up his wife which he hath taken.' " She lifted her blue eyes from the page. "It's interesting to me that this is not a widely mentioned part of Scripture."

O'Neil opened a beer and handed it to her. "I'm not sure dinner is such a hot idea."

Mary closed the Bible. "Well. Tell me about that."

He sat on the bed beside her; the cold of the outside still clung to the wool of his coat. "We could eat someplace else."

"This is true."

"I haven't been back there in almost twenty years, not since we sold it." He removed his coat and opened a beer of his own. "You know, when Kay and I got home after the accident, the first thing we found was a huge pile of mail in the front foyer. Our folks had been dead for a couple of days, but the mailman had been shoving it through the mail slot just the same. So there it was, this pile of letters and bills and magazines, all mailed to dead people." He shook his head mournfully and took a long swig of beer. All day long, Mary realized, he had been thinking about this melancholy pile of mail. She understood this was unavoidable—the mind went where it wished—and yet, deep down, she believed such brooding was profitless. O'Neil sighed hopelessly, as if he had heard her thoughts. "Now lawyers from Albany are sitting around the living room, praising the pot stickers."

"So you found out what kind of food they serve," Mary said expectantly.

"Sino-French." O'Neil sipped again and wiped his mouth. "The guy at the 7-Eleven told me. Apparently, the chef does something very nice with duck."

At eight o'clock they left for the restaurant. Mary fully expected O'Neil to change his mind at the last minute, sending them out onto dark country lanes searching for something to eat, but he surprised her and drove straight there. They parked at the curb across from the house, and sitting in the cold car, O'Neil gave her the lay of the land. The house, set back from the street, was not immediately recognizable as a restaurant, and the sign by the front door was so small it would have been possible to miss it altogether—to pass the house by, thought Mary, without knowing it was in any way different or special. O'Neil spoke quietly, as if they might be overheard, as he pointed out the details: the stone walkway his father had laid one summer, the crabapple tree that had been a sapling when his parents died but now stood fifteen feet tall, the window on the second floor that had been his room, before he had gone off to college. He spoke only of the exterior; his mind, it seemed, did not want to go inside the house.

"We sold it to a couple with kids," O'Neil said. "I think their name was McGeary. After that I just lost track."

"How does it feel?" Mary asked, and took his hand.

O'Neil looked at the house once more, taking it in, and sighed through his nose. "Strange," he said. "In most ways it's just the same. But probably the inside is all different now."

It was. They boarded the porch and stepped through the front door to find themselves in a single open area, generously lit, with fluted white columns supporting the structure where load-bearing walls had once stood. A half-dozen tables occupied the dining room, which flowed to the open kitchen at the rear of the house. From where they stood in the entryway, Mary and O'Neil could see the gleaming range, the copper pots hanging on chains. The air was moist and smelled like garlic, and quiet violin music dribbled from speakers in the ceiling.

"Son of a bitch," O'Neil said quietly.

The man whose picture they had seen in the paper came out from the kitchen and showed them to their table near the fireplace. The room was small enough that, as they sat, the other parties around them fell silent.

"I guess it's quite a change," Mary said.

O'Neil cast his eyes about the room. "You know, I think this is just about the spot where Kay and I used to play Chinese checkers on the floor. There was a sofa right there, and two chairs across from it. I don't know why I played with her, because she always beat me. So maybe that's why. It made her so happy."

Mary took a roll from the wicker basket on the table. Steam wafted up as she pulled it into halves. "I just want to know," she said, "is the whole evening going to go like this? It's all right if it is."

"They were perfectly good walls," O'Neil said. "They were the walls of my childhood, and now they're gone."

Mary held out the basket. "Try a roll, O'Neil. They're fresh."

They were finishing the bread when a young woman appeared at their table and lit the candle between them with a long match. She was pretty, with brown hair that fell to a straight line across her shoulders, and small dark eyes.

"Have you been with us before?" the woman asked.

"Not in the way you mean," O'Neil said.

"No," Mary said.

The woman handed them menus, single sheets of heavy paper written by hand. "Now, these are not menus in the typical sense," she explained. "Think of them instead as maps of what's to come."

While the woman stood beside their table, Mary and O'Neil looked the menus over. Five courses were listed: an appetizer, soup, salad, entrée, and dessert. The descriptions were lengthy and contained many ingredients that neither of them recognized, or recognized as food. The salad, for instance, contained pansies. There were no prices on anything, but the entire meal cost fifty-five dollars per person.

O'Neil handed his menu back to her. "Say, what's upstairs?" The stairs were blocked off by a velvet rope, like a forbidden wing at a museum. A brass plaque hung from the rope with the word *Private* engraved into its face.

The woman smiled neutrally. "Storage," she said.

Their courses arrived, each more bizarre than the last: grilled oysters in raspberry sauce, a watery yellow broth flecked with bits of bitter mushroom, the promised salad of endive and pansy. The endive was served as a single wedge-shaped head, laid at an angle across the plate, with pansies scattered carelessly over it, as if dropped from a great height.

When the woman had left them with their salads, Mary leaned across the table. "Maybe we should just tell her. They might be interested, you know."

O'Neil speared a pansy with his fork and chewed it, grimacing. "What would I say?" he asked. " 'Thank you for making your pretentious food in my boyhood house'? You know, if my parents were alive, I don't think they'd even eat here? Though it's sort of a moot point, because if they were, they'd be living in it."

"You can't be sure," Mary said. "They might have moved. Retired, maybe. Gone off to Florida." They would, she knew, be somewhere in their late sixties.

O'Neil took a long drink of water and frowned. "Trust me," he said. "They'd be here."

Mary didn't answer. The chef and the woman—his wife, Mary guessed—were obviously trying, and how were they to know that their place of business was, in fact, a tomb of memory? Mary had once been back to visit the house where her family had lived when she was very small. This occurred during an uncertain period in her life, the year after college, when she was working as a barmaid in the Minnesota town where she had gone to school and living in a tiny apartment over a shoe store. The house was just a few miles away from her parents' development, and yet she had not been back for many years. The address was tattooed into her memory—694 West Sycamore Lane—and she found it easily, as if guided by an internal compass: a tiny shoebox of a house, still painted Pepto-Bismol pink, on a damp patch of ground shaded by a pair of threadbare hemlocks her parents had planted twenty years before. People who had revisited their childhood homes always spoke of how small it seemed, but Mary knew it had always been that way—the house had seemed small even

then—and a flood of sensations returned to her: the close feeling
of its cramped square rooms, the thin walls and nearly weightless
doors, the smell of the airless kitchen and the way the light fell on
winter afternoons across the threadbare carpets. During the time
they had lived there, her father worked two jobs, selling used cars
for her uncle by day and moonlighting at night as a cashier in a
drugstore, selling candy and cigarettes, and one winter evening
her mother took them—Mary and her older brother, Mark, and
her little sister, Cheryl, still in a basket—to visit him. So vivid was
this memory, sitting in the car outside the house, that she doubted,
momentarily, if it had ever happened at all. Mary was four or five;
her father, standing behind his register, was wearing a smock,
dark green, with his name, Lars, on a tag over the breast pocket.
Mary knew this was his name and yet to find it this way, announced so plainly for all to see—it seemed as if he had been
stolen from her, that she had been deprived of some essential
right—amazed and frightened her. The feeling was so new, so
overwhelming in its strangeness, that Mary began to cry. There
was a general commotion; her mother had meant the trip to be a
treat, and here she was, in tears; and then her father had stepped
out from behind his register and lifted her into his arms. He was a
large and powerful man, both in memory and in fact, and held her
against his broad chest until she was calm, and sat her on the
counter beside his register. Her mother took the other children
home, but Mary stayed with him until closing time, sucking on
cherry lollipops.

Why had he done it? In Mary's experience many people
claimed to have epiphanies when nothing of the kind occurred—
insight filled you slowly, like sips of water from a cup—but that is
what happened to her, parked in front of the pink house. Her father had wanted her to know that he loved her, of course, but also
what such love as his contained: that it was made of iron, and

could work without ceasing or rest. Though he lacked the words to say this, he wanted to tell her it was all for her, everything he did in the world; whatever happened in her life, there had been one such person. She knew this, as she also knew that the pink house was a monument to this memory; that was why she had come. She hadn't knocked on the door, or even gotten out of the car. The house was inside her, that place in her heart where she was still a tiny girl, and to enter it would have stolen this feeling from her.

Mary reached under the table and found O'Neil's hand. "I'm sorry."

"It's not really so bad to be here," O'Neil said. "I only wish the food wasn't so *weird*. I wanted you to have a nice meal."

They managed to eat a respectable amount of salad before the entrée arrived: braised medallions of venison with cranberries and lemongrass, served on a bed of buckwheat couscous. After the pansies it was surprisingly good, and they ate hungrily, even O'Neil. By this time it was after ten and most of the other tables were empty. O'Neil began to talk freely about his memories of the house and the town, as he had not done since they'd arrived the day before. The stories he told were happy, and Mary understood then that part of his pleasure was his invisibility—it had been that way for her—and he would neither tell the owner who he was nor try to go upstairs. And yet she knew that was what he truly wanted: a few moments alone, in his old room.

They were the last to leave the restaurant. Outside, the winter sky was hung with a dense tapestry of stars. She waited until O'Neil was buckled in before she announced her intentions to return to the restaurant to use the bathroom.

O'Neil looked at her with a puzzled expression. How, she wondered, could he possibly fail to know what she was about to do? "The motel is only five minutes."

"I don't think I can wait," she said, and got out of the car.

She found the dining room empty, as she had hoped. Their table had already been cleared and laid out with clean linen and silverware for the next night. From the kitchen she heard the sound of pots clattering in the sink and running water, and country music playing on a radio. She waited a moment at the door to see if anyone had detected her return, then stepped over the velvet rope and climbed the stairs.

The hallway was dark, but as her eyes adjusted she saw five doors, all closed. There were three bedrooms, she knew—O'Neil had given her the basic layout—plus a bathroom and a linen closet. Cardboard boxes were stacked along the wall, and at the far end of the hall she saw a small table with a telephone on it. It was an old-style rotary phone; probably it had been there since O'Neil was a boy. She had already guessed that the chef and his wife lived up here. Turned around in the darkness, Mary had lost track of which door was which, but she guessed and opened the second one on the left.

The room was small and square, and a night-light glowed on the wall above a baby's crib. Mary stepped inside. The air was warm and sweet, like clean laundry. She saw a bureau and a changing table, and a bookshelf with toys—dinosaurs and trucks, a baseball glove, the kinds of things a boy would like. What was she doing in here? And yet she could not remove herself; the urge to remain was irresistible, as if she were soaking in a bath. She stood another moment, tasting the air, then approached the crib where the little boy was sleeping.

It was then that she saw the blinking baby monitor on the bureau. Mary's heart froze with panic, but it was too late—she had been detected. She heard footsteps running up the stairs, and then a voice, slicing through the darkness.

"What are you doing in there?"

It was the woman who had served them dinner. She pushed past Mary into the room, placing herself between Mary and the crib.

"I'm sorry," Mary said. "I was looking for the bathroom. Nobody was downstairs."

"I thought you left," the woman said sternly. "It says private, you know. Private means something to most people."

The baby had begun to fuss in its crib. The woman turned away from Mary and bent over the railings to lift him into her arms. It was then that Mary saw that it wasn't a baby at all, but a much older child—a boy in Barney pajamas, perhaps as old as five. His eyes were closed, but his mouth, which was large and wet, twisted with his soft cries. He laid his head over her shoulder; his bare feet hung nearly to the woman's knees and made a series of jerky movements. Mary noticed things in the room she somehow had not seen before: a tiny wheelchair parked beside the bureau, a white box with tubes and dials that looked medical, a shiny chrome stand for an IV. Even the crib was different—much larger, like a raised bed with bars.

The woman smoothed the child's hair. "Mummy's here," she cooed. "No bad dreams, no bad dreams."

Mary stood in the doorway. "I truly am sorry," she said again. "I didn't mean to wake him."

"He's deaf." The woman looked at Mary then, fixing her with a firm gaze. "It's not even words he hears, just a vibration."

Outside, O'Neil was waiting in the Toyota, the engine idling. He was gripping the wheel tightly, as if he couldn't wait to drive away.

"All set," she said.

He looked at her as if he was about to speak, then put the car in gear. "You'll have to tell me about that sometime," O'Neil said.

*

In the early morning, before O'Neil was awake, Mary rose from bed, seized by a turbulent nausea, and went to the bathroom to vomit. She managed to do this quietly, then rinsed her mouth out and returned to bed. But when the two of them awoke later, she found that the feeling had not passed.

"It's that goddamn restaurant," O'Neil fumed. "Pansy salad. And that awful soup. What the hell was that all about?"

They had planned to visit the cemetery that morning, but agreed this was now impossible, and O'Neil left the motel to find muffins and tea for Mary, to put something on her stomach before they attempted the drive back to Philadelphia. At the window Mary watched the car pull away, then put on her coat and walked into town. She had seen the clinic the day before, near the gallery where they had looked at pots; the sign had said it was open for Sunday walk-ins from nine to twelve o'clock.

The door was open and the lights were on, but the waiting room was empty. Mary sat down and thumbed through a needlework magazine, and a few minutes later a woman appeared, wearing a white coat and stethoscope.

"Ah," she said, seeing Mary. "I didn't know anyone was here."

"Are you the doctor?"

The woman, who had short gray hair and a handsome heart-shaped face, held up the disk of her stethoscope and looked at it in mock surprise. "Now, who put this stethoscope on me?"

The doctor led Mary into an examining room, where Mary told her about the pansies and the soup while the doctor took her temperature and blood pressure and asked her about the pain. She eased Mary back on the paper-lined table and pressed her bare stomach here and there. Her fingers were pale and slender, yet eased into Mary's flesh with surprising force.

The doctor stepped back. "Well, I don't think it's food poisoning."

"The meal was strange but I'd have to agree."

"I've eaten there. The duck is really what's special." The doctor furrowed her brow at Mary. "How late are you?"

"Ten days, give or take."

"Have you ever been pregnant before?"

"Not in many years," Mary said. "Has it changed?"

From a cabinet of supplies the doctor removed a square pink box with a picture of a daisy and handed it to Mary. Inside were a small specimen cup and a plastic wand, like an undersized thermometer, wrapped in cellophane.

Mary held up her bare wrist. "I don't have a watch."

The doctor unclasped her own—a Timex, with three hearts forming the first three links of the band on either side of the face—and showed Mary to the rest room. Mary squatted over the toilet and held the cup between her legs until she had filled it, and placed it on the toilet tank. The instructions on the box said the test would take three minutes, but the instant Mary dipped the wand into the cup, a turquoise ribbon shot up the blotter paper and filled the little window, resolving into a tiny cross. She counted off three minutes with the watch, waiting to see if there was some mistake and the blue cross would be retracted. When it wasn't, she dumped the cup into the toilet, wrapped the wand in tissue paper to show O'Neil, and returned to the office.

"These tests are pretty accurate," the doctor said, scribbling on a prescription pad, "but they're not the real thing, so when you get home, you should go see your gynecologist."

"Somebody told me this was going to happen," Mary said.

"Well, they knew something." The doctor put her watch back on. "If you don't mind my asking, is this good news for you?"

Mary fingered the wand in her pocket. "It's what I wanted," she said.

On the way back to the motel Mary stopped at a Rexall to fill her prescription. It was an old-style drugstore with a lunch counter, and the air smelled of wet clothing and fried eggs. An entire aisle of the store was devoted to baby products—fat packages of diapers, cans of powdered formula, rattles and teething toys and little spoons with kittens or puppies on the handles, all sealed in plastic—and Mary paused to look it over, this vast, hopeful inventory she had never paid any attention to. She believed it was important now to stand before it—she felt as if she had achieved some final homecoming—and when she handed her prescription to the druggist, an old man with a shuffling step who took the paper from her without comment, he, like the wall of diapers and the well-worn light of the store's interior and the lunch counter with its pies and cakes under elevated domes of glass, seemed somehow inevitable, like a figure from a dream she'd once had years ago.

The druggist handed the prescription to her in a stapled package, his face broadening with a smile. "Congratulations," he said.

Mary thanked him, bought a carton of milk at the lunch counter, and stepped outside. O'Neil would be back at the motel, pacing with worry. Where had she gone off to? Had she gotten so sick she couldn't wait for the muffins and the tea? Why hadn't she left him a note? The air had warmed; a pale and ghostly snow was falling all around. Standing by the door, Mary opened the druggist's package, which contained a bottle of prenatal vitamins. They were large orange pills that smelled like fish food, and the directions said to take one daily. The bottle contained forty pills, and the prescription could be refilled five times, for a total of two hundred—the number of days until the baby was born. *Two hundred days*, Mary thought, and removed her mittens to take the first pill, tipping her face into the falling snow and using the milk to wash it down.

LIFE BY MOONLIGHT

October 1995

FRIDAY, 9:31 P.M, a humid night in fall: Mary Olson Burke, age thirty-three—pregnant, pregnant, pregnant—pauses in the paint-rollers-brushes-dropcloths aisle of the Home Depot in King of Prussia, Pennsylvania, and knows that her water has broken.

The tear is tiny, high in her uterus; there is no splash, no bursting water-balloon of fluid, no great, embarrassing release. Mary bends to lift a gallon can of white latex semigloss from a low shelf, when suddenly her panties are damp, then wet, a release of amniotic fluid about a thimbleful; she drops her eyes to the pleats of her cotton dress and finds no stain, no mark to tell anyone what has happened. And maybe nothing has. But, no. It is six days since Mary passed her due date, silently and without fanfare, like a car crossing a desert border at night. Inside Mary the question blooms: *Hello?* And: *Soon?* Her water has broken. Mary knows.

Mary is enormous; she is a cathedral, a human aria, a C note held for ten minutes. She feels luminous, beyond gravity; she is gravity itself. Her husband, O'Neil, is crouched to examine a rack of paintbrushes. Like everything else in the Home Depot, the display is huge and confusing, like a menu that is ten pages long. There are thick brushes and thin brushes, sleek brushes and hairy brushes, brushes with tips so delicate they could be used to stroke liquid gold on Fabergé eggs. O'Neil is all details, a man overwhelmed by the tiniest purchases; it will take him an hour to buy a paintbrush, but thirty minutes to buy a car.

"O'Neil . . ."

He tilts his head to the sound of Mary's voice. His face lights up in a grateful smile; she has broken his trance.

"Who cares, am I right? You were about to say I should just pick anything so we can get the hell out of here."

Mary gently lowers herself onto the can of paint, perching like a child on a potty chair. "Roger wilco, honeybear." Now that she is off her feet, exhaustion folds over her like a heavy cloth. Repainting the kitchen now seems like madness, the dumbest idea of their marriage. "Please, can we just pick something and go? Can you take care of this while I sit here?"

O'Neil rises. "We'll need a cart."

"Make it two." Mary tries to smile, and when she can't, she realizes for the first time that she is afraid. "Just dump me in and wheel me home."

They push their purchases outside, into the soupy heat and the sound of traffic on the turnpike. O'Neil leaves Mary under the concrete overhang and disappears across the parking lot, still full of cars at this late hour. Mary stands, clutching her side; under her fingertips she feels the baby shift position, feeling this also inside of her, like the sensation of her lips and tongue when the dentist has numbed them with Novocain, woozy and not quite real. Then she sees it: in the sky beyond the parking lot, the highway, the roofs of the buildings, a fat, yellowish light is emerging. Mary thinks at first that it's a helicopter, or a searchlight, but then she sees that it's the moon—a full moon, a harvest moon. It creeps up the cluttered horizon with amazing speed, leaking its liquidy light on everything. She is still watching it when the car pulls up.

O'Neil stops loading the paint and supplies into the trunk and follows her gaze to the horizon.

"I know what you're thinking," he says finally. "A moon like that. What else? It means you'll go into labor tonight."

Mary looks again. Somehow, the moon seems even larger than before, and weirdly bright. It is almost too bright to look at. She wonders why she hasn't told O'Neil about her water yet, and then she knows. It is the last secret she has; she will not surrender it yet, though soon.

"There's always a chance," Mary says.

"Ten bucks you have this baby before breakfast," O'Neil says.

In the passenger seat Mary dozes, and by the time they pull into their driveway she is surprised to look over the lights of the dashboard and find her own house. For a moment she thinks the baby has already come but then realizes this is a dream she has had—that she was breaking open a hard-boiled egg and found a tiny person inside. Mary climbs the stairs, undresses, puts on a nightgown, and washes her face. Below her she can hear their front door opening and closing and knows that O'Neil is bringing the supplies inside. She finds him collapsed on the sofa in the living room, drinking a beer and watching television, the sound turned off. On the screen a group of divers in yellow wetsuits are lowering a small submarine from a crane into a choppy sea. These are the kinds of shows O'Neil loves.

"And zo," O'Neil says, "ze brave men of ze Calypzo dezend once more into ze inky deep." He pushes his glasses onto his forehead and rubs a hand over his tired face. "I think they're looking for the lost continent of Atlantis. Apparently, it iz near ze Canary Islands."

Mary bends to kiss O'Neil; he returns the kiss, then puts his beer on the coffee table, takes the round mass of her stomach in his hands, and kisses that too.

"Let me know if ze brave men of ze Calypzo stop by to paint ze kitchen," Mary says.

Upstairs, Mary lowers herself into bed, leaving the shades open to fill the room with the night's strange moonlight. The clock says it is just past midnight; three hours have passed since her water broke, and still nothing. She finds the position she likes, on her left side with a pillow between her thighs to straighten her back, and remembers the dream she had in the car, replaying its images in her mind like a prayer, hoping that she can return to it. It is a pleasant dream, and this time it begins in her parents' kitchen in Minneapolis. Mary is alone, seated at the table, and there is an egg in her hand, still warm from the boiling water. Mary taps it with a butter knife, pausing to scrape away the flakes with her thumbnail. Crack, scrape, crack, scrape. But something is wrong; the egg is plastic, a plastic Easter egg. She pops it open, and inside she finds a slip of paper, like a fortune cookie, on which someone has written the word *Atlantis.*

Then she is in a different house, not a house she has ever seen before. In one of the bedrooms a monkey is living, left behind by the previous owners. Mary and O'Neil discuss what to do about the monkey. Should they feed it? Is it their monkey now? In the fridge they find a wedge of cheese, and they put it on a plate and take it into the bedroom. The room is dark, the shades drawn tight against the windows, and Mary can hear the monkey moving around, scratching itself, making tiny monkey noises. "Here, monkey," Mary calls softly. "Here, little monkey." Then the monkey is in her arms. She is nearly weightless, clinging to her. She has a soft, human face, with green eyes like O'Neil's. Mary is happy, very happy, holding her, and does not mind at all that the monkey has urinated, soaking Mary's nightgown, her thighs, her bare feet on the carpet. They will have to get a diaper for the monkey.

Then it is 2:00 A.M., and Mary awakens in a puddle that smells like straw, a strong contraction moving through her, and she goes to O'Neil where he has fallen asleep in front of the TV to tell him the moment is here, the baby is coming, that they have to go to the hospital, *now*.

O'Neil at 5:00 A.M., asleep and dreaming: a brief, unhappy dream in which he watches his parents fly over a cliff into darkness. The image plays before him like a movie on a screen, his parents moving away, and he can do nothing. He is pinned to his chair in the theater, and when he looks down he sees his wrists are tied; when he looks up, his parents are gone.

Then a new sound reaches him, distant and familiar. O'Neil thinks at first it's a lawn mower, then that it's the telephone, then that it is his wife, Mary, vomiting; they have been to a party, a weird and marvelous party where all the guests wore bedsheets and carried small faceless dolls, and Mary is drunk, and throwing up in the bathroom.

"Ooooooo . . . Neil."

He opens his eyes, and at once he remembers: he has fallen asleep in the hospital, his head rocked back in a chair pulled close to Mary's bed; he understands that he is in the hospital, and also why. Mary is on her side, facing away, and the ridges of her backbone are exposed where the sides of her gown have opened. It is O'Neil's job to press his hands against this place when her contractions come. He has dozed only a moment.

"Jesus, O'Neil, what's going on back there?"

O'Neil rises on his toes and leans in. The memory of his dream, of darkness and flight, flits over his consciousness, like the shadow of a bird crossing a field. Was it his parents? He and Mary? He remembers terror, and the sound of water below. His arms feel like rubber, his eyes like little balls of lead. He has been pressing Mary's back for three hours, first in the front hallway of their house, again in the backseat of the car where it was parked in the driveway, and so on, right until this moment.

"I'm sorry," O'Neil manages. "It's your body. You have to tell me."

Mary groans, her breath catching in her chest like a hiccup. "Is that what you think?"

The nurse, whose name is Rachel, brings in some extra pillows to prop up Mary's knees. She has brown hair and a pleasant smile; on the lapel of her white jacket is a button that says, We Deliver. As she slides the pillows under Mary, she asks them if they know the sex of the baby.

They do. The baby is a girl. When Mary doesn't answer, O'Neil tells Rachel they're not sure.

"I think it's better like that," Rachel says. "You can be happy either way."

Rachel leaves again. Outside the sun is rising, and O'Neil knows he won't sleep again until after the baby is born. He would like to leave the room, the building even, to take a quick walk in fresh outdoor air, just once around the hospital. But he knows he can't, that this desire is selfish and can't even be mentioned, like the wish to buy a sports car or spend a summer in France.

Mary's obstetrician arrives a little after seven. She is a pretty woman, very small, who always dresses nicely; this morning she is wearing a blue chalk-stripe suit under her white coat, and a pair of gray flats. O'Neil would like to call her by her first name, which is Amy, but since she's never invited them to do it, he has always called her Dr. Sullivan.

She reaches under Mary's gown to examine her. She feels around inside her, her eyes pointed upward and away, like someone cracking a safe. She finishes the exam and removes her gloves.

"Five centimeters."

On the bed Mary groans. "God. That's *all*?"

Doctor Sullivan lifts her tiny shoulders in a shrug. "Five is pretty good. It could be eight an hour from now."

Mary lets her head fall back onto the pillows. "I feel like I've carried a piano up the stairs."

But at ten o'clock Mary is still at five, and she is still at five at noon, when Dr. Sullivan examines her again. The baby is in a good position, she tells O'Neil, but Mary's cervix won't dilate. She speaks in a low voice, and uses the word *stubborn*. Mary has been in labor now for ten hours, fifteen if they count it from the Home Depot. Her face is damp and flushed from exertion, and golden strands of hair cling to her neck and cheeks—the long, rich hair of pregnancy. Mary's contractions come just two minutes apart now, and between them she has little to say, to him or anyone. She seems to doze, although O'Neil knows she is actually concentrating, putting her mind in a state of readiness to ride out each contraction like a surfer paddling in front of a wave. It is a lonely feeling, he realizes, watching your wife have a baby. With each passing hour she moves farther away from him, into a place where all her strength comes from.

"I know it seems like days, but technically, it's not all that long for a first labor," Dr. Sullivan says. The pager clipped to her waist begins to beep, and her hand darts to her waist to shut it off. She peeks at it quickly, frowning. "Well. I have to take this." She lifts her eyes once more to O'Neil. "Her blood pressure is fine. The baby's in great shape. But without the epidural, as I said, this could get hard. She could run out of gas."

All along, Mary has been saying that she wants nothing, no Demerol, no epidural, not even an aspirin. It is history she is thinking of, and O'Neil has seen the pictures: faded black-and-whites of the women of her family, a lineage of stern Germanic matriarchs who bore their children in covered wagons in the middle of blizzards on the Minnesota plain. O'Neil knows that having her baby without painkillers is part of Mary's conversation with these women, with the past itself. But all along he has hoped that, when it came time, Mary would opt for something to make it easier.

"No epidural," Mary says from the bed. "Are you kidding? I've seen that needle. It's like something designed by the Pentagon."

Dr. Sullivan leaves to take her page, and Mary and O'Neil are alone again. O'Neil hasn't set foot from the room since dawn; somewhere in the late morning his body turned a corner, leaving exhaustion behind and taking him into some new state where night and day have lost their meaning and nothing else will happen until Mary has their baby. The way his body feels reminds O'Neil of the night his parents died, when O'Neil was just nineteen. They had just been up to visit him at college, and on the trip home their car missed a turn and went over an embankment. This is the memory he often returns to. O'Neil was coming back from a party, and when he opened the door to his room and saw the college chaplain there, and his roommate, Stephen, and then noticed behind them his track coach, talking in a low voice to the dormitory's resident advisor, and their eyes, a luminous chorus of compassion, rose all at once to meet his own where he stood in the doorway with his keys in his hand, he knew something awful had happened, and also what it was; before anyone could speak, a hole appeared in O'Neil's heart where his parents had once been. Though he has gone on to live his life, to choose a profession and marry and start a family, he is not certain he has ever left it, this pause—a gap in his life like the valley of rocks and trees where his parents' car, upside down and wheels spinning, came at last to rest. It was three days before he slept again. This is the way he feels now—suspended, like a balloon that will neither rise nor fall—and he wonders if there are other men in the building who feel the way he does.

The doctor has suggested that Mary walk, and O'Neil helps

her out of bed and into her robe. He is uncertain how much weight he should bear, and he settles for letting her take his arm, like a couple walking down the aisle. For four hours more they shuffle the short hallway of the hospital's labor and delivery unit, from the empty operating room where cesareans are performed to the front doors and back again, pausing whenever Mary has a contraction so she can brace herself against the wall. Most of the other rooms are empty, though as they pass one door they hear a woman's deep, throaty moans, and a man's voice telling her to push. When they pass it the next time they hear a baby crying.

When Mary can walk no more, Dr. Sullivan examines her again. Mary's contractions are so tightly spaced that it is hard to tell where one ends and the next begins. The day has turned to late afternoon, and someone has drawn the drapes in Mary's room to shield her face from the low, sharp light streaming in. O'Neil misses his wife, who seems to have gone far, far away from him.

"Have you eaten anything?" Dr. Sullivan asks him.

O'Neil can't remember. He guesses he hasn't. He is holding Mary's damp hand and wiping her face with a cloth he has moistened in the pitcher on the table by her bed.

"Well, you better get something if you're going to." Dr. Sullivan snaps off her gloves and speaks in a bright, loud voice. "Ten centimeters, Mary. I think we're off to the races here."

A fresh energy fills O'Neil, and he decides he can make it; there's a candy machine in the hallway, and he asks Rachel—back for the night shift, still with her happy smile and jokey button—if she'd mind getting him something, anything, to tide him over. O'Neil telephones Mary's parents in Minnesota from the phone on the bedside table to tell them the baby is coming. Rachel hands him a tiny cellophane tray of yellow cheese and stale Saltines while the phone is ringing in his in-laws' house, a thousand miles away, and a burst of saliva washes down the insides of his mouth;

he hadn't realized he was so hungry. When the answering machine picks up, O'Neil decides not to leave a message, because his mouth is full of the cheese and crackers. He would rather call later to tell them that their granddaughter has been born, anyway.

In bed Mary raises her thighs with her hands and bends her chin to her chest. "Can I push now? *Oh please . . . I . . . want . . . to . . . push.*"

O'Neil takes her hand. "Can she?"

"I'd say you already are," Dr. Sullivan says.

Mary in labor, dreaming of crows: she is on her knees, vomiting into the snow and corn stubble, and when she looks up she sees them—their glistening beaks and dark eyes on her, on the terrible thing she's done. Her car idles on the side of the road behind her. At the clinic they told her she should not drive. A baby, she thinks; I am twenty-two and *it was a baby*.

The vision scatters; her next contraction comes, obliterating her, every memory she has ever contained. It bears down on her in a black cone, a roar enveloping her like a subway bursting from its tube into the station, only the train does not stop. It roars and roars, full speed past the platform, the air around her shuddering with the heat and weight and noise of it. A chorus of voices tells her to push, and Mary knows she is. Like a flock of birds, every atom of her body turns and points itself toward pushing, but the place where force must be applied is deep within her, a point of light that moves whenever she looks at it. If she can find it, she knows, the light will become a face, her daughter's face, and the baby will be born.

How much time has passed, she does not know. Behind the drapes the sun has set, but Mary cannot remember if it is the first evening of her labor, or the second, or even, impossibly, the third. She has been doing this forever, trying to push the baby out.

Another contraction comes, and she counts the cars as they blow past—twenty, thirty, forty. O'Neil is telling her to push, and she wishes she could do something for him, tell him not to be afraid. Between the contractions it is like dreaming, what she feels; her body seems scattered and broken, pieces of a puzzle spread across the floor, each one a different picture of something that has happened to her: waiting in the rain for someone to pick her up after a dance at school; O'Neil diving into a lake, his arms and legs flailing as he laughs and then is swallowed by the water; the crows and the corn stubble and their glistening gaze upon her. It is only a moment, this oasis of the past. She opens her eyes then and sees O'Neil, his glasses fogging, and beyond him the silver edge of the portable steel lights that have been brought into the room so the doctors and nurses can see the baby coming; she hears her own voice, howling, almost hooting, and knows that it is O'Neil's hand she feels in her own, and that soon she will return to him. She closes her eyes again, letting the contraction take her: *Louise,* she thinks, *Louise.* She named her, the first one she did not, could not have, ten years ago, when she was twenty-two; in her heart she had given her the name Louise, there in the wintry field where she knelt with the crows' eyes on her, telling Mary what she had done and what it meant, and that nothing—not even the pain she feels now—would take this burden from her. *Louise,* she thinks again. Then: *Nora. Nora.* A voice, O'Neil's voice, tells her the baby's head is crowning, and that her hair is blond, like Mary's. The roar swallows her again, for what Mary knows is the last time. It is a train, a comet, the moon set loose and sailing down to her, taking her over, and at once it becomes the light that she has worked to find. Her body wraps around it, this light that is first two faces and then just one, a great calm fills her, and Mary pushes the baby out, safe and well: alive.

*

It is after eleven by the time Mary and the baby are settled down in their new room, where a cot has been wheeled in for O'Neil to spend the night with them. Their little girl is small, just six and a half pounds, and wearing a diaper and T-shirt that looks to O'Neil as tiny as doll clothes. Propped up in bed with Nora in her arms, Mary opens her robe and guides her to her breast; the baby latches on at once, her pink mouth pulling at Mary's flesh in a languid rhythm that seems to O'Neil a pure force of nature. He strokes Mary's hair, then gives one finger to Nora, who wraps her fingers around it and squeezes. She tugs at it to match the cadence of her mouth. O'Neil feels his knees buckle. "Wow," he says.

When Rachel comes to change the baby's diaper, O'Neil leaves the two of them in the room and takes the elevator down to the ground floor to find something to eat. But the truth is, he's too tired to eat, or even sleep. What he wants is a moment alone with the idea of the day and what has happened: that he has watched his wife have a baby, and that her name is Nora. He wouldn't mind standing a minute outside, someplace quiet and ordinary, even if it means standing by the Dumpsters. He passes the cafeteria, which is closed, and beyond it a room with vending machines, and a small lounge where someone in a white coat, a doctor or nurse, is lying on a sofa reading a *People* magazine in the dark. Then someone comes through a door O'Neil hadn't noticed, and he realizes he has found what he is looking for.

The door opens onto a little portico, with a wheelchair ramp leading down to the lawn and a large ashtray full of butts. More cigarettes are scattered on the ground. O'Neil looks around, and sees that he is at the back of the hospital. It would be the right time, he thinks, to smoke, but he doesn't; he wishes he did. There is a stretch of grass beyond the portico, and what looks like a garden with beds of flowers and a bench. The moon has risen, and everything is very still.

In the little room of vending machines O'Neil finds a pay phone and calls his in-laws in Minneapolis, who use the other telephone line in the house to make travel arrangements while O'Neil is still talking with them, giving them all the news, and by the time the call is over they have booked a plane to Philadelphia, arriving the next evening. As he hangs up he realizes that he is woozy with hunger; he buys a peanut butter sandwich from one of the vending machines and puts it away in four bites, washing it down with a pint of milk as he sits at a Formica table in the empty room. *My wife and daughter are asleep upstairs,* he thinks, and then he says it: "My wife and daughter are asleep upstairs." O'Neil rises again and returns to the pay phone. His parents have been dead for sixteen years, but he still remembers their telephone number, and without thinking he dials it, surprised to be doing it, and by the way it feels and sounds: a sequence of bright tones that resonates inside him like an echo on a canyon wall, as strange and familiar as his own heartbeat. O'Neil intends to listen to the phone ring a couple of times and then hang up, but then there is a click on the line.

"Hello?" It is a woman's voice, groggy with sleep. "Honey?"

"I'm sorry," O'Neil says. He thinks at first she is an older woman, then that she is young, then neither; old or young, he doesn't know. "I didn't mean—"

"Honey? What time is it?" He hears the woman turn over, and then the scratch of the alarm clock on her bedside table as she pulls it toward her. "Is it midnight?" she asks. "Where are you?"

For a moment O'Neil does not answer. The phone is slick in his damp hand. "It's late," he says finally. "I'm sorry. I shouldn't have woken you."

The woman's breathing in the receiver is deep and even, like sighing, and O'Neil thinks she may have fallen back asleep.

"Mmmm. I was having the strangest dream. Are you all right?"

"I'm fine," O'Neil says. He hesitates, then speaks again. "I think everything's working out just the way I wanted it."

"That's nice to hear. It's nice when everything works out like that." The receiver rustles against her face as she pulls the covers close. "Honey? You sound . . . I don't know. Far away."

"I'm really okay," O'Neil says. "A little tired. It's been quite a day. I have some news too."

"I know," the woman says sleepily. "You love me."

The answer is easy to give. "I do. Of course I do."

"I wish you were here, honey. Let everybody else handle things for a while. Can you? Just come home."

"I will," O'Neil says. "As soon as everything's taken care of here, I'll come straight home."

"Come home, my darling. Say it: I'm coming home."

"I'm coming home."

"And you miss me."

O'Neil thinks of his parents, gone so long, taken from him when he was just a boy in college, standing at the door with his keys in his hand. "Yes, I miss you. It's awful, missing you."

"I miss you too," the woman says, and then—so gently O'Neil doesn't realize what has happened—she hangs up the phone.

Back in the room O'Neil strips to his shorts in the dark, and lowers himself onto the little cot. He would like to wake up Mary, to tell her about the call, but he closes his eyes instead and is instantly asleep.

Then he is awake again, and wondering where he is. It takes him a moment to collect his thoughts, and to realize that what has awakened him is the sound of crying: not Nora, as he first thought, but Mary.

"I'm so sorry," Mary says. She is speaking softly to herself, to baby Nora, to O'Neil. She hugs the child close. "I'm so sorry."

She is sitting on her bed with Nora in her arms, and O'Neil knows that she is thinking of the other baby, the one from years ago. It happened long before they'd even met. The baby's father was her boyfriend at the time, a judge's son who wanted to be a painter. He was serious and clever but had no idea what to do with himself, let alone Mary and a baby. In the end he had fallen apart completely; Mary had driven herself to the clinic.

O'Neil gets into bed behind her and Mary moves a little to let him hold her, as he always does when she is sad. In the dark room he can smell his wife's tears, mixing with the smell of their new baby. His family fills his arms.

"I'm so sorry," Mary says again, rocking. "I shouldn't have done it."

"It's her," O'Neil says. As he says it he believes it. He had meant only to comfort her, to offer words, but he knows at once that this is true.

"It is," O'Neil says. "It's the one you lost, come back to you."

Mary doesn't answer, and O'Neil holds her that way a long time, until her crying has stopped. He wishes she could believe it too. Around them the hospital is silent, like a house after everyone has gone to bed.

"I want to leave," Mary says finally.

"Go home, you mean?"

Mary shakes her head. In her arms Nora makes a tiny mewing sound. She gives a startlingly human-looking yawn. "No, just for a minute. Let's take her outside."

By the supply closet O'Neil finds a wheelchair and a blanket, and pushes it back to the room to the edge of Mary's bed. He holds the baby while she eases herself into it. In his arms she feels like a loaf of bread. She fusses a little when he gives her to Mary, but then is quiet again.

"How do we do this?" Mary whispers.

"I think we just do."

He wheels her into the hallway, past the empty nurses' station to the elevator. The clock on the wall beside the elevator says that it's a little after 2:00 A.M. Downstairs, they pass the empty cafeteria, the lounge with its vending machines and pay phones. He is on the verge of thinking he's gotten them lost when he turns a corner and sees the door.

"Ta-da," O'Neil says.

He wheels them up to it and pushes the metal bar. Silence meets them, and a draft of cool night air that smells of grass. O'Neil turns the wheelchair around and backs through the door. Tomorrow it will be different, he knows. Tomorrow there will be papers and forms to fill out, and a visit from the pediatrician, and luggage to be packed; there will be more calls to make, and the nervous drive home through backstreets with no traffic, and Mary's parents arriving from Minneapolis, their arms full of large, unnecessary presents. There will be meals to cook and beds to make and diapers to be changed. There will be a thousand details, and then a thousand thousand more, and at the end of it all, on a day far, far away, one of them will be alone.

But now it is easy, the simplest, brightest wish fulfilled: the three of them, and the cool moonlight silvering down the green grass on their first night together.

"I just wanted her to see it," Mary says, and O'Neil wheels his wife and daughter outside, down the ramp, into the garden that lies beyond the lights of the hospital.

If you had seen them, you might have thought they were ghosts, or angels. You might have wondered if they were really there at all, these glowing bodies on the lawn. You would have known they were happy.

A GATHERING OF SHADES

March 1999–September 2000

THE FIRST TIME, after the surgery, O'Neil drove. Kay had told him not to come, that the doctors would soon know more and then he should visit if he wanted to. But on he came anyway, arriving in the early morning darkness at the hospital, a citadel of light surrounded by dense green woods. The air was cold and very still, and smelled of the tall pine trees that were everywhere beyond the lamps of the parking lot. Eight hours at the wheel of his tiny car: he'd stopped only once, at a McDonald's south of Albany, to empty his aching bladder and call Mary, who was already in bed. The baby had a cold, she said drowsily; it would be a long night.

The nurse was expecting him, the brother from Philadelphia; his sister was awake, she said, and waiting for him. She smiled with heavy lids when he entered the room. She wore a gown, of course, thin as a pillowcase, which embarrassed her; an IV was threaded into her arm. Someone was sleeping in the next bed, a dark form O'Neil glimpsed as he entered, shielded by a vinyl curtain. He helped Kay out of bed and into a robe, and down the hall to a small room where they could talk.

She had lost a breast to cancer eight years ago. There was some correlation, not well understood, between cancers of the breast and colon, and that was what was happening to her now. Fatigue, weight loss she welcomed at first and then worried over, some bleeding that she thought was hemorrhoids; it had happened slowly and then all at once, like anything. She hadn't put all of it together, until two weeks ago. The cancer had moved outside the colon, she explained, into adjacent lymphatic tissues, though her liver and lungs were clear; that's what the tests had shown. Her hair was grayer than the last time he'd visited, eight months before. In other ways she looked the same. He'd brought photographs of his older daughter, Nora, who was three, and baby Leah, just six weeks old, whom they called Roo; he brought a small CD player he'd purchased on his way out of town, and some disks for her to listen to: Bob Marley, whom she had loved in high school, Miles Davis's *Birth of the Cool, Sticky Fingers* by the Rolling Stones. He told her that he had bought the last recalling a time, many years ago, when he had seen her dancing to "Brown Sugar" at a summer party. She was the big sister home from college and had smuggled him into a party at the house of friends, and he had stood in the kitchen doorway, a glass of warm beer in his hand, and seen her dancing. Why did some images stay with us that way, he wondered, arbitrary flashes of life seared into memory, while others vanished without a trace? Kay thanked him for the gifts, and when she said she was tired he walked her back to the room and kissed her good-night, the first time in years he had done this. I'm glad you're here, she said sleepily, and squeezed his hand. The boys will be happy to see you.

It was late March, the sky sodden and gray. The mountains around the town were dolloped with white, and all the cars on the streets had ski racks. O'Neil slept on a foldout in the den that had been Jack's office before the divorce, and spent the days of his visit with his nephews—ice-skating, pizza, trips to the movies and the mall. The oldest, Sam, was fifteen, Noah twelve, Simon six. O'Neil did not think he would ever have a son, and he welcomed this time with the boys, especially Sam, who was the same age as many of his students and had grown into a boy of surprising sweetness and touchingly mature enthusiasms: the flute, which he played expertly, and Scouts, and helping with his younger brothers, especially Noah, who was autistic and required almost as much looking after as Simon. Evenings, after dinner, O'Neil returned to the hospital. The room was awash with flowers, cards, gifts. Visitors came and went constantly, mostly women but some men, even Jack's colleagues at the college. It was hard for her to rest, but good to see she had so many friends. I have the most famous colon in the Lower Champlain Valley, she said. Everybody here knows everybody else.

The rule was, she had to pass gas; it would mean that everything was working again. This happened on the fourth day after the surgery. The boys were at a hockey game with their father, and O'Neil and Kay were reading the Sunday *Times* together. She put down her paper and frowned. Honey, she said, I do believe I farted, and laughed. How wonderful to see her laughing! He hugged her, kissed her. Pull my finger, he said. Like they were kids again.

Her surgeon said she could be released the next day. It seemed too soon, but Kay was determined. O'Neil offered to stay longer, to help with the boys until she was really well, but she would have none of it. "Don't they need you back home?" she said. "Don't you have classes to teach? I'm fine. I miss my boys, I want to get back to work. Go home." He brought them with him the next morning and found her up and dressed and looking well. The flowers that had not wilted were boxed in their vases to be carried down, wedged into place with the books and magazines and cards and the photos of her sons and O'Neil's daughters that she had kept on the table by her bed. The boys flew into her arms. "My babies, my babies," she said. Light poured from her face. "Did Daddy do fun things with you? Did Uncle O'Neil? And look at you, Simon. So big, in just a week!" The little boy puffed with pride. He had his mother's hair, his father's nose, eyes that were completely his own, iridescent and knowing. She hugged them again, each in turn, and then together. "It's so good to see you all."

He wondered how they would manage. She would begin her chemotherapy in three weeks, once the surgery was completely healed; it would last six months, each round taking a greater toll on her strength. Jack lived in a small apartment on campus, and though he and Kay shared custody, the boys had never spent a single night there. How would she make sure the boys got fed, that the bills were paid on time, that the complex enterprise of a house with children did not collapse into chaos? Already, the effects had started to show: the boys were living on pizza and hamburgers, Noah had worn the same sweatsuit three days running, the bathrooms reeked of piss. One of the boys' rabbits—there were three or four, O'Neil could never be sure—had wriggled under the wire of his hutch and left droppings all over the garage. Before he left, O'Neil did the only helpful thing he could think to do, scouring the house from top to bottom and washing a dozen loads of laundry. He was angry at himself for failing to do these things before, for letting Kay come home from the hospital to a filthy house.

He planned to leave that evening; he could drive through the night, go home to shower and see Mary and the girls for breakfast, and then go straight to school. He had already missed five days of teaching. His students would be behind in everything, happily bewildered by this unplanned vacation; it would take him at least a week to get them back on track. He worked all day on the house, then loaded his car after dinner and went to Kay's bedroom to say good-bye. Noah and Simon were under the covers beside her, listening to her read from *Treasure Island;* Sam, lying diagonally at their feet, was listening with earphones to the CD player O'Neil had brought for Kay and punching numbers into a calculator, recording them on a yellow legal pad. All eyes rose as he entered the room.

"Kiss your uncle, boys."

They did, even Sam, though he also shook O'Neil's hand. *Fifteen years old*, O'Neil thought. *Now you're in charge*. He bent over the bed to embrace his sister. She was wearing a flannel nightgown, and he felt, against his chest, the doleful space of air where her left breast had been. He couldn't imagine having to go through such a thing more than once. Their parents had died, swiftly, together, years ago, when O'Neil was still in college; it was Kay who had carried him through that awful time. A piercing loneliness touched him, and he realized, with a start, that it wasn't his parents he was thinking of, or even Kay. He was thinking of his wife and daughters. He longed to hold them in his arms.

"Will you be . . . ?" he began.

"We'll be fine," his sister said merrily, "won't we, boys?" and waved him out the door.

After that he flew: when she began the chemo in April, in mid-May when the worst of the sickness set in, again in early June when her white count crashed and she finally asked him—Would you come? For the boys? He flew on Fridays, always taking the same 5:00 P.M. flight and renting a car in Burlington so that she would not have to send someone to get him, and because an extra car was always helpful: trips to the grocery or hardware store, to her doctor's, to Noah's therapist—he was always driving somewhere. His glimpses of Jack were cordial and fleeting, always in doors or driveways, when one or the other was delivering the boys. The divorce, two years ago, had been amicable; as Kay explained it, Jack had simply drifted away, like a comet slipping into a progressively wider orbit. O'Neil believed her but also knew this wasn't the whole story. Though no one had said as much, he could tell there had been other women.

"In a way we're better friends now than we were before," Kay told him. They were folding warm towels at the kitchen table; it was early summer, and the boys were at the pool with friends. "All those years, I waited for him to get the hang of it. When I stopped asking for that to happen, I could appreciate him for what he is."

"Okay, what is he?"

He'd meant it as a joke, but O'Neil could tell he had startled her. She snapped a towel into form and folded it across her chest with her thin arms. "He's the boys' father, O'Neil. He's not a bad man. I know you think he is, but he's really all right." She sighed and looked away. "He just can't face this sort of thing."

Every three weeks she returned to the hospital for her infusions, and if one of these weeks coincided with his visits, O'Neil would take her. For the hour before these trips Kay would say nothing; an expectant quiet fell over the house, and O'Neil knew it was time to go when he saw her in the hallway putting on her coat or, in summer, a light sweater and a scarf, for the chills that came after. The hospital had a special parking lot for cancer patients, and inside there was a room of upholstered easy chairs facing a large television, though in all of O'Neil's visits he had never seen anyone turn it on. O'Neil had heard some of the other patients call this room "the gas station." It had been decorated to suggest a den or basement rec room, but the floor was bare linoleum and beside each chair there was a rolling tray of supplies: gauze and tape, needles holstered in cellophane, basins. Many of the other patients chatted away with one another like customers at a hair salon, and scheduled their treatments to coincide with one another's. They introduced themselves to O'Neil by citing both their profession and their illness—Peter, for instance, was a mechanical engineer with chronic lymphocytic leukemia, Delores a lawyer with the state's attorney's office who had ovarian cancer—and when next they saw him, they always asked him specific questions about his life: his daughters, his teaching, the movies he had seen and the books he had read. Then a nurse would set up the IV of clear liquid for Kay, and while the medicine dripped into her arm, the two of them read magazines and listened to the new CDs O'Neil brought with him each time he visited: Charlie Parker, the Beatles' "White Album," a new recording of the Brandenburg Concertos. Sometimes Kay received an injection first, to control the nausea, and fell asleep at once, leaving O'Neil to watch over her, listening through his headphones to the same music on which his sister floated into dreams.

Her weight plummeted, stabilized, plummeted again; by midsummer her hair was mostly gone. In August there was a break in her treatments, and O'Neil rented a house for all of them on the Jersey shore. He had taken it sight unseen, over the phone, but it was perfect: a charming cottage on a quiet street that ended at stairs and the beach. He had lied to his sister about how much it cost, which was fifteen hundred dollars for the week. It took him two days before he realized his mistake. Her bony body, one breast gone, her balding head impossible to really hide, no matter what hat she wore: of course it would break her heart to be at the beach. She took off her T-shirt or robe only to swim; everywhere she looked she would see golden, healthy bodies in the sun. The next morning he drove around town, looking for a barbershop, but had to settle for an expensive salon called Trendz.

When his turn came, he sat in the chair. "Short," he instructed.

The girl was slowly chewing gum; she was very attractive, with hazel eyes and silver bracelets all up and down her bare arms.

She held her comb and scissors slightly raised, like a conductor preparing to lead an orchestra. She spoke to him through the wide mirror.

"How short, exactly?"

O'Neil nodded. "All of it," he said.

She used scissors, then clippers, and finally a safety razor to scrape his scalp clean. At the first touch of the blade O'Neil felt the coolness of air on skin that had not felt it since the first days of his life. When she was done, he ran his hand over it again and again, amazed. And yet his face in the mirror was the same.

"I don't get many requests for something like that," the girl said, bewildered. "A lot of older guys come in here and actually want me to somehow make it *longer*."

He paid her, tipping generously, and returned to the house. It was lunchtime, and Mary and the children were making sandwiches in the kitchen. Sam, reading at the kitchen table, saw him first and started to laugh.

"Holy shit, O'Neil," he said. "You look like a white Michael Jordan." But his face was proud—he understood what O'Neil had done.

Nora giggled. "Daddy lost his hair," she sang. "Bald man, bald man."

"Hush," Mary said. She put down the knife she had been using to spread peanut butter onto sandwiches for the children. She wiped her hands on a dish towel and looked at him. "O'Neil?"

He shrugged. "It's just something I've been meaning to try for a while. What do you think? It *feels* great."

She narrowed her eyes, tilted her head this way and that to examine him. "Well, I think I like it. I really do. Turn around and let me see the back."

He did, pivoting toward the doorway in time for Kay to enter the room and meet his gaze. She stepped forward and touched his bare scalp. Tears floated in her eyes, and O'Neil's heart constricted: another mistake?

"Oh, honey," she said, and laughed. "Is that what I look like? You look just *awful*."

That evening the two of them went down to the ocean to swim. Kay had asked him if he could get some marijuana for her, to help her appetite, and he brought it with him to the beach—three joints, tightly wrapped in green and red paper, like little Christmas presents. It had been years since he'd smoked it; he'd bought it from a friend of Mary's, a sculptor she'd known in graduate school, who knew someone who knew someone else—the road it had traveled to him was obscure. Why had Kay thought that he, of all people, would be able to get it? And yet he had, and done it with ease. O'Neil had planned a big meal to follow it: spaghetti with clam sauce, a salad of mixed greens, fresh sweet corn slabbed with butter, and a key lime pie for dessert. He'd told her nothing about this; the meal was an ambush. The joints were in a Baggie, and after their swim, he took one out and lit it, somehow, in the wind.

"I feel like I'm in high school," she said, and took the joint from him. "I mean that in a good way."

The smoke tasted like pepper on his tongue. They finished about half the joint before the wind blew it out, and O'Neil returned it to the bag. The pot he'd had in high school and college was all stems and seeds—sometimes they smoked through the night and barely caught a buzz—but everything he'd heard told him that, these days, half a joint would probably be more than enough for his purpose. Sure enough: he looked around and discovered that, already, the scenery seemed a little fluttery, like a movie just slightly out of synch. This fact was also elusively funny.

"How are you feeling?" he asked.

She was sitting cross-legged on the sand, her legs covered by a towel. He saw her eyes had closed. "Choirs of angels are soaring from the heavens, singing the Hallelujah Chorus." She turned, wide-eyed and grinning, to look at him. "No, but seriously, I am *stoned*. It's like 1979 all over again. Where did you get this stuff?"

O'Neil shrugged. "Apparently not much has changed in this regard. A few calls, next thing you know, a car's in the driveway and money's changing hands."

"Interesting." She looked out over the water, blinking. The sun was behind them, low against the buildings, which saw-toothed the light. "Really, it's fucking marvelous, O'Neil. I wish I'd had it the last time, though Jack probably would have disapproved. Does Mary know?"

"Mary *helped*."

"Good for Mary. Thank her for me. No, I'll thank her myself." She straightened her back and touched his bald head again. "You didn't have to do this, you know. Make sure you wear sunscreen. You wouldn't believe how fast you can burn."

"Hungry?"

She thought for a moment and nodded. "I could eat."

She packed it away: two helpings of the spaghetti, three ears of corn, seconds on the pie. O'Neil was elated, but later that night he awoke to a sound he recognized at once. He crept down the hall and waited by the door until Kay finished, as he had learned to do, then entered the room and prepared a moistened washcloth for her face.

"I tried," she said dispiritedly. "I really tried."

"It was my fault." He dabbed her face and mouth with the cloth. "I let you overdo it. It was just so good to watch you eat."

Sam came in, wearing boxer shorts and rubbing his eyes. Down the hall Leah had woken up and was calling for Mary. It would be just moments before everyone in the house was prowling the halls. "Is Mom okay?"

Sitting on the closed toilet lid, Kay managed a smile. "I'm all right, honey. Go back to bed."

The boy looked warily at O'Neil. "Is she really okay?"

"She's fine, son," O'Neil said. "Just a few too many clams."

They didn't smoke again. By the day the trip ended, his head, despite Kay's warning, was tender with sunburn. Already it was prickly with stubble; he would have hair again by the start of the school year, just three weeks away. They drove back to O'Neil's and Mary's house in Philadelphia, and the next morning, in smothering heat, O'Neil took Kay and the boys to the airport for their flight home to Vermont. At the gate, when Sam took his brothers off to the bathroom, he took the Baggie from his pocket and slid it into her purse.

She wrinkled her brow. "Is that safe? I don't want to get arrested."

"You just don't check it through," O'Neil explained. "We did it all the time in college." This wasn't true; he'd done nothing of the kind. But when it came down to it, he couldn't believe that anyone would search such an obviously sick woman.

"You're lying," Kay said after a moment. "But it's all right. What could they do to me? I'm a public relations nightmare." She paused and gave a little laugh. "The good thing about cancer, sweetie, and I mean the only good thing, is that you don't sweat the details."

Their plane was announced. Sam emerged from the men's room, holding each of his brothers by a hand. Noah, almost as tall as his brother, was clutching a paper bag of seashells he had collected on the beach. O'Neil saw that Simon had had some troubles; one buckle of his overalls was undone, and both his sneakers were untied. All three were deeply tanned and wearing souvenir T-shirts O'Neil had bought for them, neon-blue with a picture of a surfer and the words *Sea Isle, New Jersey* printed on the front. Kay rose and waved to hurry them up.

"Mary's friend," she said quietly. "The sculptor. Is it Mike?" O'Neil nodded; he knew what she was about to ask. "Can he get some more?"

"I'll bring it," he said, and kissed his sister and then the boys, and watched them all fly away from him.

In September, Mary did not go back to teaching; they had discussed this all through the spring and summer, weighing the pros and cons, but in the end it was money that made the decision for them. Though O'Neil's salary was modest, his parents had left him a small inheritance, and over time these funds, which he almost never touched, had done very well, most of this in the last two years. It seemed foolish for Mary to continue working if she no longer wished to now that her paycheck wasn't necessary. Mary had abandoned her Ph.D. years ago, a decision she had always regretted, and in August she telephoned her old advisor to see if it was still possible for her to return. It was; her advisor even laughed at the question, asking, What took you so long? We always had the brightest hopes for you, Mary. They converted an attic storage room into an office and hired a woman to look after the girls in the afternoons while Mary worked on her dissertation, and though the effort came at first with difficulty—the muscles that had once been so strong and limber atrophied after ten years of teaching high school French and advising the debate team and the horticulture club—soon she was writing away. When O'Neil returned from school in the afternoon, Mrs. Carlisle presented the children to him like a gift she had been wrapping all day—it was not unusual to find the three of them actually baking something,

Nora gleefully licking chocolate batter from the spoon while baby Leah, freshly changed, burbled contentedly in her bouncer—and as the old woman put on her coat and hat and scarf in the hallway, Mary would descend the stairs, yawning, a pencil tucked behind one ear or holding her bun of hair in place. Was it four? she would ask, her face glazed by hours of concentration. Five o'clock already? They spent their evenings together, and once the girls were fed and washed and put to bed, they made a pot of tea and took it to the living room to spend a quiet hour trading stories of their days: the students he had won and lost, the running battles with Nora over television and Leah's persistent earaches, Mary's research and her quarrels with the library over certain manuscripts and her hopes for a travel fellowship to France. She had decided to shift her focus a little, she explained. The most exciting work was being done now on women writers of the sixteenth and seventeenth centuries, the early moderns. Literally dozens of them had only just been discovered, though of course they had been there all along; that, she said, was the point, the very thing that made it so exciting, the fact that they had been so *overlooked;* all the research was new. O'Neil had never seen his wife so happy. Working hard, it would take her two years, she conjectured. Certainly not more than three, even if they went to France. Then she could go back to teaching, or have another baby, or whatever else she wanted to do.

Some of O'Neil's colleagues also had money—a woman in the math department, a Wanamaker, drove a Benz and owned a summer house in Sienna; the dean of the upper school was the husband of a Main Line plastic surgeon; one of the secretaries, it was said, had won a million dollars in the lottery, but given it all to the church. Their situations were not the same, but O'Neil knew that, like them, he was lucky—who would have thought that a company named Yahoo would do so well?—and that such good fortune was best kept secret. When people asked him about Mary, he said only that she had decided to stay home with Leah a while longer, suggesting with his silence that this new arrangement was temporary and soon she would return. Well, that was certainly understandable, they all agreed, with a baby who was still so young. Tell her we miss her. On the last Friday in October the school held its annual Halloween parade, and as the crowds of parents and teachers assembled, O'Neil found himself standing beside the headmaster, a tall, athletic man who was fifty-five but looked forty. The low stone buildings of the campus were arranged in a U-shape around a spacious quad, and under crisp autumn sunshine everyone watched while the lower-schoolers, dressed as fairies and mermaids and pirates, some of them holding hands, marched three times around before their teachers whisked them inside so that they wouldn't be frightened by the costumes of the older children, who followed. Psychotics in hockey masks, rotting corpses, vampires with trails of ketchup running down their chins, an accident victim carrying a severed limb in a basket of smoking dry ice: one of O'Neil's students, a precocious ninth grader who loved to torment him over the most delicate distinctions of grammar, waved to him as he passed, dressed as if for an ordinary day at school but with an ax apparently buried in his bleeding skull. "Mr. Burke, Mr. Burke!" he called. "You're giving me *such* a headache!" When all the prizes had been awarded, the headmaster turned to O'Neil, agreeing that it had been one of the best parades ever, and asked, as if the thought had only just occurred to him, So tell me, how is Mary? And the girls? O'Neil assured him that all was well, that she missed the old place, but on the whole he had to say it was good for her to have some time at home. Well, the headmaster said, he was certainly glad to hear it. He shuffled his feet on the gravel. He had two kids of his own, one in college, the other grown and gone. It all goes so quickly, he said, shaking his head. She should enjoy this special time. Tell her I asked about her, won't you? It's not the same without her here. Tell her she can come back whenever she's ready.

His students were bright, sometimes alarmingly so. For many years O'Neil had doubted his worthiness as a teacher and waited for his fraud to be unmasked. But somehow, over time, he had come to be, he understood, beloved, a fixture of the institution and its memories. Khakis and loafers, an oxford shirt frayed at the collar and the wrists, a fifteen-year-old tie—that was his costume. His other life, his real life, was a mystery to them. Nearly every year he received a letter or postcard from a student he had taught years ago, thanking him for all he had done. He understood these letters were written in a mood of nostalgia (many began, "Today I am graduating from Harvard/Penn/Princeton/Yale . . ." and went on to describe some small but life-changing generosity he did not recall), and yet they touched him deeply. He kept them together in a manila folder in his desk, knowing that someday they might save him.

The Sunday after the parade his nephew Sam telephoned. O'Neil was doing an art project with Nora in the kitchen, and Mary and the baby were napping. Leah had become Leah: the nickname Roo had failed to stick.

"Mom doesn't want you to know, but there's something wrong."

He gripped the phone tightly. His nephew's voice was taut with fear; he knew the boy had been crying.

"Where are you?" O'Neil asked. A ludicrous question: the boy was many miles, and hours, away.

"I'm upstairs." He lowered his voice to a desperate whisper. "They say it's in her liver, O'Neil. She can't stop throwing up."

He thought to tell the boy to call his father, but stopped himself. "I'm coming," he said.

He caught a plane that afternoon, arriving at the house a little after eight o'clock. It was Halloween night; all the houses on her street had decorations up. Groups of children still prowled the neighborhood, pillowcases of candy flung over their shoulders, the beams of their flashlights volleying through the trees. But Kay's porch was barren, the lights doused. He wondered if she had taken the boys out trick-or-treating, but as he climbed the steps, the door opened to meet him. His sister stood in the doorway, bathed in darkness.

"I told him not to call," she said and hugged him, shaking and fiercely weeping.

She fell swiftly. After Christmas, Jack moved in to look after the boys; three weeks later Kay went into the hospital, knowing she would not return. A haze of airports and rental cars: each week, O'Neil taught his classes and then caught the five o'clock plane on Friday afternoon, driving straight to the hospital in spotless, mid-sized American sedans that all seemed, somehow, to be the same car. Some weeks he didn't even unpack. His lessons were scattered, but his students seemed not to know or if they did, to care. Some days he simply turned off the lights in his classroom and read to them—*The Grapes of Wrath,* which the ninth graders were hacking their way through like explorers in a jungle—or sent them to the library with assignments he knew he would only pretend to grade. Are you all right? they asked him, barely hiding their pleasure. What's gotten into you, Mr. Burke? Whatever it is, they assured him, we like it. He slept fitfully or not at all, and yet his body and mind were filled with a strange energy he could not express. At lunchtime, when this internal churning became too much to bear, he put on sweatpants and went running on the paths of the sanctuary behind the campus, his mind drifting formlessly. The winter was snowless and mild; many of the trees were still dropping their leaves, though the autumn was long gone and the first of Mary's bulbs, the crocus and hyacinth, had appeared. Had he simply failed to notice it in winters past, this anachronistic overlapping of the seasons? The woodlands where he ran were bisected by a weedy creek, and one blustery day in February he paused on the old stone bridge that crossed it, while all around him a showering of leaves, light as paper, came down. He turned his face upward and closed his eyes, receiving them. He had not been to church in years, having long forgotten how. Leaves fell on his shoulders, into his hair. Suddenly he knew that this was prayer, standing in a cathedral of falling leaves.

Later he asked a colleague, who taught science, about what he had seen.

"They're white oaks, O'Neil," he replied, his voice incredulous. His classroom was like a greenhouse, filled with every kind of plant. "Didn't you know? They keep their leaves all winter."

Weekends, he stayed at a motel on the highway that led to the hospital. Many of the other guests were there because someone they loved was dying, or so he imagined. Surely, he believed, there must be others who were living the same divided existence, one foot in each of two worlds. He spent long days at the hospital with Kay: shuttling the boys back and forth for visits, eating off a tray in the cafeteria, hoping for some glimmer of good news but knowing none would come. At night he fell into bed, exhausted but still humming with wakefulness; sometimes he would talk to Mary for hours, finally falling asleep with the telephone resting on the pillow beside him. For Simon the time was almost happy: their father was at home with them again. Noah regarded it as he regarded everything, with a vague but neutral interest; Mama was sick, Daddy was sleeping where he used to sleep, it was winter, he had to wear gloves and a hat. Sam was trying to be brave, but underneath, O'Neil felt the strain, a disturbance that rippled through his body like a flush of fever. On a Sunday in early March, O'Neil had caught him in a moment when he thought no one was watching. Sam was standing in the snowy yard; at his feet, he had built a pile of snowballs, perhaps a dozen of them, expertly spherical and perfect for throwing. As O'Neil watched from the window, Sam had hurled these snowballs one by one, as hard as he could, at the wall of the garage. The target was unmissably large; accuracy was not the point. Nor was the grace of his throw; he released each one with the full force of his entire body, nearly falling over every time. When he was through, he leaned over, his hands on his knees, panting with exertion. Then he made more snowballs and did it all again.

O'Neil waited to hear from Sam. Finally he did, two weeks later. It was Saturday morning, an ice-cold day at the end of March. O'Neil was driving him to band practice at the high school. After, they would meet Jack and the other boys at a McDonald's, and O'Neil would ferry the three of them to the hospital.

"I think we should come and live with you," he announced.

He meant after his mother had died. Of course it was impossible, even if O'Neil had wanted to. He pulled the car over.

"Sam—" he began.

"He doesn't care about her!" the boy burst out. "He never did!" His face fell. "Nobody told me, but I knew what he was doing."

What could he say to the boy? That marriage was complicated, that there was more to it than he could understand, that the things that made a man a bad husband did not, necessarily, make him a bad parent? How could he explain something he didn't really know himself?

"He's your father," O'Neil said. "He loves you."

"He's an asshole," Sam said. He sighed and breathed deeply, his mouth curling with anger. "So are you. You don't want us either. I can tell."

The boy was trying to hurt him, to hurt anyone. "Sam, listen to me. That's not it, not at all. If it made even the slightest bit of sense, I'd tell you. But it doesn't. Not legally, not in a hundred other ways."

"He thinks you're going to try, you know. He's talking to his lawyer."

O'Neil was astonished. "Well, that should be a very interesting conversation. Trust me, it won't amount to anything."

They drove in silence to the school. Sam got out and carried his instrument case toward the entrance, but at the door he stopped.

"Sam?" O'Neil said. "Aren't you going in?" But the boy was frozen, stockstill.

"You know, I think I'm done with band," he said calmly, and turned to face O'Neil. "Fuck band. And fuck you. I'm done with everything."

At home O'Neil called his attorney. She was a friend's wife who had become a friend herself—a composed, slyly beautiful woman who exuded an air of magisterial competence. The walls of her tiny office were plastered with degrees: law, social work, urban planning, even a master's in art history that she had, in her words, "picked up somehow along the way." He described the situation, not even sure what he was truly asking.

"I can't be very encouraging," Beth said. "It might be different in Vermont, but in Pennsylvania the law is pretty clear. You'd have to prove that he was an unfit parent, just for starters, and that can be difficult."

"Well, he isn't. He's not going to win any medals, but I wouldn't call him unfit."

She thought a moment. "The only thing I can see happening here is, he might ask your sister to sign over full custody. People do it all the time, in situations like this. With full custody there'd be no question. There isn't anyway, not really." She paused. "Tell me this, O'Neil. When did you last get a decent night of sleep?"

He almost laughed. "What month is it?"

"Forget about it," Beth advised. "His lawyer is probably saying the same thing. Get a good night's sleep, and forget about it."

Through the spring Kay faded, like a picture going out of focus. Her body was frail and gray. When she had gone into the hospital in January, her doctors had told her it was a matter of a month or two, perhaps less. Her liver, her lungs, the bones of her spine—everything was suddenly involved. And yet it was April, then May.

"I'm like that old Volvo," she told O'Neil. It was a car she and Jack had driven for years. "That goddamn thing would not be killed."

He nodded at such remarks, or laughed if she wanted him to laugh. He never knew what to say. Some days he got into her bed beside her, careful of the tubes and wires and her own brittle bones, to read her the paper or brush her hair, which had, after the summer, grown back.

"Remember when you shaved your head?" She said this as if it had happened years ago. "You looked so terrible."

"I think Mary kind of liked it."

She closed her eyes. "I hate to break it to you, but she was humoring you, sweetie."

Sleep dropped on her like a blade. One minute they would be talking, the next she would be falling away. He watched her sleep for hours. Then, without warning, she would be awake again, seamlessly picking up the broken thread of conversation as if she had excused herself only a moment to tie a shoe or answer the telephone. "Noah will do better if they let him nap after lunch," she said, or "I don't care if they cost sixty dollars, Sam needs new sneakers," or "The thing about Jack is, he's absolutely brilliant. He's living proof of the sociopathic effects of brilliance."

Finally she said, "O'Neil? I'll want one person here."

It was on a day very near the end that Jack arrived at the hospital, carrying under his arm a large envelope that O'Neil knew, without looking, contained the papers Beth had described. The boys were downstairs in the lounge, playing pinball. Kay was sleeping, and before Jack could say anything, O'Neil pulled him into the hall.

"What's in the envelope?"

Jack did not meet his gaze. "I don't see that this is your business, O'Neil. You've been a great help to all of us. But this is a private family matter."

"Stop this, Jack. Think about what you're asking her to do."

His brother-in-law sighed with nervous irritation. "Okay, since you seem to know what it's all about. Let me ask you something. What would you do if you were me? Since you don't know, I'll tell you. Exactly the same thing."

"I don't want to be you, Jack. I just don't want you to do something everyone will feel sorry about later on."

"For Godsakes, O'Neil! It's just a formality, a few papers to sign!" He made a face of exasperation and lowered his voice. "You and I both know she's never leaving here. It's awful to say it, but those are the facts. I have to think about what's best for the boys. I have to make plans. She'll understand that."

Would she? O'Neil looked toward the room, where Kay was sleeping. Perhaps she would. But it didn't matter. She would never have to.

"Let's just go someplace to talk about it," O'Neil said. "She's sleeping now, anyway. Just hear me out. Listen to what I have to say, and then you can do whatever you want to do."

Jack folded his arms over his chest. "You're not talking me out of it," he warned.

"Trust me," O'Neil said. "That's the furthest thing from my mind."

He walked with Jack to the parking lot, letting his brother-in-law get three steps ahead of him. Jack would wonder where he was taking him, which was exactly what O'Neil intended, and when Jack turned to look for him, O'Neil took two steps and hit him, hard, just below the left eye. O'Neil had never hit anyone before, and the sensation was not at all what he would have expected if he'd thought about it, which he hadn't. His hand sailed through Jack's face easily, without a trace of pain, and seemed to pop him right off his feet. As Jack went down, a second surge of adrenaline passed through O'Neil's body, and his fist clenched again, ready for more.

"Jesus Christ, O'Neil!"

O'Neil relaxed his fist and went to where Jack was sitting, his back braced against the tire of a minivan. One hand covered the spot near his eye where O'Neil had made contact. O'Neil crouched beside him.

"You fucking asshole!" Jack's sneakers kicked at the pavement. "Get away from me!"

"Oh, stop it," O'Neil said. "Let's see that eye."

A nurse in the ER gave O'Neil a plastic bottle of alcohol and a bandage for Jack's cut, and some tape for O'Neil's knuckles, which were split and bleeding after all. Back in the parking lot O'Neil sat Jack on the bumper of the minivan and swabbed his eye clean with a Q-Tip.

"Aw, hell, O'Neil, I probably deserved that. I told my lawyer it was a dumb idea."

"Dumb is the least of it, if you'll pardon my saying so." A purposeful calm had filled him, a feeling beyond exhaustion or anger or fear; he wasn't threatening, merely stating the facts. He pasted a bandage to Jack's clean cut.

"There, good as new. Now, give me those papers or I'll hit you again."

With a sigh of defeat Jack removed the now-crinkled envelope from the pocket of his jacket and handed it to him. O'Neil opened it to look the contents over. As he'd expected, the document was an agreement giving Jack full custody of the boys. There was more to it—four pages of mumbo-jumbo he was too tired to wade through—but that was the gist. Jack had already signed it, and on the last page, at the bottom, beside his signature, was a place for Kay to write her name, marked with a red arrow. O'Neil saw that Jack's signature was dated two weeks before. So at least he had waited before deciding to go ahead with it.

"I won't fight you, if that's what you're worried about." O'Neil folded the agreement and put it in the pocket of his coat. What would he do with it? Burn it? Shove it in a Dumpster somewhere? "If you'd asked me, that's what I would have told you. They're your children, and they need you. But I don't want you to tell Kay anything about this. She's never going to know you even *thought* it. Agreed?"

Jack frowned hopelessly. "Why should I believe you? You just assaulted me, for Chrissakes."

"Yes, but that's all done," O'Neil said.

At the hospital entrance Jack stopped. "Let me ask you one last thing. Do you even have the faintest idea why I did it?"

"Actually, no."

"Fucking Saint O'Neil," Jack said, shaking his head. "So perfect he doesn't even know it."

O'Neil left Jack with the children and went up to Kay's room. "Breaking news. I just punched your husband."

"Did you kill him?" Kay smiled weakly. "You look so happy."

He showed her his bandaged knuckles. "Just minor damage. Would you like me to?" A joke: but he would do it if she asked.

Kay shook her head. "Maybe later." She sighed deeply, haltingly. Two sentences, and already she was exhausted. "Right now I'd like to see my children, please."

He brought the boys to her and waited outside with Jack. It was noon when they emerged: Noah and Simon looking confused and uncertain, Sam holding his face bravely so they wouldn't know what was happening. Be strong, Kay had whispered to him. Help your brothers. O'Neil left Jack with Kay and took the boys to the cafeteria and tried to feed them, and an hour later Jack came down. O'Neil saw him first, as he passed through the door and stood a moment, drying his glasses and then his face with a handkerchief. Then he strode briskly to the table.

"Okay, boys," he said, rubbing his hands together.

When O'Neil returned to the room, Kay was sleeping. The morphine button was in her hand, her thumb resting on it. Without opening her eyes she pushed the button. O'Neil watched as the morphine moved through her, like rings on a pond, easing her into a state far deeper than sleep and yet of little use. For years it had been just the two of them. Now, for the first time since Kay had gotten sick, he felt her exhaustion as if it were his own. He knew what she wanted, and wanted it too; he wanted her suffering to end more than he wanted her not to die.

"I'm not leaving," he told her.

The nurse brought him dinner; he left the room only to go to the bathroom, and once to call Mary from a pay phone. It was happening, he told her. He couldn't talk for long. Later that evening Kay awoke, moaning. "God, honey," she said. Her eyes were open but unfocused. Could she see him? Did she know where she was? Her voice was etched with pain; her words seemed to hang in the air, not sounds alone but things with form and substance. "*God,* honey, *God.*" Then she was silent.

He spent the night in a chair by her bed, and the night after, and just as he promised, was there in the room when she died the next morning.

They went to Paris after all. O'Neil had thought to cancel the trip, but when, at the last minute, Mary's fellowship came through, he agreed to go; there was no telling if she'd ever get the grant again. With the help of one of her professors they rented an apartment for the month of July in Saint-Germaine, a small town near the end of the Metro line where O'Neil had stayed with friends on a trip after college. O'Neil looked after the girls while Mary wrote or worked at the library, and on weekends they took long drives through the countryside in the car that came, unannounced, with the apartment—an ancient Fiat that stank of stale cigarette smoke and had an engine the size of a milk bottle. At night, when Mary stopped working, he cooked for all of them, trying new recipes with ingredients he'd picked up at the open-air market down the street. Even these simple excursions required a constant vigilance that left him dazed with adrenaline; trying to manage the girls and his awful French besides, he often asked for the wrong things entirely, or else bought gigantic quantities of the right ingredients by accident: a loaf of pâté the size of a shoe box, a liter of salt, an entire wheel of Roquefort cheese. It didn't matter; Mary was working, the girls were enjoying themselves, Nora laughing herself senseless as the dog shit all over the sidewalks, Leah chatting away in a mishmash of French and English that sometimes seemed to be a language all its own.

"I feel so guilty," Mary said to him one evening. They were lying in bed, a huge four-poster with a curtain. "Cooped up with Nora and Leah all day. You haven't even been to the Louvre."

He couldn't have cared less about the Louvre. "What's at the Louvre?" he said, laughing. "I'm fine, I'm perfectly happy." He hugged her to reassure her this was so. "It's nice just to be here, to spend so much time with the girls. I've been away too long."

Nevertheless, he decided to go. The car would be too much trouble; he planned to use the train. It took him two hours to assemble his supplies and get the girls dressed and ready, and by then they needed lunch. After he fed them, Leah went down for a nap; by the time she woke up, whining for the cup of heated milk that was her habit, Nora was beginning to fade. She slept two hours, until four o'clock, while O'Neil read the *Tribune*, bouncing Leah on his knee. Then he heard Mary's footsteps on the stairs.

"How was it?" she said happily. She piled her books onto the table and hugged the girls. "Did you like the paintings? *Aimiez-vous les peintures?*"

"Mona is in top form," O'Neil said. "You know, I somehow always thought it would be *bigger*."

Mary, crouched, studied him with her eyes. Her face fell with sympathy. "It didn't work out, did it?"

O'Neil shrugged. "It's not important," he said.

Their last night, they hired a baby-sitter and went to eat at a café down the street. While they waited for their meal, they wrote their final postcards to friends back home: Mary's family in Minnesota, Mrs. Carlisle, the couple next door who were watching over their house. O'Neil hadn't seen the boys since the day after the funeral, when Jack had told him that he would be taking them back to St. Louis in August. O'Neil thought at first that he meant for a visit, but realized as they were talking that Jack meant permanently, to live. All of Jack's family was there, and he would need their help raising the boys, especially Noah and Simon. He had found a teaching job there—a temporary appointment, but one which, with luck, could turn into something long term. He had already submitted his resignation and arranged to put the house up for sale. The move would be hard for Sam, he conceded, but in another year he would be off to college anyway.

O'Neil saved the last postcard for Sam. The boy had barely spoken to him since the day in the car when he had asked O'Neil—what? To be his father? O'Neil had never fully known what to make of the request. The boy had been in pain, no doubt, and still was. Sixteen years old, and all his life people had been asking him to be strong when others could not. Noah's problems, the divorce, his mother's illness. Perhaps all he had wanted was for someone else to carry his load. But what could O'Neil have done? He looked at the blank postcard—on the other side was a picture of the Eiffel Tower—waiting to find the words. But none would come.

"O'Neil?" Mary looked at him quizzically. "What's wrong?"

"It's nothing." He capped his pen and did his best to smile. "I'll see him when we get back. Whatever I have to say, I'll think of it then."

Mary offered her hand across the table. "I just want you to know how much this month has meant to me. I know how difficult it's been for you this last year, and now, spending so much time without me to help, taking care of the girls . . ."

"Really, I was happy to do it. We've had a great time together. You've wanted to come back for years."

"Still, it means something, O'Neil." Her face and voice were serious, almost scolding. "It means something to *me*. I'm just telling you how thankful I am. With all you've done, I don't think anyone has said that to you."

It was true. No one had.

He traveled north one last time, the week before the summer ended and school began. He took the car, as he had done the first time, all those months ago. The weather was clear, the sky a flaw-less blue; he treated himself and did not cut east from Albany into Vermont, the quickest route, but instead drove north along the lake, and took a ferry across it. The boat ride from New York to Vermont was forty minutes; he passed it lying on the hood of his car, his eyes closed, the sun spilling on his face, his ears and body tuned to the throb of the engine and the slap of water against the steel plating of the ferry's hull.

A moving van was parked in the driveway, and two men in jumpsuits were carting out the contents of the house: furniture, appliances, clothing, toys. A thousand crates of books. Jack had set aside some things of Kay's for O'Neil to take with him—a single cardboard box, containing mostly photographs. In the box O'Neil also found her Phi Beta Kappa key, the engraved silver hairbrush she had had since she was a baby, and her senior thesis from col-lege, a slender, yellowed volume entitled "Wayward Women: The Poems of Sylvia Plath and Anne Sexton." The last pleased him the most. Reading it, he knew, he would hear her voice.

"It's not a lot, I know," Jack apologized. He was wearing shorts and a T-shirt circled with sweat; he had been packing for days. "Really, if there's anything else you want . . ."

"It's perfect," O'Neil said. All his anger had left him, long ago. "Thank you."

The next day he took the boys to Friendly's for lunch. The house was empty, a silent, ghostly hall. His nephews would spend another day in town, and on Monday Jack would put them on a plane to St. Louis. Then he would drive west to meet them, and together they would begin their new life.

"What's St. Louis like?" Simon wanted to know.

"Let's see." O'Neil thought a moment. "Well, it's a lot like here. It's warmer, that's one difference. It almost never snows."

"No snow!" the little boy said, shocked.

"Well, it *can* snow," O'Neil explained. "I'm not saying it *never* snows. It just doesn't, most of the time. And plus, your grandparents are there. And all your uncles and aunts and cousins."

"Will you move there with us?" Noah asked.

"No, but I can come to visit. Or you can come to visit me."

"Where's Pennsylvania?" the littlest boy asked. He pronounced it deliberately, like a new word he had just learned: *Pencil-vay-nee-a*.

"Well, it's not so far."

"Mom's in heaven," Noah stated. He was doodling with crayons on his place mat, and did not look up as he spoke.

"That's right," O'Neil said. "That's where she is."

"With her mommy and daddy. Our other grandparents."

"Yes, they're all there together."

"Cool it, Noah," Sam said. "Let him eat." He looked at his uncle. "I'm sorry, O'Neil."

"No, it's all right," O'Neil said. "We can talk about it. I don't mind at all."

"Did they die too?" Simon asked.

"Yes, they did, a long time ago. But that doesn't matter. You see, in heaven there's no yesterday, or today, or tomorrow. It's all the same in heaven. So, you're there already, too, with your mom. Think about it. How could it be heaven if she didn't have you there?"

Noah frowned. "But I'm alive," he said.

"Yes, you are. And you'll live many, many years. Your whole life. But when you get there, it will be like only a day has passed. Not even a day. No time at all. That's heaven."

Noah eyed him skeptically. "How do you know?"

O'Neil looked at him, then at Sam. If they had been alone, he would have thrown his arms around the boy and told him how sorry he was, how much he loved him.

"Your mother told me," O'Neil said.

It happened in September. O'Neil had been back teaching four weeks. He had just turned forty; later, he would wonder if this fact had something to do with what occurred. As the day approached, Mary asked him if he wanted her to plan a party, and though he said no, he knew she would do something. That night, a Friday, he came home to a darkened house. As he opened the door he assumed he would be stepping into the party he had refused, but found only Mary and the girls, coloring with crayons on construction paper at the kitchen table. Happy birthday, Daddy, the girls cried, and hugged him tightly. They showed him what they had made: a picture of the two of them, enclosed in a heart. Go shower, Mary said, as he was admiring it. We have a dinner reservation at seven; Mrs. Carlisle will be here any minute. They dressed and drove to the restaurant, and only when they were seated at their table did O'Neil notice the balloons and the gifts and lift his face to find all his friends there, laughing at him, the oblivious O'Neil.

Forty: how unlikely it seemed. As a boy O'Neil had computed his age in the year 2000—an impossibly distant future—and discovered, to his astonishment, that he would be forty years old. Under the eaves of his bedroom he had wondered, What would the world be like then? Would we be living in outer space, in bubbles under the sea, soaring to work in helicopters? Would he even be able to enjoy these wondrous things, being so old? Yet here he was, the same person, living in the same world, none of it truly changed. He drove a car to work, lived in a house twice as old as he was, looked at the stars when he cared to, feeling only the vague appreciation one gave to anything beautiful and useless and far away. Every day he went to school, just as he had as a boy. Amazing.

Was your birthday all right? Mary asked, driving home from the party. Was it what you wanted? Dozens of old friends had come, some he hadn't seen for years. His college roommate, Stephen, had even driven down from Boston. O'Neil told her it was; it was perfect, he said. You know, in this light, you don't look forty, Mary said, and squeezed his hand promisingly. My gift to you comes later, handsome man.

She meant she was pregnant. She did not tell him that night, but he thought she would soon; that was how it had been the first two times, Mary keeping the news to herself until she was sure, living alone with her secret like the answer to a question she wasn't sure anyone had posed. Well, he thought as sleep came to him, perhaps it wasn't so. She would tell him, or not. She was, or she wasn't. He would wait to hear. So, in the meantime, his be-lief—for that's what it was—would be a secret too.

Monday he drove to work, his mind buzzing with happiness. Everything he saw—the morning sunlight rebounding in the turning leaves, the bright yellow school buses and dutiful crossing guards, a woman putting on lipstick in her rearview mirror at a stop sign—filled him with a strange delight. It flowed through him like a benign electric current. So much joy! So much to look forward to! The awful months were over; he had stepped back into life. In the faculty workroom the morning talk among his colleagues was still of summer pleasures, of gardens planted and trips taken, of books read and movies seen, of mountains scaled and rivers kayaked and long, unhurried days doing nothing at all. They were teachers, with more time than money; their enjoy-ments, modest to a fault, seemed to O'Neil to possess the same unassuming purity of green grass, summer light, and flowers in a pail, and he listened to their stories with a feeling like kinship. This life they described was, after all, the same one he had chosen.

"O'Neil, what's gotten into you?" someone asked—the science teacher who, so long ago, had explained the leaves to him. "Nine months to go," Paul said. "What's there to be so happy about? You're grinning like an ape."

"Was I?" O'Neil laughed and sipped his coffee; he didn't know.

"Forty years old," another said, shaking his head. He was a young man, just a few years out of college, who had joined the faculty a year ago. He had spent his summer teaching sailing on the coast of Maine, and was as brown as a shot of scotch.

"It's not so bad," O'Neil reassured him.

The young man helped himself to a cookie off the tray. "I don't know about you, but I'd want to go hang myself." He lifted his face and smiled so everyone could see he was joking. An embarrassed titter ran through the room.

"Trust me," O'Neil said. "You won't feel like that at all."

The bell rang; off they went to class, sliding into the river of students that flowed through the hallways. Clanging lockers, books, and backpacks strewn everywhere—huge piles of them, heaped under stairways and in every open corner—the urgent din of voices, the girls erupting in shrieks, the boys croaking and wailing: it was like stepping into chaos itself. *Let's hurry it up now,* O'Neil heard himself saying. They darted from his path like minnows in the shallows. *Let's move it along, people.* How like a teacher, he thought.

His ninth graders were studying the *Odyssey.* It was, by the standards of the school, a rite of passage; his department chair liked to say that students at the academy had been reading it since the Trojan War itself. Even in the lower grades the students spoke of this task like a terrible fate that awaited them all. The *Odyssey!* they cried. All of it! It's, like, a thousand pages long! And yet most of them came to like it, even as they refused to admit this. War, magic, adultery, ruination, betrayal; nymphs and cyclopses and men turned into pigs; a long trip and the yearning for home. What was it, in the end, but a metaphor for the trials of growing up? They had read to Book Eleven, "A Gathering of Shades," in which Odysseus and his men, blown to a dark and nameless shore by Circe, queen of Aeaea, filled a trench with blood to summon forth the spirits of the dead.

"What are we seeing here?" he asked them. "Is Circe doing him a favor, or not?"

Half a dozen hands went up. "It's like Odysseus is getting another chance," a girl said. "Tiresias tells him everything that's going to happen to him, so he can avoid it. It's like he's reading Cliff Notes." She smiled. "Like he's cheating on a test."

Others disagreed; one boy, a passionate rationalist, thought it was a dirty trick.

"What good can it do him?" he asked. "How can it help you to see the future, if you can't change it?"

"Well, that's just the question," O'Neil said. "What do you think? Is the future fixed, or isn't it?"

The boy was immovable. "The future is what it is," he said.

The discussion was spirited; they moved through the text line by line. As the end of the period neared they came to the part where Odysseus was approached by the ghost of his mother. Though he had taught the book a dozen times, this scene remained, for O'Neil, a moment of the deepest poignancy—the great hero, so full of arrogance, reduced to a childlike yearning for his mother's touch. He rose, took his copy of the book from his desk, and read these lines to them:

> *I bit my lip*
> *rising perplexed, with longing to embrace her,*
> *and tried three times, putting my arms around her,*
> *but she went sifting through my hands, impalpable*
> *as shadows are, and wavering like a dream.*

Wavering like a dream. O'Neil stopped, the book cradled in his hand; he knew what was about to happen. All along he had hoped it would happen when he was alone, or else with Mary. He entered an interval of time that felt suspended, and in that instant he found he was at once aware of who and where and when he was—the physical parameters of his consciousness—and all the weeks and months that had brought him to this moment: the planes and airports and rental cars, the long white hours of the hospital, the jaws of the open moving van. He knew that soon he would begin to cry, and that the force of it would blind him. He would cry and cry and cry, and struggle for breath like a man who was dying, until another moment came when the tears separated on the surface of his eyes, and he would see again—see the world through tears. He felt all this coming toward him, a rumbling in the hills above, and then it did, more powerfully even than he had imagined it. His hands found the table so he would not fall.

"Mr. Burke, what's wrong—"

"Shut up, idiot," someone said. "Didn't you hear? His sister died."

His children: why had he thought they would not know? Of course they would know. And then he realized: everyone knew. They had only been waiting for him to tell them. The bell was ringing, but he sensed no stirring, no familiar shuffling of feet or papers or books. No one moved. Others would come—the changing period was moments away—but then he heard the sounds he longed for: the shade being drawn over the small square window, and the quietly locking door.

"Shhhh," a small voice said, and he felt their hands upon him. "It's all right."

His children were around him. They had sealed themselves away. The moment would pass, but until it did, no one was going anywhere.

Acknowledgments

The author wishes to express his gratitude to the following:

Susan Kamil and Carla Riccio; Ellen Levine; Stephen Kiernan and Susan Chernesky; Andrea McGeary, M.D.; Students 1–7; The Pennsylvania Council on the Arts; the College of Arts and Sciences of La Salle University; The MacDowell Colony; and K.M., for the inspiration of her courage.

JUSTI
Work
Unive
ary jc
Cresce
He li
Philac